A FAMILY FOR RAFFI

Praise for previous books by Lara Rios.

CONQUEST

Her characters come to life right before your eyes from the very first word.
Robin Peek - Under the Covers

Lara Rios pens an enjoyable romance with a unique premise in Conquest.
Rickey R. Mallory - Painted Rock Reviews

Ms. Rios humanizes Tess and Logan by showing their family relationships and the forces that made them the people they are. She shows their strengths and vulnerabilities, their tenderness and passion, and intersperses the serious with the humourous.
Jane Bowers - Romance Reviews Today

Ms. Rios succeeds in bringing out the best in both characters and leaving the reader wanting more.
Fatin Soufan -Addicted2Romancebooks.com

Lara Rios has a nice breezy style to her writing that keeps you interested in her charming characters.
Suzanne Coleburn -The Belles and Beaux of Romance

Praise for WINNER TAKE ALL
To be released January 2002!

Lara Rios delivers a dynamite story rich with emotion, deeply passionate characters, and breath-taking sensuality!
Best selling Temptation author Janelle Denison

"Unforgettable characters in a compelling story about the enduring spirit of the heart."
Meryl Sawyer - author of TRUST NO ONE

ACKNOWLEDGMENTS

I've got to start by thanking my husband, a wonderful father, a kind, supportive husband, and a man whose enthusiasm for life and gift for business has encouraged me to become more daring in pursuit of my dreams. I hope you know I could do none of it without you, honey!

Next on my list have to be my dear friends Susan and Wanell who introduced me to the glorious world of adoption. I could never thank you enough. I love you both and I adore your sweet, beautiful, intelligent daughter.

My mother in law, Pat, who thinks all her kids and grand kids are perfect. I think you're perfect! Leo, Kenny, Leah, Bob, and Rene - thanks for being my brothers and sisters. I love you all.

Thank you to all my teacher/school friends who have been so enthusiastic about my writing career. You have made it all the more fun! Aiko, Alice, Arlene, Barbara, Capri, Carol, Cory, Debbie, Donna, Evey, Gloria, Jean, Katherine, Maria, Mr. T, Nancy, Rosa, Steve, and so many others – Thank you! People ought to stop and ask you for your autographs -- for giving every day, part of yourself to help mold the future. You're the real life heroes. I miss you all.

Thanks to everyone at the Arrowhead Credit Union for, uhm, ahh, well, you know. I'll put a quarter in the cup, next week.

My writing colleagues at IVRWA and OCCRWA. Through the years, I have gained so much from my association with many of you, from help by critique partners, to words of wisdom from speakers, to personal chats filled with advice and 'tips'. Thank you all.

Linda, my talented friend who took on the awesome, 'rush' job of editing this entire book. I have to admit I gasped when I saw the amount of corrections, but one of the things I admire most about you is your eye for perfection. So I dove into rewrite heaven. You helped make this book what it is today – Thank you!

Laurie and Kate at Kensington, thanks for allowing me to print a preview of WINNER TAKE ALL. You are the best!

I'd like to thank my mother who performed the thankless job of motherhood expertly and without complaint. You have this way of turning injustice or obstacles into learning experiences. You always look at the glass as if it's half full, and you find the good in everyone. I don't know how you do it. I've learned so much from you. Most of all, you've taught me how to be a good mother. I hope I do half as good a job as you've done. I love you.

And thank you, God, for my two beautiful children. It's probably way more than I deserve. They are absolutely, without a doubt, the best gifts in my life.

For Marshall and Emily:

May you always know the pleasure you have brought to my life. Every smile, every kiss, every hug is a priceless gift you give me daily and that I will cherish forever.

Don't ever doubt how much you were wanted. Although you had no choice about joining our family, (a higher, wiser power made that decision for all of us), I want you to know you are right where you belong.

Reach for the stars as you make your way along the path of life. As long as you follow your dreams and believe in yourself, you will always be a success.

Remember that I'll always be there to support your aspirations. If you ever lose your way, reach back and take my hand until you have the strength to continue on your own.

And most importantly, remember that **I love you.**

A FAMILY FOR RAFFI

Published by
Pristine Publishing
P.O. Box 10816
San Bernardino, Ca. 92423

ETERNAL books published by Pristine Publishing.

This novel is a work of fiction. Names, characters, places, and incidents either are the product of the author's imagination or are used fictitiously. Any resemblance to actual persons, living or dead, events, or locales is entirely coincidental.

Rios, Lara, 1967-
A family for Raffi / Lara Rios. – 1st ed.
p. cm.
LCCN 2001090476
ISBN 1-931627-00-2

1. Adoption–Fiction. 2. Los Angeles (Calif.)–Fiction. 3. Family life–Fiction. 4. Love stories.
I.Title.

PS3568.I5895F36 2001 813'.6
QBI01-700586

ISBN 1-931627-00-2

First Eternal Printing: October 2001
10 9 8 7 6 5 4 3 2 1

Printed in the United States of America

Chapter preview of WINNER TAKE ALL by Lara Rios, forthcoming book to be published January 2002 by Encanto Books, an imprint of Kensington Publishing Corp. Printed by permission of the publisher.

CHAPTER ONE

"Hey! What do you think you're doing?" Dale Curtis crossed the luxurious, expertly maintained Pacific Sands Country Club lawn.

The raggedy little boy bent over the spectacular welcoming flower bed at the entrance of the hall looked up in alarm. He stood abruptly with a handful of pulled flowers in his filthy fist. The dirt under his fingernails had obviously been packed in from digging, but from the look of the boy, Dale guessed he'd already had enough dirt under there to make little difference if he added more. His unkept appearance angered Dale. What parent would let their child run around like that?

The boy looked like he might bolt at any second.

"I asked you a question. What are you doing

here and who gave you the right to pull those flowers and destroy private property?"

"I, I din't do notin'." The boy's expression turned belligerent.

"Raffi! What's going on, sweetie?" A female voice called from behind them.

Dale watched an athletic, young woman, who looked just as unkept as the boy, marching toward them. She gave Dale an apprehensive look then turned her attention to the boy.

"I din't do notin'," the boy repeated to her this time.

"What do you call those flowers in your hands?" Dale challenged.

"They're for you." The boy held out the fist full of flowers to the woman.

Her face softened and she bent down on one knee. "That's so sweet, Raffi. How can I ever thank you?" She accepted the flowers and kissed his dirty cheek.

"Thank him?" Dale inhaled sharply. "Is this your kid?"

The woman tilted her head, glancing at him. She patted the boy's head full of long, black curls, and stood to face Dale. "My name is Tamara, and yes, he's with me."

Dale ignored her outstretched hand, examining instead her torn, stained jeans, about two sizes too big for her, and her equally spotted, once white, T-shirt with the logo 'just do it' written across her chest. "You and your son do not belong here. Now I suggest you leave before I have you thrown out."

Tamara's full, voluptuous lips curved into a start of a smile. "He just pulled a few flowers. It didn't hurt anyone. You don't have to be so nasty about it."

"He yelled to me," Raffi pouted, reaching for Tamara's hand.

She took his small hand into the protective cover of hers. "Don't worry, sweetie, they can afford more flowers."

"Is that what you teach your son?" Dale asked, getting angrier by the second. He was tired of people who didn't teach their kids to take any responsibility for their actions. "Stealing from rich people is okay?"

Tamara tossed back her unruly brown hair and held the boy close to her leg. "Look mister, he didn't steal. Haven't you ever picked a flower for someone?"

"No, I usually buy them like I'm supposed to."

She brought the uneven bouquet to her nose, sniffed, and closed her eyes, bringing a look of pure ecstasy to her face.

Dale was unnerved at the way his body reacted to her simple yet sensual act.

"Mmm, you ought to try picking some yourself someday." She opened her eyes and treated him to a sexy, wide smile.

Dale looked at the boy who turned his face away, focusing instead on the opulent angel fountain in the middle of the flower garden. Dale felt some sympathy for the child. What chance did he have to grow up right, if this was what he had for a mother? "How did you get here?" he asked Tamara.

"Car," she said.

"Which is . . . ?"

"Over there." She let her hand float upwards and her index finger flicked up.

A piece of junk, Volkswagen bug, with half its paint peeled off, sat abandoned on the red curb.

Dale sighed. "Well, get back in it and leave."

"It died. I expected it to eventually since it hasn't been running well, but I didn't know it would be today. I'll call a mechanic to come fix it. Don't worry."

He wasn't worried, just annoyed. What was she doing driving in a private country club anyway? At the board of directors meeting last week, they had discussed getting better security, perhaps installing electric gates or closed circuit cameras. In past years such measures hadn't been necessary. A couple of patrolling security guards had been enough, but lately vandals snuck inside and had gotten caught in the pools, tennis courts, or strolling through the property. Of course, he'd always pictured the vandals as punk teenagers, not poor mothers with little boys.

"I'll call a tow truck. A mechanic will cost you a fortune if he has to come out here to work."

"No thanks, Prince Charming, I'll call my

mechanic. Come on Raffi, let's go." She headed for her car.

Dale followed behind. "Stay off the grounds while you wait."

She ignored him and continued to stroll leisurely toward the VW Bug.

Dale watched the sexy sway of her hips and imagined how much better she'd look if she wore better fitting clothes. His entire body temperature rose a few degrees. He followed a respectable distance behind her until she reached the curb.

She opened the back door. "Oh, damn. This isn't my day." The vinyl head liner lay on her back seat. She crawled in and began stretching it back up, taping it with double sided sticky tape.

Dale leaned inside, and shook his head. Her car was a hazard. "You need to reupholster it."

She laughed. "It's not worth the cost. The tape works well for months, then it falls again and I just add more tape."

He exhaled, part from frustration, part from annoyance, and reached his hand inside to help her hold one side while she taped the other. She sat on the car seat, while he leaned inside. Both had their hands on the roof. A corner slipped and they both reached for it at the same time. Dale leaned in too far, lost his balance, and fell inside - on her.

She fell hard on her back, a choked yelp escaping from her lips. Her arms landed above her head.

He stared into her obviously stunned eyes,

noticing the almost golden shade of brown, hating to admit how appealing she looked in this position.

She placed her hands on his shoulders and lifted her head. "I've had lot's of guys make strange passes at me, but this tops them all," she said a little breathless.

He'd apparently knocked the wind out of her. Dale braced his arms on either side of her head, lifting his upper body off her. "Don't flatter yourself. I prefer my women clean, with less denim, and more lace."

Tamara frowned and for the first time looked angry at his antagonism. "And when was the last time one of those women gave you a night you couldn't forget?"

Dale felt her shift under him, parts of her rubbing intimately against his already aroused body. He lifted himself off her. "I'll let security know you're here. If your mechanic doesn't get here within the hour, I'll have you towed away."

Tamara watched that arrogant, pampered, rich jerk walk away in his two hundred dollar golf shirt and hand tailored tan slacks. His shoes alone probably cost half of her weekly salary. In fact, the hard earned couple thousand dollars she made a month, he probably threw away in a day.

Every time she met one of these obnoxiously wealthy men, she remembered why she had chosen to leave her family's money behind, and had built a life separate from these types of people. For the most part, she stayed as far away as she could. Unfortunately, today she couldn't miss her best friend's bridal shower, so she'd put her personal dislike aside.

Tamara took her cell phone out of her purse, called her mechanic, asked him to fix the car then tow it to her work place. Then she took little Raffi to the women's locker room to wash his face and hands. She signed him up for swimming lessons for the afternoon, so she could attend the shower. Only then did she herself shower and go to the beauty salon to have her make up applied, hair made up, and dress fitted.

She finished everything just in time for the start of the shower. When she walked in, she spotted Daphne already at the head of the table deep in conversation, waving her hands around as she talked.

Daphne smiled when she saw Tamara, excused herself, stood, and reached for Tamara's hands. "Oh Tam, how are you?"

Tamara kissed her friend on both cheeks and smiled. "I'm here."

"You sure are and I couldn't be more pleased."

"You look marvelous, as always, Daphne."

Daphne beamed and introduced Tamara to the others, although Tamara knew many of them already from previous functions. She politely greeted everyone, offering her fingertips for a handshake to the older aunts as a sign of respect.

The bridal shower was as oppressively formal as Tamara knew it would be. Tuxedoed waiters swarmed the tables, pouring iced water with lemon. As soon as Tamara sat, the first waiter approached her and asked, "Champagne?"

"Yes, please." Tamara shifted her shoulder so he could reach her glass more easily. If she were in one of her favorite, casual restaurants, she would have lifted the glass so the waiter could fill it, but in this setting, it wasn't proper for guests to acknowledge the waiters, much less help them.

Another waiter arrived seconds later with the menu choices. Tamara accepted the menu and placed it on her plate without looking at the items on the list.

Four long tables were placed in a horseshoe shape so everyone could see the guest of honor and each other. Tamara guessed about one hundred and fifty women were invited.

She made polite, inconsequential conversation with the ladies beside her.

"Still doing that social work job, Tamara?"

"Yes, I am."

"Isn't that sweet? Tamara's so kind hearted. She works with the poor," the woman said in a type of hushed manner as if she were telling a dirty joke.

"Ohhh," the other women said trying to hide the distaste and lack of understanding from their faces.

Tamara smiled and explained what she did. They all nodded and smiled back. Tamara could tell from their faces they understood even less after she explained it than before. She resisted the urge to sigh. Why did she waste her breath on these obviously superficial women?

The meal was exquisite, the champagne plentiful, the atmosphere extravagant in every way. Tamara noticed the bouquets of yellow Angel trumpets and purple crocus in beds of baby's breath adorning the tables. Above, golden and Ruby Pothos hung from beams, decorating the ceiling and adding an open, outdoorsy ambiance to the room. The flowers reminded her of Raffi and his thoughtful gesture. Of course, that brought to mind that hateful man who had made an already abused boy feel even worse for attempting to perform a kind act.

What did Raffi know about flowers and which were okay to pick and which weren't? Easily three or four thousand dollars worth of flowers adorned this room alone. What was the harm in Raffi picking a few from the garden? Tamara shook off the unkind feelings she had for the mean-spirited jerk. She'd kept her cool out there so why dwell on it now? She would take Raffi one of these bouquets when she left the shower, she decided.

After the drawn out meal, the shallow conversations, and the classical music flowing from hidden speakers paused, Tamara was grateful for the intermission, allowing the waiters to remove the tables and bring the shower gifts. Comfortable chairs were brought for the ladies to sit and watch

Daphne open her gifts while they enjoyed cake and coffee.

The break gave Tamara a chance to walk around and stretch. She set out for the head of the table to speak with the one person she cared about here. "I had your gift shipped, Daphne," Tamara explained to her friend as she took her hand.

"Tamara, I know how busy you are. Don't worry about it."

"It's for your new house. I had it sent there."

Daphne's mother joined them and they excitedly talked about the wedding and their honeymoon cruise to Europe.

"When will *you* get married, Tamara?" The older woman clasped Tamara's arm and slid her hand down its length, raising Tamara's fingers. "No ring yet."

"Not yet, Edna. I'm too busy to find a husband."

Edna waved her hand in distaste. "Too busy with that dreadful job, I take it?"

"I'm afraid so, Edna. It takes all my time, but it's important. Lots of children depend on me."

"Let them depend on someone else, I say. Your poor mother must be horrified to tell her friends what you do for a living."

Tamara knew her parents weren't very happy about her choice of work, but at least they were outwardly supportive. They never cared much what she did anyway. "I doubt Celeste discusses me over tea with her friends."

"And if she does, I'm sure she's as proud of her as I am." Daphne smiled. "Oh, there's Dale," she said, touching her mother's shoulder.

Tamara glanced across the room and noticed the man from the flower garden strolling their way. She felt bitter distaste building inside her at the sight of that horrid man. "You know him?"

"Know him?" Daphne laughed. "He's my brother Dale. I told you about him in college, remember?"

Brother? *That* spoiled socialite was Daphne's kind, charming brother Dale? Boy, did he have Daphne fooled.

Dale strolled toward them with the grace of a giraffe, nodding politely to women along the way; women who responded with swooning smiles. Elvis would not have gotten a better reaction. Tamara admitted he wasn't bad looking. No, actually, he was attractive. His wavy, blond hair fit his coloring perfectly. His face was almost too beautiful for a man, yet it had a hard, masculine edge. His height, maybe six feet, weight, body frame . . . everything well proportioned. Yes, she could see what women might like about Dale, as long as he didn't open his mouth and spew out all his venom, that is.

Daphne hugged him and then Edna did the same. Dale's olive green eyes shone with appreciation as he looked at the two women, then his eyes shifted to Tamara. His smile, coloring, and good humor faded.

Tamara noticed the awareness of Dale's response to her on Daphne's face. Daphne looked from Dale to Tamara, shifting her glance back and forth a couple of times, then introduced Tamara to Dale.

"Nice to meet you, Dale." She held out her hand. She remembered doing the same outside earlier, and he refused to take it, refused to touch her.

This time he did accept her fingers, squeezing them almost painfully. "Likewise."

"I didn't know men were invited to bridal showers," Tamara said sweetly, refusing to flinch or pull her hand away.

"He's not a guest," Daphne intervened jovially. "He's a board member here at Pacific Sands and helped Mother make the arrangements for the shower."

"I see." Tamara nodded, keeping her smile in place. "A board member. Such an important position must make you feel like you own the club."

His jaw stiffened and moved from side to side. His thumb slid over her knuckles, and she finally relented and glanced at their still joined hands. Ahh, yes, one more beautiful attribute for Dale Curtis, strong, large hands with sleek, long fingers, just like Daphne.

At her inspection, he released her hand. "I do my best to keep it the upper class treasure that it is."

Ouch. "You do a marvelous job. I've been a member for years precisely for that reason, Dale."

Daphne and her mother excused themselves.

They must have sensed they were being practically ignored. Once they left, the same frown she'd seen by the flower garden returned to his face. He buried his hands in his trousers, and ran a sweeping glance down her cocktail dress.

A lacy outer layer which went down to her knees, covered the white satin fabric inside. "Enough lace for you, Dale?"

As if her words were an invitation, he stepped closer, lifted a hand from his pocket, and reached around her to press his palm on her back. "Don't tell me you had this hidden in your car." His firm, warm hand moved from her shoulder blades, down her spine, and stopped at her lower back, in such a bold, intimate manner, she had to fight not to jump back and put some distance between them.

"Sure, didn't you see it in that brown paper bag on the floor of the back seat when you were laying on top of me?"

He began to walk, forcing her to move her legs and go with him, leading her out of the main hall. He let up the pressure on her back when they turned out to a veranda covered with vines of fragrant, white trumpet shaped Easter lilies. Then he faced her. "When I was laying on top of you, I was trying not to touch anything to keep from getting as dirty as you were."

She smiled at him. "Don't worry, Dale, you were a perfect gentleman. You didn't soil yourself at all."

He took a step away from her, obviously getting flustered if the color rising on his face meant what she thought it did.

"Who are you?"

"I'm your little sister's best friend, she told you."

"My sister doesn't hang out with sloppy women with filthy mouths."

Tamara nodded. "You're right. She hangs out with over indulgent, high society types."

"And you're trying to tell me that's what you are?"

"Not when I can help it, but I'm afraid it's in the breeding."

"Meaning?"

"Meaning my ancestors owned half of Los Angeles and our family has been selling off bits of land ever since, making them filthy rich for doing nothing."

Dale frowned, keeping his eyes glued on her. "Did Daphne say your last name was Cassetti?"

She smiled. "She did, and it is."

"As in Cassetti Inc., as in Cassetti Cultural Center in down town, as in The Cassetti's?"

"Surprise."

Dale looked baffled. "Yeah, you could say that again."

She shrugged. "You see, you have nothing to worry about. Daphne hasn't lowered herself and become friends with an unworthy commoner. I'm just another spoiled rich girl."

He moved closer and gazed at the curls scattered around her head.

The hair stylist had done a terrific job,

Tamara had to admit. Her hair had been a filthy mess. Now it was pinned up with strands let loose for effect.

He reached for a curl and wrapped it around his index finger. For the first time, he gave her a lopsided grin. "A beautiful rich girl at that."

She smiled back even though she felt like slapping him. A few hours ago, she had been the scourge of humanity and he'd practically run her off the grounds. She really couldn't stand men like him. "Oh Dale, you're going to make me blush."

He let her hair go and frowned. "Why were you driving that sorry excuse for a car, which was towed by the way, and who was the miserable looking kid, and why--"

"Oh give it a rest, Dale. I'm a social worker. I just pulled that *miserable* four-year old child from an abusive home, and he has clung to me like glue. He's afraid of everyone, so I can't leave him alone yet or put him in a foster home."

Dale's eyes widened. "A social worker? Rich girls don't become social workers."

"Yeah, I know, your mother tells me that every time I see her."

"Never mind my mother. Why --?"

"Because I chose to."

His eyes returned to normal, then actually began to narrow. "So this boy, you brought him with you today because you had no where to leave him?"

"Right. I've been working on his case for months. Each time Raffi has been in worse condition and more terrified. I couldn't miss the shower, but I couldn't leave Raffi either."

"So where is he now?"

"Swimming. He's probably a lot cleaner now, so you won't have to wrinkle your nose at him."

"I only stopped him from doing something wrong. You're the one who should be teaching him to behave properly."

"Look, Dale." She poked his chest with her acrylic fingernail. "Don't stand here in this multi-million dollar country club with your designer everything and tell me how to deal with a poor, abused boy. Maybe you should learn a thing or two about how to speak to the other two-thirds of humanity."

"Can't you admit he did something wrong?"

"Yes. He should have given you back those flowers, shoved them into your nice, expensive pants pockets."

Dale shook his head. "I won't apologize, Tamara. And look at yourself. Aren't you being a little hypocritical? How much did your dress cost *you*?"

Tamara did what she could, but she couldn't deny who she was. Yes, it was hypocritical, perhaps, but she was part of two worlds, and neither one understood the other. "I need to return to your sister's shower. Nice meeting you after all these years," she said in the sweetest voice possible.

He placed his hand on her shoulder to detain her. "Why did you let me believe you were some poor, white trash woman?"

She stared at him for the longest time, her golden eyes seemed to delve into his conscience, making him uncomfortable. "I never described myself that way. Funny how you decided that was who I was."

"Do you blame me?"

"Oh yes, Dale. I blame you."

He invaded her personal space, and slid his hand behind her neck, rubbing his thumb along the elegant line of her throat. God, she cleaned up good. "Give me a chance to make it up to you."

"Why?"

Why indeed. Maybe because she'd aroused something in him that had been long dead. In a bold move, he bowed his head and brushed her lips. They were so soft and moist.

A small breath escaped through her lips. She didn't pull away and her soft acquiescence gave him encouragement.

He kissed her again, letting his fingers slide up into her thick, golden brown hair which smelled of sweet Vanilla. She placed her hands on his shoulders and applied just enough pressure to make him lift his head.

"Can I drive you home after the shower?" he whispered against her lips.

"I've arranged for a limo."

"Let me take you home, Tamara."

She moved away from him, apparently unaffected by his kiss. "I like men who wear more denim and less wool and cashmere. Good bye,

Dale."

He sat at the bar in the back of the room, occasionally sipping his double whiskey, knowing he should return to his office at Quest Air. He had met his obligation to his mother and sister. The rest of the shower would proceed without problems. Yet he stayed and watched Tamara from afar, both intrigued and aroused. He wanted her in a way he hadn't wanted anyone or anything in a long time. He had wanted her when he thought she was a poor street woman and had been angry with himself. But now that he knew she was from his social class, his desire was her ten times greater. Not that he wouldn't have slept with her if she had been poor, but he would have felt guilty. He wasn't into using people, and that's how he would have felt.

But now . . . he stretched his legs out in front of him, he didn't have to worry about turning a poor woman's head. Tamara, he could safely seduce, have a good time with, and not feel like he owed her anything.

She was indignant now, of course, because she perceived him as cold hearted and unsympathetic and he understood why, but he would show her she was wrong about him. He swirled the ice in his glass and smiled to himself. Yes, it had been too long since he'd allowed himself the pleasure of courting a woman. And he definitely enjoyed a good chase.

After the shower when she was saying her goodbyes to Daphne, he approached her again.

"Are you leaving, Tamara?"

She glanced at him, a look of surprise on her face. "Yes, it's time. You don't mind if I take one of these bouquets for Raffi, do you?"

Dale fought a smile. "They belong to the club."

"Dale?" Daphne looked incensed. "Of course, she can take a centerpiece if she likes."

Dale shrugged. "Yes, of course you may, Tamara. May I walk you to get Raffi?"

She began to shake her head, but Daphne interrupted, saying it was a great idea. A waiter brought her a wrap and Dale helped her cover her shoulders, purposely caressing the base of her neck.

Tamara looked unnerved and it pleased him. The little flirt had a great time teasing him earlier so now it was his turn. As they walked along the wood plank walkway to the gym area, he placed his arm around her shoulder. "Do you think you could wear a little more lace, and I could wear a little more denim?"

"I'm not interested in you, Dale."

"You're lying."

"I'm not lying. I don't go out with guys who belong to country clubs." She lifted her chin and gazed at him. "The last thing I want is to marry into this same group and be stuck being a high society wife. No, thank you."

"I wasn't offering marriage."

She smiled. "What do you want, a one night stand?"

He pulled her closer to his side. "Sure, why not?"

"I'll think about it," she said in a way which told him she wouldn't think about it at all.

They reached the gym and a now clean Raffi with still moist, shiny black hair parted on the side, greeted them with apprehensive eyes. "He gonna yell to me again?"

"No. I won't let him, Raffi." She held out the centerpiece. "Look, I brought *you* flowers this time."

He smiled, his dark eyes brightened, and reached for her hand. "You look pretty, Tamara."

"Thank you, sweetie. You look tired. Do you want to come to my place tonight?"

Raffi nodded.

Dale wished she had made him the same offer. He bent to Raffi's level. "I didn't mean to scare you today. It's just that if someone pulls out the flowers, the gardeners have to come and plant new ones, and they cost a lot of money. You understand?"

Raffi nodded, then looked up to Tamara once again. "We go now?"

"Yes, sweetie." She glanced at Dale. "Again, I'm glad we met, Dale. Daphne used to talk about you incessantly in college and read your letters to me."

Dale stood, not knowing exactly how he felt about his sister sharing specific personal details with Tamara. He knew nothing about her. But he smiled. "I've enjoyed meeting you as well."

"I'm sure I'll see you at Daphne's wedding."

"I hope it won't be that long before we see each other again."

She offered a warm, genuine smile. "One night stands aren't my thing, Dale. Especially not with my best friend's brother."

CHAPTER TWO

The next day Dale drilled his sister for details about Tamara. It appeared Tamara hadn't lied. Whether she liked it or not, she was very much a wellborn lady. She'd attended an all girl academy with Daphne, then they roomed together at Stanford. Daphne called her a dreamer who was embarrassed by all her privilege. Dale didn't care what Tamara thought of the privileged class as a whole, as long as she didn't hold her opinions against *him*.

Dale bought a pair of Levi's and a vulgar looking T-shirt. Then he drove to the child welfare office. Inside, the atmosphere was pure chaos. Phones rang, people shouted, desks were piled high with manila file folders over stuffed with paperwork. He wove between desks unnoticed, then he spotted Tamara sitting on her desk, her feet on her chair, and the phone receiver at her ear.

"I understand your frustration. Yes I do," Tamara said into the phone with the same, calm patience she had showed him when he was harassing her at Pacific Sands .

"Don't you think I'd be the first one to pull her out of that house if I could? Well, I would, and I will, but I have to follow procedure. I -- hello?"

She pulled the receiver away from her ear, shook her head and twisted her torso to hang up, and then she noticed Dale.

He gave her a sympathetic grin. "Having a bad day?"

She stared at him with no expression for a couple of seconds then smiled. "Every day is a bad day around here, Dale."

"I'm sorry to hear that. Perhaps I can take you to lunch, and you can get away from the problems for a while."

She rubbed her hands on her jean clad thighs and seemed to mull over his invitation, while making an obvious appraisal of his clothes. As if she'd made a sudden decision, she jumped off her desk and opened its bottom drawer, pulling out her purse. "Come on, I'll buy *you* lunch."

They went to a crowded, noisy deli where they had to shout their order to the harried man behind the counter, then stand and wait until their number was called. When it finally was, a bag of chips was hurled at them and an overfilled cardboard cup was pushed into their hands.

They found a corner, bar style table and a

couple of high backed stools to sit at.

Dale cast a glance around the place. "You brought me here for retribution, didn't you?

Tamara bit into her sandwich and he watched her luscious lips become wet and oily from the dressing dripping off the edges of the roll. The sight made him want to touch his lips to hers.

She chewed with a hint of a smile on her provocative mouth. "Take a bite, you'll love it," she said between the first and second mouthful.

Dale dragged his attention from her and began to eat. The sandwich was good, but it was a sandwich, no big deal, certainly not worth putting up with all the commotion. But he kept his opinion to himself. She watched him as she ate, and Dale tried to pretend he didn't notice.

"How's your sister?" Tamara asked finally when only a few bites of her meal were left.

"Fine, I guess."

"I gather she told you where I work."

Dale shook his head. "I just looked for the most run down, dirty building I could find, and knew you'd be inside."

Tamara nodded apparently taking his teasing in stride. She lifted a chip to her mouth, pausing before eating it. "So, why did you bother?"

He took the chip out of her hand and fed it to her.

She accepted the chip, chewed, then licked the salt off her lips, stirring Dale's own appetite.

He lowered his hand from her face and covered her right hand. "I bothered because you looked very good in lace."

"I don't wear it often."

"You could."

She pulled her hand out of his, the look of amusement and teasing gone from her face. "Dale, I told you I wasn't interested."

"You lied."

She crossed her arms across her chest. "Why would I do that?"

"Because you think you don't want to involve yourself with a rich guy, but you're being overly simplistic. Just because a guy has money or belongs to a country club doesn't make him one dimensional."

"No, but when *he* all but throws an apparent down on her luck, poor mother and child out of *his* country club because *their* kind doesn't belong there, it makes *her* not interested." Tamara stood and lifted her purse off the back of her stool and onto her shoulder.

Dale didn't know what he saw in her, maybe it was her wildness, but he couldn't give up. "How is Raffi, by the way?"

Her features softened, but she eyed him warily like she didn't believe Dale would care. That annoyed him even more. What kind of heartless creep did she think he was?

"He's all right. He has nightmares, and is apathetic in school, but that should fade with time." She shrugged. "Before long, he'll be put up for adoption."

Poor kid. Dale couldn't understand anyone

mistreating a child. When he had seen him by the garden picking those flowers, he'd thought the boy looked neglected and was sickened to think a parent could be so irresponsible. But Dale had no idea his home life had been so bad. "Where is he now?"

Tamara pointed toward the door. "Let's get out of here."

He followed her out. She hadn't answered his question, but that was okay. It was none of his business anyway. They strolled back to her building. She was quiet, somewhere in her own world. Dale took her hand, and she didn't resist. He caressed her inner wrist with his thumb, amazed that just touch of her skin had the power to arouse him. "I'm sorry we got off to a bad start, Tamara, but I'm attracted to you and would like to see more of you."

She shook her head. "I don't think so."

He stopped walking and pulled her up against a store window away from the flow of pedestrians. "Give me one good reason, why not." Their bodies were close, and he smelled the scent of lilacs coming from her hair.

"We have nothing in common."

"Sure we do."

"Name one."

He didn't really know her, but he had to think of something. "We like my sister."

Tamara laughed. "Your sister is a good, loving person."

"So am I."

"That's not what I've seen." Tamara's eyes darkened.

"Give me another chance, you'll change your mind."

"Dale, I'm definitely the wrong girl for you, trust me."

"I'd rather trust me, and my body's telling me I want you."

"Your body? You're going to let a physical attraction guide you?"

Dale moved in closer, and reached around to caress her back and pull her against him. She didn't resist nor did she bring her arms to him to embrace him.

"Dale, come on. Back off." She smiled as if she thought his little seduction scene was cute.

He tilted his face and lowered his lips to hers. He touched them with the tip of his tongue as he had wanted to do in the deli. They were still a little salty and silky soft from the Italian dressing on her sandwich. "Kiss me," he whispered then locked his lips to hers and felt a surge of satisfaction when she did return his kiss, meeting his tongue with hers. Her hands went to his hips and she hooked her thumbs on the belt loops of his jeans.

Dale deepened the kiss, thoroughly exploring every crevice of her warm mouth. He also pulled her harder against him, making her aware how attracted he was to her.

She began to withdraw though, and it happened a little at a time. She removed her hands from his hips, then her face moved away from his, and only her lower body stayed pressed against him.

"Man, Dale, you don't give up easily, do you?" She braced her hands on his upper arms.

"Come to my place."

"You're very presumptuous too."

"Come on, Tamara." He rubbed his hands along her shoulders. "I can feel you're attracted to me."

"That doesn't mean I want to jump in your bed."

"You don't?"

"No." Now, she pushed completely away.

"Damn."

She gave a shaky laugh. "Daphne never told me you were so . . ."

"Desirable?"

"I was going to say brazen."

"I'm sure there's a lot my sister hasn't told you about me. So what do you say you find out for yourself?"

She shrugged. "Fine, but don't say I didn't warn you, Dale Curtis. I'm not a Barbie doll and I never want to be one, do you understand?"

"Well, I'm not exactly Ken."

"But you are." She shook her head and sighed. "That's the problem."

Tamara's job was draining, and having the added burden of caring for Raffi in her home made her regret telling Dale she'd see him. She really didn't see the point anyway, she and Dale were total opposites. She had been curious when he showed up at her office, tempted when he began to kiss her, but to take this any further was senseless. Though he *was* a great kisser and turned her knees to rubber. She rationalized accepting his invitation, telling herself he was Daphne's brother and since Daphne was her friend, Dale could be too. Friends, that's all. What could it hurt?

In fact, compared to dealing with Raffi, Dale was totally easy. She tried to explain to Raffi how he would have to stay with a foster family until he was adopted, but he refused to listen. He threw his dinner all over her kitchen floor and ran into the guest room where he was staying for the time being. Raffi was afraid to trust many adults and the thought of going into a foster home of strangers, terrified him. She understood, but what could she do?

She was cleaning the broken plate and Spaghetti-O's when Dale rang her bell. She dumped the dirty paper towel into the trash and went to open the door, hoping she didn't reek of tomato sauce though she knew she did. "Hi, come in," Tamara muttered and returned to the kitchen, leaving him standing outside her door.

Once she finished, she washed her hands and went out to her living room where she found him examining her trinkets. Most were modeling statues she made in college art classes. They were truly terrible.

"Sorry, I was cleaning some spilt food."

He looked up and gave her a magnificent smile. His jeans were gone and he was dressed in casual slacks and a button up shirt. Tamara hadn't had time to get ready yet.

"I didn't know you were the clumsy type."

Know. That was the operative word, he didn't know anything about her. "If you don't mind waiting a bit, I'll go get ready."

His lips moved into a crooked smile. "You mean you're not going like that?"

"I think I can do a little better than this." Since she never knew what kind of day she'd have at work, she always dressed like she was going to go play at the city dump. A few times, she literally had to track kids down in alley ways between abandoned buildings.

He sauntered over to her and hooked his fingers on the waist of her pants. For a second she thought he was going to undo the top button and a threatening thrill shot through her body. But he tugged on her pants just a little and winked at her. "You could take it all off, and we could stay here."

Tamara pried his fingers from her waistband. "Actually, I planned on us staying here."

"Really?" He looked shocked, and suddenly he wasn't so flirtatious anymore. "I made dinner reservations."

She could see Dale had a certain order to how the night should proceed. "Well, I expected Raffi would be in a foster home by now, but there were complications."

"Raffi? What does he have to do with our date?"

"I'm still supervising him. He's been staying here with me."

Dale looked completely surprised.

Tamara sat on the couch and suggested he do the same, but he didn't.

"What kind of date will it be with a kid in the next room?"

"A nice quiet one, with a candlelight dinner, soft music, and a lot of talking."

He placed his hands on his hips and looked gorgeous. Tamara hoped he would understand.

"You should have told me that kid was staying here."

A slow, cold anger started to build inside her, just as it had at the country club. The way he said 'that kid', as if Raffi were from a loathsome subhuman species. "Does it make a difference?"

His stare was almost hostile. "What is it with you, Tamara? Why the hell are you doing this kind of work, dressing like a slob, and living in a run down apartment in this part of town?"

She sat on the edge of the couch, her hands gripped the cushions, and stared back. "What should I be doing, Dale?" She kept her voice calm, empty of the strong emotions brewing inside. "Hanging out with my own people?"

"Yes. Don't you care about your family? You know," he pointed a finger at her and scowled. "My mother says you're quite an embarrassment to them."

Tamara stood. "Get out."

"You're throwing me out?"

She strode to the door, opened it, and waved her arm out.

Dale's face was red, but he came toward her.

She purposely averted her gaze, afraid of the hot feeling threatening just below the surface. So she was surprised when he grabbed her elbow, pulled her away from the door, and slammed it shut. "You're doing this on purpose, aren't you, just so you can say you were right, that you and I have no chance?"

"Oh, sure, I'm making you act like a rude, arrogant, selfish--"

"Stop! Leave her alone!" A small, constricted voice came from the hallway. Raffi came running toward them and began kicking and hitting Dale with all his might.

Both Dale and Tamara were stunned. Dale reacted first, lifting the child and placing him on the couch. "Calm down. It's okay, Raffi. It's okay."

The boy cried and called him more curse words than Tamara remembered existed. "If you hurt her, I'll kill you."

Tamara's breath caught in her throat, shocked by the young boy's intensity. She sat next to Raffi on the couch and pulled him into an embrace. "He wasn't hurting me, sweetie."

Dale placed a hand on the boy's leg. "Raffi, I'm sorry. I'd never hurt her. I like her, I came over to have dinner with her . . . and with you."

Tamara held the boy's head against her

bosom and rested her chin on top of his head. She glanced at Dale from the corner of her eye. "That's right, Raffi. Dale came over to apologize for snapping at you about the flowers and to have dinner with us."

Dale smiled. "So, do you forgive me?"

The boy pulled away from Tamara. "No, I don't like you. Go away."

Tamara saw Dale's chest deflate. "Raffi, that wasn't nice. I *do* like Dale. He's my best friend's brother, and he's really sorry for what happened the other day."

"But he'll hurt you." Raffi's pleading face almost scared Tamara into agreeing with Raffi.

Dale might indeed hurt her, but not the way Raffi meant. Dale was an odd intrusion into her life. A complex mixture which both excited and terrified her. How long had it been since someone had pursued her this aggressively? Maybe never.

She shook her head. "Not everyone hurts other people, Raffi. Promise me you'll try to trust him."

Raffi shook his head.

"Do you trust *me*?"

The boy hung his head. "No, you want to get rid of me too."

"I don't want to get rid of you. I can't keep you, sweetie. I have to let you be adopted. It's my job."

Raffi didn't look convinced, but he turned to Dale who watched the exchange with a strange expression on his face. "You can stay, but I'm not hungry."

Dale nodded. "How about if we skip dinner and go out for some ice cream? Would you like that?"

Raffi shrugged. "I guess."

Tamara smiled at both guys. "Well, ice cream sounds terrific to me. Let's go."

Dale buckled both Raffi and Tamara into his Mercedes and drove clear out of town to Beverly Hills. He bought them ice cream and they strolled along the recently rain saturated street looking in shop windows.

Tamara loved cold, chocolate ice cream on chilly days. Probably because she enjoyed going against the grain.

Dale draped his arm on her shoulder. "I didn't mean to spook him."

She shrugged, surprised at how natural his arm felt on her shoulder. "I should have known better than to argue with him in the apartment. Most arguments he's witnessed have ended with someone going to the hospital, usually him."

Dale winced. "Poor kid."

Tamara lifted her face to get a better look at Dale. He was very attractive. He was also like a fish out of water when it came to understanding what her job - her life - was all about. She forgave him for sounding so selfish earlier. He couldn't have sympathy for something he had never been exposed to. "He'll be all right. . . eventually."

"He doesn't want to be adopted?"

"He doesn't want to leave me. Being in my

home has been the only peace and stability he's experienced since he was born."

"Can't you keep him until he's adopted?"

"I'm not a foster parent. I shouldn't have him now, but child welfare has made an exception because he's been so afraid of everyone else."

Dale nodded and hugged her closer. "You're an exceptional person, Tamara."

She placed her arm around his waist. Yes, he was forgiven. Later that evening, when Dale bought Raffi a book he saw in a store window, Tamara decided not only did she forgive Dale, but she would definitely go out on another date with him if he wanted - a real date.

But unfortunately, he didn't ask. When he dropped them off, he kissed her cheek and wished her luck with Raffi.

Tamara didn't sleep well that night or the next or the entire week. Damn Dale, why did he have to push himself into her life and get her thinking of romantic possibilities? She seldom dated anymore, and when she did they were friendly dinners which led no where. Dale made her remember what it was like to date someone who made her insides vaporize.

CHAPTER THREE

While throwing himself into his family business at Quest Air, Dale kept telling himself to get Tamara off his mind. She was all wrong for him. Although a kind person, and extremely good looking, she would never do. He wanted a woman who would accompany him to business dinners, and enjoy the lavish holiday parties both his company and his family hosted yearly.

Tamara made it clear she didn't care for that lifestyle. Still, he couldn't seem to get past those kind eyes of hers or that soothing voice. No wonder the boy felt so safe with her, she had a calming effect on people.

Dale managed to stay away for two weeks, then his curiosity won out, and he called her.

"Ms. Cassetti's desk. May I help you?"

"Hello, Ms. Cassetti. How have you been?"

The line was quiet for a few seconds. "Dale?"

"You recognized my voice. I knew this was true love."

She laughed. "Of course, what else could it be?"

His anxiety eased at the sound of her laughter. "What are you doing this weekend?"

"I've got a hot date."

Dale gripped his cell phone tighter. Hot date? He didn't like hearing those two words at all - unless she was talking about the two of them. "Nothing important then. How about we catch the end of the March winds and go sailing tomorrow? You, me, and Raffi."

Tamara laughed harder. "First of all, if I had a date, I wouldn't cancel it. Second, Raffi has been placed in a foster home."

"So, you don't have a date?"

"No, I was kidding. Thought it might make you furiously jealous, but obviously it didn't work."

He chuckled. "Oh, it worked. What's this about Raffi?"

"He was very unhappy, but he had to go to a foster home."

Dale felt a twinge of guilt at being relieved Raffi was gone, but the feeling faded as he realized he also felt sad for the boy. He had wanted to stay with Tamara so badly. Dale knew how difficult it had been for him, a grown man, not to call Tamara these past two weeks, it must have been pure hell for the boy. "How about we take him with us anyway?"

"Sailing?"

"Sure. Is he allowed to spend the day with us."

"Are you sure you want him to?"

No. He didn't want the kid to go with them, but he knew Tamara liked the boy. And he wanted to do something nice for them both. "I do."

"Well . . . I've got to check in periodically and see how he's doing. Why don't you meet me at the foster parent's house in the morning and we can leave from there?"

"Give me the address."

Dale drove to the middle class neighborhood. Raffi's new place was a small, square box of a house. Chain link enclosed the front yard, and bikes, tricycles, and other toys littered the grass. Dale checked his watch. Tamara said she would be here at ten, but her car was not parked outside the house.

He lifted the forked handle which made a shrill screech. He grimaced and let himself into the yard, hoping a rabid dog wouldn't jump out at him. No dog, materialized, and he made it all the way to the front door. Before he could knock, the door flew open and three kids who appeared to be around ten years old ran out, all talking at once. Dale watched the two boys and one girl run down the street.

He leaned inside the house, knocked on the

open door and called out, "Hello?"

No one answered. He called out again, saw a door bell, and pressed the button. It rang and rang, but still no one came to the door. Dale wondered if maybe the people were in the back yard. He walked into the living room which was just as littered with toys as the front yard. The TV blared, but no one was in the room. Dale walked through the house toward the back and looked out the den sliding glass door. No one was in the back yard. Again he called out but got no answer.

He was about to leave, but decided instead to walk down the hall and see if anyone was in the bedrooms. The house had four bedrooms from the look of it, and only one bathroom. He didn't see anyone in the bedrooms either.

Dale sighed. Who leaves a house empty and unlocked, with three young kids inside who obviously haven't learned to turn off the TV or any lights before leaving? Dale rubbed his temples and turned to leave, but he heard a faint moan. It came from behind the bed.

Dale hurried over and saw Raffi on the floor with his eyes closed. A large, steel, yellow truck about twice as big as his head lay on the floor next to him, and a huge red spot marked Raffi's forehead. Dale lifted the boy and placed him on the bed. "Raffi," he said and patted the boy's face.

Raffi moaned again and lifted his hand to his forehead. Then he opened his eyes, saw Dale leaning over him, and in a startled defensive move, pushed himself to a sitting position and slid backward, away from Dale.

"Hey Raffi, it's okay. What happened, kid?"

Raffi frowned and tears filled his eyes.

Dale's heart broke. Was it just him Raffi feared or was he afraid of everyone? "I came to pick you up and found you lying on the floor. No one else is in the house."

"Donny, trow the truck."

"Donny? He threw that truck at you?"

Raffi nodded. "Hit my head."

Dale looked down at the heavy, steel truck then at the red spot on Raffi's head. It hit him all right, and knocked him out. He placed his hand on Raffi's forehead. "That must have hurt."

Raffi nodded again.

"Is Donny a boy who lives here?"

"He hates me, and I hate him too."

"You guys fight a lot, huh?" Dale sat beside Raffi on the bed.

"He likes to beat me up."

"Have you told anyone?"

He shook his head. "Can't, he hurt me more. But I don't cry, even in night when he burn me with cigarettes and matches."

Dale tried not to show the shock or anger bubbling up inside him. His fingers fisted around the bed coverings. How could some bully be hurting this child and the care giver not notice? "Can you show me where he burns you?"

Raffi shrugged, then he pulled down his pajama bottoms which he still wore in the middle of the day, and on his hips were several burn marks.

"On my bottom feet too."

Dale looked at the soles of his feet and saw blisters formed by burns. He stood abruptly and rubbed his temples again. He forced his voice to remain calm when inside he fumed. "Get your things, we're leaving."

Raffi didn't move.

"Did you hear me?" He remembered not to raise his voice. "Oh forget it, we'll get new things, come on." Dale took the boy's hand and pulled him up.

Raffi followed him out meekly.

Dale checked his watch again as Raffi climbed into his car. Where the hell was Tamara? He called her at home and got her answering machine. She was probably on her way. He swore and hung up.

First he drove to a family doctor and had Raffi's head and burns checked. That taken care of, he took him to his condo and showed him to a guest room.

Raffi looked around, uncertain.

"What's the matter?" Dale asked.

"Noting."

"You can stay here as long as you want, Raffi. This will be your new room."

"Tamara won't let you keep me."

Keep him? That's not what Dale meant, he couldn't keep the boy. Well, what *did* he mean then? Dale didn't know, but he did know Raffi wasn't going back into any foster home. Tamara better get him adopted and fast. To the boy he only smiled and said, "You let me worry about Tamara."

He left the boy in the room, and called Tamara again. This time she answered.

"Are you out of your mind, Tamara?"

"Dale? Where were you this morning? I waited about an hour for you and –."

"What do you people do, take kids away from bad parents and then put them it worse situations?" He paced behind his sofa.

"What are you talking about?"

Her calm, patient voice only angered him, today. "I'm talking about that shit hole you stuck Raffi in."

"I know it's not one of the mansions you're used to living in, but I assure you--"

"Don't give me that, Tamara, I'm serious."

She sighed. "His foster mother has eight kids, and she's been doing this for years. She took him as a favor to me, Dale. What could possibly be upsetting you?"

"I just came back from visiting a doctor who treated Raffi for a concussion and cigarette burns, *that*'s what's upsetting me."

"What?" Now she sounded concerned. He could picture her straightening her back and holding the phone tightly against her ear.

Dale explained everything he'd seen or not seen inside the house and carefully detailed Raffi's condition.

"But how . . . ? This morning his foster mother said he was playing at a friend's house."

"No, when I got there he was passed out

beside his bed, and now he's at my place. She didn't even know I'd taken him. See what I mean?"

"You can't just pull a child out of a foster home, Dale. You have no authority. I'll have to investigate and see what happened."

"Fine, you investigate, and in the mean time, he'll stay here."

"You can't do that."

"Just watch me."

She sighed. "I'll find out what happened, and I'll be over later. Give me your address."

He gave her directions to his place. But as soon as he hung up, he called his lawyer. The lawyer told him he was crazy and not to get involved, but Dale already was involved. The day that boy pulled those flowers from Pacific Sands Country Club garden he'd become involved, dammit, with both Raffi and Tamara. Tamara might see this everyday, and it might have become old hat to her, but to Dale this situation was unacceptable.

By the time Tamara showed up late that afternoon, Dale and Raffi had already eaten an early dinner, and Raffi looked more at ease. When Raffi saw Tamara walk in, his eyes lit up for a second and then he lowered them. A frown appeared on his bruised forehead.

She looked fresh, smelled of rich vanilla, and her hair was swept up away from her face. She wore a pair of white Capris, a light tank top, and sandals - all evidence she had planned to spend a relaxing day on his sailboat. Dale couldn't resist staring.

She didn't wait to be invited in, she entered, caressing Dale's forearm as she walked inside his home. "Hey, sweetie," she said to Raffi.

Raffi turned away from her.

She looked at Dale and smiled.

He thought she'd be hurt by Raffi's rejection, but she wasn't.

"Wow, Dale you have a nice place."

"Thank you."

"Much nicer than mine." Her gaze returned to Raffi's profile. "Isn't that right, Raffi?"

No answer from Raffi.

"Yes, well, I think it is. Is it a family condo, Dale?"

He took her hand and led her to the couch where Raffi stood with his back to them. "No, I bought it when I moved out of my parent's home in Palos Verdes."

She sat so close to Dale, their thighs and shoulders touched. She looked up and Dale looked into her eyes. She moved her lips and mouthed, 'thank you.'

He wanted to dip his head and kiss those lips in answer, but instead he nodded and looked at the boy. "Raffi, I called Tamara over so we could discuss where you're going to be staying. Don't you want to talk to her?"

He pivoted and shot an accusing glance at

her. "I want to go wit you again."

Tamara leaned forward on the couch. "I'm sorry, Raffi."

Dale wondered what she was sorry for, putting him in a substandard home or because she wouldn't take him in again.

"You can keep me if you want." Raffi's high pitched voice cracked.

"That's not true, I explained it all to you before."

There was that patient tone again, but Raffi wasn't buying it this time. He kicked the sofa and looked away with tears in his eyes.

Dale remembered what Raffi said about not crying when that Donny kid burned or hit him, but Dale suspected he would cry if Tamara didn't agree to take him back. *Yep, you're learning at a young age, boy. It's always women who can make you cry.*

Dale decided to intervene. "Well, I've decided Tamara isn't going to take you anywhere, Raffi. You're staying here."

"I want to go with her."

"If you stay with me, you'll see lots of Tamara. We'll go see her together, I promise."

Raffi seemed to think it over, obviously weighing the advantages of the proposal.

Dale saw his frown slowly disappear, and then Raffi nodded his head.

Tamara looked from Dale to Raffi, then smiled. "For tonight it'll be okay. Dale, may I speak with you alone?"

Dale turned the television on for Raffi, and

led Tamara into his bedroom.

She glanced at the bed first then at the other items in his room, before turning to him. "I appreciate . . . I know you're trying to help . . . ."

Dale closed and locked the door, then he hooked his fingers behind her neck and took the kiss he'd been wanting since he opened the front door. She placed her hands on his hips and kissed him back, but with some reluctance. When he lifted his face, he saw sadness reflected in her eyes.

"You shouldn't have told him he could stay. He can't."

"Sure he can." Dale kissed her cheek, her chin, her nose. "I've tried not to think of you, Tamara, but it hasn't worked."

Tamara shook her head. "Dale, please, concentrate on what I'm telling you. I have to find another foster home for him."

Dale moved his lips to her neck, leaving a trail of hot kisses down to her shoulder blades. She smelled delicious. He had to have this woman. Maybe if he kept touching her, kept kissing her silken skin, she'd agree to let him bed her. Not tonight obviously, but he could give her a taste, a glimpse of what they might share together.

She shivered, and leaned her head back.

Oh, yes. Dale walked forward until he was at his bed, then he slowly lowered her on it. She looked terrific on his bed. He came down on top of her and kissed her more passionately this time.

She broke the kiss. "Dale? Did you hear me?"

"You've got a foster home, Tamara. He'll stay here," he muttered and began to unbutton her top.

She placed a hand over his. "No. I have to find him a real foster home, Dale. I'm sorry."

Dale sighed, gazing at the concerned expression on her face. "I called my lawyer. I'll fill out the papers to be a foster parent. Raffi's not leaving until you find some loving adoptive parents who really want him. Now, can we forget about him for while?"

She frowned. "You called your lawyer?"

"Yes."

"So he could tell you how to deal with me?"

"I had to know where I stood."

She pushed Dale off her and slid off the bed.

He rolled over on his back and ran a hand over his face. "Tamara, come on, you want what's best for the boy, don't you?"

"You're not it."

Dale sat, holding his upper body up with his arms. "Oh, and where you put him was?"

Her body tensed and a look a pure frustration replaced her normal easy going nature. "The foster mother was at a neighbor's house when you got there. She had no idea the other boys were picking on Raffi. She's a good foster parent."

He stood. "Oh really? Your standards are too low if that's what you consider good."

"You don't know what you're getting yourself into." She placed her hands on her hips.

He didn't want to argue with her, in fact, talking of any type was the last thing he wanted.

What did he have to do to connect with her? He stood in front of her again and gripped her shoulders.

"You're a tough woman, Tamara. I'll do whatever you say, but if you're willing to help me, I'll keep him with me until you can arrange an adoption."

"Boys his age don't get adopted quickly."

Dale swallowed. *Take the out, she's offering you an out. You don't want to get stuck with a kid for years. You didn't ask for this.* "Sometimes things happen in our live when we don't expect them to, Tamara. They happen for a reason, and we can't turn our backs on them."

She lowered her eyes. "You could be making a big mistake."

He returned his hands to the buttons on her top and started undoing them again. "Yeah, but I'll take that chance. How about you?" The conversation had shifted, and neither of them were talking about Raffi anymore. Could they, should they, take a chance on each other?

Her chin lifted and her gaze held an almost vulnerable skepticism. "Dale, why do you want me?"

"Hell, I don't know."

"You figure if we sleep together once, you'll get me out of your system?"

He didn't think so. "Maybe."

"It won't work out for the long term, you know?"

"I don't know that, and neither do you."

She pushed his hands off her and rebuttoned her shirt. "Well, we won't find out tonight. You need to put Raffi to bed, and I need to go home. I'm going to have a lot of papers to fill out tomorrow, and we need to get you registered as a foster parent as soon as we can." She paused, "You're sure about this?"

Dale wasn't sure about anything, Raffi, Tamara, anything. "Get all the bureaucratic paperwork done, I'll keep Raffi."

"All right." She nodded, stared at him a little longer, then walked to the door, placing her hand on the door knob, but she didn't leave.

Dale stood in place, frustrated from want. "What's wrong?"

Still facing the door, she said, "I don't know what you thought you were doing tonight, putting your hands all over me, or why I let you --."

"Because you're as attracted to me as I am to you." *And he so loved the feel of her skin.*

She glanced over her shoulder. "Maybe. But Dale, we have to stop this, really. We can't do this."

He laughed. "I'm not letting up, Tamara. I want you, it's that simple."

She frowned. "I can not have an affair with you. Please understand."

"You're the one who has to understand, it will happen. Next time you step inside this bedroom, you'll stay all night, I promise you."

"I'm sorry." She whispered and left his room.

Dale heard her talking with Raffi for a few

minutes, then heard the front door close.

Well, he'd sealed his fate, he now had a kid. Why had he done it? Was it to please this woman? Tamara would have found Raffi a new place to stay. Dale didn't need to get involved.

He walked into the living room and sat next to Raffi who eyed him curiously.

"I guess we're stuck together now," Dale said.

"Guess so," Raffi answered, not exactly looking pleased with the fact.

Dale leaned his head back and stared at the ceiling. What had he been thinking? He didn't know one thing about raising a boy.

"I won't cause you no trouble," the small voice beside him said.

Dale rolled his head, facing the boy. "You promise?"

"Yep."

"Good." Dale faced the ceiling again. "And I'll never hurt you," he said, unable to look at Raffi.

"Thanks," Raffi answered.

Dale swallowed the lump in his throat, and then understood why he'd agreed to take on this responsibility. Raffi had no one. At four years old, he didn't have a soul in this world to care for his needs, to love him. Well, now he had Dale, and Dale would do his best to be a good foster dad, even if it scared him to death.

That night, Dale and Raffi fell asleep watching television together on the couch, both scared, both uncomfortable with each other, and both dreaming of one woman -- Tamara.

CHAPTER FOUR

Usually, Tamara made sure she didn't work on weekends. Those were her days to recover and keep her sanity, but for Raffi she made an exception. The next day, she was in her office early preparing the paperwork to transfer Raffi from his current foster mother to the temporary care of Dale Curtis.

She had stayed up half the night trying to figure out why Dale was doing this. Taking in an abused child like Raffi was not going to be easy, and shouldn't be done on a whim. She hated to think he was doing it to win her sympathy, but she couldn't help wondering if that was his real motivation. The fact that Raffi would have to live with Dale when he didn't even like the man, worried her.

But what she knew of Dale, mostly from Daphne's comments in the past, he was a good man. At least Raffi would be well fed, and no one would hurt him. So Tamara finished all the paperwork necessary to give Dale temporary custody, then packed her briefcase and headed to Dale's place.

She was blown over with surprise when she got there. Dale and Raffi had spent all morning shopping. Raffi had an extensive, brand new wardrobe, a toy box full of toys, a book case full of children's books, and they were in the process of moving the current furniture out of Raffi's room to make room for his bedroom set which was due to arrive.

Full of excitement, and with an illuminated face, Raffi relayed the events of the day and showed her all 'his' new things.

"Looks like you went a little overboard, Dale."

"He had to get some things. He didn't have anything."

Later, she would have to warn Dale not to spoil Raffi and get him used to living in too much luxury. Whoever adopted him would surely not have the ability to spend as freely as Dale had. But for now, she smiled and sat on the bed to read Raffi one of his new books. The small child climbed on her lap, and listened contently as she read, and her heart melted.

She was getting too emotionally involved with this child and she knew she shouldn't. For some reason, Raffi tugged at her heartstrings more than others had. Maybe because he'd clung to her so desperately when child welfare pulled him out of his home.

Dale leaned on the door frame and listened to her read the book. Tamara knew he watched her. When she finished reading, she looked at him. His sun browned arms with shiny, blond hairs were crossed at his chest. He looked perfect, and she felt her heart strings being pulled again, but this time for a beautiful blond man who was all wrong for her.

Tamara kissed Raffi on top of his head, and returned his book. "That was a good story, did you like it?"

Raffi lifted his face and gave her the most adorable doggy eyes she'd ever seen. "I like any book you read, Tamara."

She tipped his chin. "Well, I'll just have to read you more, won't I?"

Raffi smiled and nodded his head.

She got off his bed. "Maybe before I go, I'll read another."

Tamara and Dale left Raffi to play with some of his new toys while they went into the kitchen. Dale handed her a glass of iced tea. Ice cubes clinked against the sweating glass.

She sipped the cool drink. "He looks much happier than he did yesterday."

"I told you we'd be fine together."

Tamara nodded. "Have you told Daphne and Edna yet?"

Dale's face sobered. "No, not yet. Why?"

"They'll think you've gone as crazy as me."

"Maybe you're not so crazy after all. I felt great buying that kid all those things today. No one's ever bought him anything new before, you know that?"

"It doesn't surprise me."

"He was kind of shy at first, reluctant to ask for anything, but I kept telling him he could have whatever he wanted and finally he loosened up and we had a blast shopping."

Tamara smiled. Dale had a classically handsome face, and now that he was so excited and passionate, his skin had a ruddy color to it which made him even more attractive. The more he talked about bringing Raffi a little happiness, the more intense was het urge to go to him and kiss him. "I'm glad you two had fun."

Dale sat across the table and stared at Tamara.

She stared back, wondering what he was thinking.

He finally leaned forward and slid the back of his fingers down her hand which was wrapped around the iced tea glass. "You're gorgeous, Tamara."

Tamara didn't want to let their conversation turn personal. "Even without lace?"

"Without lace." Dale chuckled. "Without anything would even be better."

She clicked her tongue doing her best not to blush. "Dale, I'm now your social worker. You better be careful how you speak to me."

His fingers encircled her wrist. "I'm a lucky guy to have such a hot social worker."

Tamara pulled her wrist loose and stood. "Dale, we really should avoid confusing the issue. We have a business relationship now."

"And what kind of relationship did we have before?"

Tamara shrugged. "An antagonistic one, I guess."

"Well, my social worker or not, I still want to take all your clothes off."

"Of course you do," she said, still trying to keep the provocative conversation from effecting her. "But stripping isn't in my job description."

Dale came around the table and began to crowd her against the hard, tiled kitchen counter. "You wouldn't have to strip, I'd take every stitch of clothing off you myself."

Tamara wondered how serious he was or was this a little seductive word play he engaged in regularly with women. "Well, in that case, I guess it wouldn't violate any ethical standards."
She picked at a piece of lint on his shirt.

He captured her hand and brought it to his warm lips, kissing her knuckles suggestively, making her wish he'd continue up her arm. He smiled. "I was looking forward to going sailing with you. I guess now that Raffi will be living here for a while, we'll have an opportunity to take the yacht out another time."

"I'm sure he'd enjoy that."

"But as far as doing something together, just

the two of us . . . I guess we'll have to wait."

The way he said those words - so deep, so intimate -- sent a shiver up her spine. Something together, like what? What exactly did Dale want from her and why was he so sure she was willing to give it to him? "Raffi will need a lot of attention, that's true."

"How about you, Tamara? Don't you need some attention every once in a while?"

She pulled her hand free and broke eye contact. "I'm doing fine."

He was about to say something when the door bell rang, announcing the furniture delivery. Then they spent the next few hours setting up Raffi's bedroom, organizing his things, and cleaning the mess of cardboard boxes and plastic coverings.

Dale had the old furniture from Raffi's bedroom hauled away. By that evening, Raffi had a sparkly new room, put together in one day.

Tamara knew she should feel happy for Raffi and grateful to Dale, but some of her old resentment toward the wealthy prevented her from feeling as she should. The rich handled everything so easily, just throw enough money out and Raffi gets a ready made bedroom. This was fine on the surface, but was Dale prepared to handle things which would not be fixed so effortlessly by the almighty dollar? Raffi needed love, understanding, a family. Tamara wasn't sure Dale could give him any of those things, not even temporarily.

She left early, refusing their invitation to dinner. The two of them needed to spend time alone, without her interference. Both guys seemed disappointed. But Tamara was glad to get away, especially from Dale.

Throughout the next week, Dale realized it wasn't so easy to have a child in his home. He couldn't work late at the office even though he needed to deal with demands from maintenance workers for more money. Everyone in the airline industry seemed to be demanding more and yet their ticket prices had to be maintained at an all time low.

Despite his overwhelming workload he had to find time to take Raffi to pre-school, pick him up and then stay home with the boy in the evenings. He had to plan for dinner when he usually either stopped somewhere on the way home or fixed a quick bite. Worst of all, he couldn't find any thing to do at home with a four year old boy.

Dale also realized how much the boy disliked him. Raffi was polite, but never went out of his way to bond. Dale tried to consult with him on meal decisions, T.V. programs, and offered to read to him, but nothing sparked any interest in Raffi.

Everyday he thought of picking up the phone and admitting to Tamara he'd made a big mistake, but pride and sympathy for Raffi kept him from doing so.

Instead, he decided to spend evenings working on Raffi's manners and vocabulary. They played board games, filled notebooks with the alphabet which Dale was astounded the child didn't know. At what age did kids learn to read anyway?

By Friday, Raffi drew a picture of an angel and wrote a capital A on top of the page. He handed it to Dale.

Dale lowered his newspaper on the table. "This is very good."

"Ah, huh," he mumbled.

"You mean, 'thank you'."

Raffi nodded. "Thank you."

"Can you make a lower case 'A' beside the capital one?"

"Ah huh."

Dale gave him a sharp look.

"I mean, yes."

"Let's see."

Raffi stuck his tongue out the side of his mouth and drew a perfect lower case A.

"Good job." Dale smiled.

"Thank you."

Dale ran his fingers through the boy's feather soft, black hair. They'd been to the barber and trimmed his hair, cutting the curls and leaving gentle waves.

"It's Tamara," he said.

"Tamara?" Dale glanced at the picture again. Who? The angel was Tamara? Is that how Raffi thought of her? He lifted the paper, and placing his elbows on the table, leaned closer to Raffi. Dale supposed if she had pulled him out of a scary, violent home, he would think of her as an angel too.

"Yes, you know, I see the resemblance."

Raffi frowned, and Dale realized he didn't understand.

"That means, it looks just like her."

Raffi smiled. "Can I hang it on my wall?"

"Sure, and get ready for bed, okay?"

"Okay." He ran off.

Dale made a mental note to get a bulletin board for him to hang his drawings or Dale would have tape all over his white walls.

Dale left the table and stretched out on the sofa. He called Daphne and after exchanging a few pleasantries, he told her what he'd done.

She was silent for an eternity before she finally filled his ear with laughter.

"What's so damn funny?"

"Don't tell me you let Tamara talk you into this?"

"Not at all, it was my idea. As a matter of fact, she didn't want me to do it."

"And probably for good reason. How long do you plan on taking care of this child?'

"I don't know. I look at it as temporary big brother type of thing. The kid needs some guidance."

"What are you going to tell Mom?"

Certainly, not the truth. His mother donated to charities as a tax strategy, not because she cared about the poor or less fortunate. It was a fault of hers, but Dale loved his mother and had no intention of upsetting her. "As little as possible."

"Dale, darling, when you show up with a

child, you'll have to say something."

"Yes, I suppose I'll have to come up with something."

"Do me a favor and don't mention this had anything to do with Tamara. Mom dislikes her enough already."

"That's too bad, because I kind of like her."

"Don't get too close to her, big brother. Tamara's a free spirit and she won't form any permanent attachments. Take it from someone who knows, remember I roomed with her for five years. I saw her break a lot of hearts."

Dale didn't want to hear this. He was dreaming about her on a regular basis now. She hadn't called all week to check on how things were going and that had disappointed him. "Why is she so distant?"

"I don't know." She sighed. "All I do know is her parents never really wanted her. They sent her more money in high school than she could possibly spend, and she would take most of it and give it to the homeless in front of fast food restaurants or on street corners. She wanted her parents to come visit her or show they cared, but their idea of caring was to buy her things and that just killed her."

"Well, Mother sent you away too."

"She did *not.* She sent me to a quality school. I always came home on long weekends and holidays, and Mom visited me all the time."

"Didn't Tamara's parents do the same?"

"No, Tamara went home for Christmas, but stayed at school for other holidays. Her grandmother was the only one who wrote her regularly or called on the phone."

"Too bad," Dale said. Tamara was pretty much raised by institutions then. How lonely she must have been.

"Just don't get too involved with her, that's all," Daphne warned. "I love her, but sometimes I think she's on self destruct mode."

"Sure, thanks for the tip."

After hanging up from the conversation, Dale couldn't help wanting Tamara still. She was different from most of the well-bred, boring women he usually dated. Tamara had a spark inside that drove her and filled her with life. Dale was as attracted to that spark as a moth to light. He hoped he could keep that distance Daphne warned him about or like a moth, he would end up getting burned.

Tamara worked late everyday all week. She had finally been able to pull a two year old girl named Cindy from an abusive home and place her into temporary foster care. It gave her great satisfaction to know she'd at least accomplished something concrete this week, rather than shuffling through tons of tiring paperwork. But by Friday, she was drained. She went home, showered, changed, and drove to Daphne's new house in Pacific Palisades. Daphne had already moved in, furnishing and decorating before she officially started her life with her new husband.

Tamara rang the bell at the large iron gates outside Daphne's home. After verifying who Tamara was, a faceless voice allowed her to enter. Once she got to the front door, the servants let her in.

"You're not even moved in, and you've already employed a crew of people?" Tamara asked, exasperation ringing in her voice.

Daphne smiled and kissed Tamara, inviting her to the perfectly decorated sitting room where she asked for tea to be brought in. "This is quite a surprise, Tamara."

"Well, you'll be married soon, and we won't have anymore days where it'll just be the two of us. I was hoping you didn't have any plans this weekend, and we could spend it together."

Daphne shrugged. "I don't have anything to do that I can't change. You okay?"

Tamara sank into Daphne's plush sofa, letting her shoulders sag. "I'm tired."

"That all?"

"Yes, that's all. And, I miss our old talks at night in the dorm. Has it been five years since graduation already?"

The tea was brought in along with shortbread cookies - sugar free, of course. Daphne thanked and excused her help. Tamara hated to see her looking so proper, like a stranger she didn't know.

"Amazing isn't it?" She lifted her cup of tea to her lips and sipped delicately. "Well, we can talk all night if you'd like."

Tamara nodded. "I'd like to order a pizza, get into some shorts, go for a swim and relax. Remember how to do that, Daphne?"

Daphne sighed. "Tamara, don't start in on me, I remember you getting me into a lot of trouble in school. I'm through with my rebellious stage. When are you going to get over it?"

"What makes you think it's a stage?"

"I hope to God it is."

"You sound like your mother."

Daphne frowned. "Why do you say that like it's a terrible thing? My mother is a good woman."

"She's also . . . " She cut off her response and took a tired breath. "Forget it."

"I won't forget it, Tamara."

Tamara stretched back on the luxurious, loose pillow back sofa and closed her eyes, not wanting to discuss Edna with Daphne. Daphne loved her mother and she should. "Are you sure you want to marry this guy, Daphne?"

"Of course I do. Why would you ask?"

"How about your singing? You used to be so passionate about it."

"I got your wedding gift. A baby grand piano?"

Tamara turned her head, opened her eyes, and looked at Daphne. "I don't want you to forget your dream, Daph. If you want to be a singer, you should go for it."

"I want to marry Adam more."

"Do you?"

Daphne nodded.

After studying her friend's face, Tamara believed her. Daphne looked happy, and she conceded that everyone may not be like her and feel stifled by the rigidity of the privileged lifestyle. Tamara swung her legs down and sat, reaching for Daphne's hands. "You do like the piano, don't you?"

Daphne smiled. "I love it."

They didn't order pizza, but they did go for a swim. Later that evening Adam showed up with his friend, Charles. The four went out to eat dinner at Pacific Sands Country Club.

Tamara found herself wondering what Dale was doing. She rationalized her thoughts, telling herself she'd only thought of him because she was in the same place they met. But part of her knew that wasn't true, Dale had been on her mind all week. She'd pushed him back each time he moved to the front of her thoughts, but it never worked for long.

Adam's friend, Charles, was nice, and he showed definite interest in Tamara. She was polite because he was Daphne and Adam's friend, but resisted encouraging him. At the end of the evening, he asked to see her again.

"I'm sorry, I'm seeing someone else."

"I'm sorry to hear that." He gave her a disappointed smile. "Is it serious?"

Tamara could have kicked herself for the lie. Why hadn't she just said she wasn't interested in dating? Because, she reminded herself, men never took no for an answer. "It all depends on him."

"Well, if he has any brains, he'll keep close reins on you."

That night as they curled up in Daphne's king size bed Tamara told Daphne about Charles' amorous intentions. They both laughed like they had in school over dates that hadn't gone well.

"Poor Charles. He couldn't have zeroed in on a worse target."

Tamara laughed. "See what happens when I pretend to be respectable? These poor men get fooled into thinking I'm one of them."

Daphne turned around in bed and touched Tamara's arm. "Is Dale one of those fooled men?"

Tamara's laughter faded. Oh, why did she have to bring up Dale? "I know he's your brother, Daph. But he knows exactly who I am and what my life is like."

"He's still interested in you though, isn't he?"

Tamara propped her head on her hand and leaned on it. "I don't know what Dale wants from me. Honestly, I think he just wants to sleep with me."

Daphne laughed. "I can't believe my big brother is hitting on my best friend."

Tamara laughed too. If only Daphne knew how strongly Dale was 'hitting on her'. Suddenly, she wanted to confide in her friend, as she had in the past. "If I tell you something, will you promise not to tell him?"

Daphne propped herself up as well, moving

closer to Tamara in the muted light. "I promise."

"Your brother has me all tied up in knots. I can't stop thinking of him. I wouldn't need much persuading to spend the night with him."

Daphne dropped back down on her side of the bed, shaking her head on her plush pillow. "I hope you two know what you're doing."

But Tamara didn't know what she was doing, not if she was falling for Dale Curtis. Edna Curtis' children were raised to be proper, upstanding citizens who complied with their social positions proudly and obediently -- Daphne being a perfect example.

CHAPTER FIVE

The next morning Tamara enjoyed an early morning swim while Daphne slept in. She had slept peacefully for the first time all week and awoke early, feeling refreshed. Spending time with the only person other than her grandmother she had ever been close to felt wonderful. As Tamara walked inside with a towel wrapped around her, Daphne stumbled out of the bedroom in a silk, lavender robe.

Tamara smiled, mostly at her own thoughts as she compared herself to her friend. Daphne looked like a princess. She even smelled of fragrant perfume, while Tamara was all wet, in a towel, and smelled of chlorine. How they'd changed, or more precisely, how Daphne had changed, reverted back to her expected persona.

And that was exactly how Dale found them a

few seconds later when he walked in with Raffi, perfectly dressed beside him.

"Tamara!" Raffi ran to her and wrapped his small arms around her legs, causing the towel to slip down enough to expose the top of her breasts.

"Oh Raffi, sweetie. I'm glad to see you too, but let me get rid of this towel and dressed in real clothes." She held her towel up with one hand and patted the boy's head with the other.

"Tamara, did you go skinny dipping?" Daphne looked at her incredulously.

She felt like a naughty teenager caught in a reprehensible act. "It's not like anyone saw me. You were sleeping and . . . ." She dared a glance at Dale who watched her through hooded lids. "And I didn't know your brother just showed up at your place so early on Saturday mornings."

"He doesn't usually. In fact, he never does." Daphne turned her attention to Dale. "What are you doing here?"

Tamara began to breath easier, feeling less noticeable.

Dale sat back on a bar stool, looking slightly amused. "I came to take you to breakfast. Raffi and I were bored."

"At--." Daphne looked at the grandfather clock. "Eight-fifty in the morning, you were bored?"

"And hungry. I didn't know Tamara would be here . . . and in such an appealing state." He practically leered at her. "She told me her job description didn't include stripping, but I guess she made an exception for you, Sis."

"She's not one of my foster families," Tamara said, and immediately regretted it since her comment brought Dale's complete focus on her.

His eyes held her in a kind of arctic contempt. "I didn't realize I'd be punished for becoming a foster parent."

"What did you expect, special privileges?"

He stiffened and lifted himself off the stool. He walked forward until they were almost toe to toe, but instead of looking or talking to her, he turned and smiled at Raffi. "Would you like Tamara to come to breakfast with us?"

"Sure." Raffi smiled back at Dale.

He actually smiled, Tamara notice in amazement. She knew exactly what Dale was doing, and though she should resent him using Raffi to get her to spend time with him, she didn't really mind.

Dale swung his glance to her face. His strong, fully dressed body made her feel vulnerable, and she clutched the towel harder against her breasts. "I'll only be a few minutes." Then she turned and went into Daphne's bedroom.

Swinging his gaze away from the closed door, Dale noticed Daphne standing beside the bar with her arms crossed.

"What?" he asked.

"Didn't you listen to a word I said yesterday?"

Dale could feel himself getting angry. His right eye twitched, just like it did every time he got frustrated. "Who does she think she is avoiding me? I've got women waiting in line to go out with me."

"Great! Call one of them, and leave Tamara alone."

Dale looked at Raffi who watched him and his sister with keen interest. "Raffi, stay here a minute with Daphne." Then he stormed into Daphne's bedroom, not knowing what he was going to do when he got inside.

Tamara sat on Daphne's bed, thinking, still wrapped in her towel when Dale shot in and closed the door behind him. They silently stared into each other's eyes.

Tamara swallowed the lump in her throat. Such a terrific looking man, so tall, so sure of himself. She had a wicked urge to drop the towel, to allow the terry cloth to slide down and pool around her hips and lap, to see the hungry look in his eyes as he took in her exposed nude body. Tamara wanted him to touch her, to feel his hands lifting her breasts, his fingers grazing her aroused nipples. It was wrong, impossible between them, but God help her, she wanted all of this and more.

"Haven't heard from you," he said finally, not taking his eyes off her.

"I had nothing new to tell you."

Dale finally moved forward, reached the bed, and took a few strands of her wet hair between his fingers.

Tamara could barely breathe.

"Oh Tamara, I've tried and tried to stop

thinking of you. I've told myself the exact same things you yourself have told me. Between us, there could never be anything . . . but, there *is* something. I'm not sure what it is, but it's there and it's strong, and it won't go away."

She braved a glance at him, and realized her mistake the second she looked into his earnest eyes. She nodded slowly.

He dropped down to his knees and stared deep into her eyes without speaking for a long time, then asked, "What are we going to do about it?"

She threaded her fingers through his hair, scratching at his scalp. He closed his eyes and leaned his head into her hands like a purring cat, a dangerous, elegant, golden tiger cat. His arms slipped behind her and encircled her waist loosely.

She knew what could happen all too easily between them, and what scared her the most was she wanted it to. Tamara wanted to ask him to touch her, to tell him it was okay, but that wouldn't get them anywhere. "Dale," she whispered.

He opened his eyes. "Tell me you want me, Tamara."

"Oh, Dale," she breathed the words.

"Tell me."

"I do. I want you, but --."

"Then stop avoiding me, dammit." He pushed her back on the bed and braced himself above her, his lips hovered over hers. Then he ground his lips against hers, invading her mouth, sensually dipping his tongue in and out and tilting his head back and forth until he'd thoroughly kissed her and left her lips throbbing.

He looked between them, to her body covered in a towel. The desire in his eyes was inescapable, and they both knew with one pull he would see everything he wanted, but Dale, however brazen he wanted to be, was a gentleman after all. He lifted himself off her, wiping his lips with his thumb.

"You know, with you being Daphne's friend and our families knowing each other, this is much more complicated than I originally thought," he said hoarsely.

"Meaning that casual, one night stand is no longer an option?" She tried to joke as she lifted her upper body off the mattress.

He licked his lips and turned to the door. "I don't know what I mean exactly, Tamara. I want to see you, but I don't. Maybe we *should* spend one spectacular night making love to each other and see where it leads. Think about it."

She watched him leave and collapsed back onto the mattress. Think about it? Think about indulging in a night of passion in Dale Curtis' arms? Then what? They walk away and pretend it never happened? The offer was almost tempting. At least it would be the most honest relationship she'd ever had. No pretending they loved each other, just sex. She laughed. *I'm insane. Dale's really getting to me if I'm considering sleeping with him.*

The group of four enjoyed a full breakfast at

a pancake house which drew Tamara to the menu immediately with it's delicious aromas of coffee, sweet breads, and sizzling bacon -- nothing extravagant, nothing demanding. Raffi seemed happy, talking about his week at pre-school, and how Dale had helped him with his homework.

"But you said you were going to read me more stories and you didn't come back," Raffi complained, licking syrup off his fork.

Tamara glanced at Dale. No she hadn't gone back. "Dale can read you stories."

"I offered, but he didn't want me to read." Dale looked at her over the top of his coffee mug. "He wants you."

"Can you come over tonight, Tamara?"

This time she refused to look at Dale. "I can come over before you go to church tomorrow morning."

Raffi wrinkled his nose. "You can't come over in the morning. You have to come over in night when I go to sleep, then read me a story."

I don't want to come over at night, Raffi. Don't you understand how dangerous that would be for me? But of course Raffi didn't understand. "I guess you're right. I'll come read you a story real soon, okay?"

"Tonight?"

"Raffi, she'll come when she decides she wants to, now leave her alone," Dale said, his voice too loud and obviously annoyed.

Raffi frowned at Dale, apparently not appreciating his intervention. "If you'd be nicer, she'd come over."

Tamara couldn't resist. "Yes, Dale, try being nicer." She smiled and batted her eyelashes.

He chuckled. "I'm trying, Tam. I really want to be nice to you."

"So you'll come," Raffi pleaded.

Tamara turned her smile to Raffi. "We'll see."

That wasn't what he wanted to hear, but he let up. Tamara and Dale listened to Daphne talk about her upcoming wedding.

"I really wish you could have been my maid of honor, Tamara. It won't be the same without you standing beside me."

"My heart will be beside you, but you know I couldn't handle all those pre-wedding social events."

"I know, but I still would have liked it if you were."

Dale picked up the bill and pulled out his wallet from his back pocket. "I thought you two were best friends."

"We are," they both said.

"Then," he said, facing Tamara. "Couldn't you make an exception and attend the 'social events' just this once? It's Daphne's wedding."

Tamara felt like telling him to mind his own business, but she didn't. "I am making exceptions. I attended her bridal shower. I'll be at the wedding."

Daphne placed her hand over her brother's. "That's right, she is and I do appreciate it. Shall we go, Dale?"

Dale took the cue from his sister to drop the subject. He nodded and turned to Raffi. "What now?"

Raffi looked longingly at Tamara.

Dale's stomach tightened. *Yeah, I know, if you could have it your way you'd go with her and never set eyes on me again, but it's not going to happen, pal, so forget it. She's finished with you. You've been placed in a good home, and now she's off to save someone else.*

"Tamara?" Raffi's voice was so quiet she barely heard him.

"What, sweetie?"

"Is my mama okay?"

All three adults stared at the small child, plainly each equally shocked at the unexpected question.

Tamara recovered first, taking his small hand and leaning her forehead into his. "She signed the papers to let you be legally adopted. That had to have been hard for her, but she understands it's the best thing she could do for you."

He wrapped his arms around Tamara's neck and buried his face in her shoulder.

She caressed his head, and looked at Dale. "Would you mind very much if I spent the day with Raffi? I'll bring him by your place tonight."

Still baffled and emotionally pained at watching the two of them, he could manage nothing more than a nod.

Dale decided to do some of the things he couldn't get done during the week because of Raffi. He went to Pacific Sands Country Club to check on it's status and make sure there were no troubling incidents needing his attention. He thought about going into work, but decided, at least for the weekend, not to worry about air schedules, wage disagreements, or expansion routes. He played racquetball with his friend Bill, then took his clothes to the cleaners.

But the whole time his mind was on Tamara and Raffi. How could she work for the state - dealing with such painful cases? Didn't it break her heart to work with children like Raffi? Every time he saw her, he gained more respect for what she chose to do with her life and for her personally.

Dale thought of what he did and realized how little importance his job actually had. If Quest Air went bankrupt tomorrow, who would really care? His entire existence mattered little. But not everyone could do Tamara's job, he concluded.

Hours later, he found himself at home waiting for them to arrive. He made a batch of macaroni and cheese and set the table for three. Only after he had finished did he realize Tamara might not stay for dinner. He'd been pursuing her rather ruthlessly, and purely for selfish, physical reasons. No wonder she'd been staying away.

Dale sighed. She had been so flirtatious and sexy when they first met he'd been turned on and eager to accept what she seemed to offer. But he was beginning to understand she wasn't an easy woman who slept with anyone for the thrill of it as he'd originally thought.

Just the opposite. Tamara kept men at a distance, afraid to ask for the love she had never gotten as a child, and now acted as if that type of affection didn't matter. Except around children. She was loving and open with children.

He heard their voices outside his door just before Raffi burst in to show Dale his super dooper lollipop he'd purchased at Disneyland. He excitedly told Dale about all the wonderful rides he'd been on. Dale listened, smiling, and wishing Tamara had invited him to go along with them. He realized the outing sounded so much better than what he'd done today.

"Here," Raffi said, handing him a Disney bag.

"What's this?" Dale took the plastic bag and rustled inside to find a T-shirt.

"Tamara picked it out for you," Raffi explained. "I wanted to get you a train, because you said you liked trains but she said 'no'."

Dale smiled. "It's a great shirt. Thanks for thinking of me, Raffi." He glanced up. "Tamara."

She'd been very quiet, and now smiled. "You're welcome."

"I made us all some dinner. Nothing special, just some macaroni and cheese."

"I love macaroni and cheese!" Raffi jumped up and down.

Dale guessed it had turned out to be a very

good day for the little boy. After Raffi washed up, Dale served them all their dinner.

Tamara told him again and again how terrific the meal was and helped him load the dishes into the dishwasher. Then she went into Raffi's room, put him to bed, and read him a book.

Dale watched, trying not to intrude on Raffi's moment. A small part of him liking the domestic scene they'd just played out.

When she came out to the living room, she looked sad and tired. She sat on the couch without saying a word.

"It was a long day, wasn't it?" Dale sat beside her.

She leaned forward and brushed her lips against his. "Sometimes working with these children tears me up inside."

Dale nodded and caressed the side of her face. "I can imagine that day after day of seeing cases like Raffi's would leave you drained."

She met and held his gaze. "I've been thinking over what you said, and I want to spend the night with you. I want to be held and caressed, but I don't think I can handle a casual affair with you, Dale."

Her affection caught him off guard. "I understand. I probably couldn't either." But was he ready to offer anything more? And if he was, was she ready to accept more?

Her lips curved up sensually at the corners. Then her fingers began to work the buttons on his shirt and when she got to his waist, she tugged at the ends of his shirt, pulling them out of his trousers.

"Tamara."

Her kisses fluttered along his jaw. "Hmmm."

"You're just feeling lonely tonight."

She shrugged and pushed his shirt off his shoulders. "So help me feel less lonely, Dale."

He caught her hands and eased them away from him. He couldn't believe he was doing this. Hadn't he been dreaming of this every night for the past few weeks? But he'd learned a lot about her since then, and he no longer wanted to have meaningless sex with her. Obviously she didn't want that either. "You'll regret it come morning."

She smiled patiently. "I'm not a fool. I know what I'm doing."

"Do you?" He raised an eyebrow and looked at her. "You said you didn't want a casual affair. What do you think this would be?"

She pulled back. "I thought . . . I hoped it could be the beginning of something more."

"More? You mean long term?"

She smiled. "Maybe."

"Look, I want you. I've wanted you from the first time I saw you."

She nodded.

"But now I know you and I like you, Tamara, a lot."

The color in cheeks deepened. "Well . . . ."

"And, you were right when you said we're from different worlds. When it comes down to it, I don't know how compatible we really are. We lead vastly divergent lives."

Her eyes flickered down. "I see. All you really wanted from me was sex."

He couldn't lie. "Yes, that's what I wanted when we first met."

She gazed at him again, her eyes had darkened. "Well, that's what I'm offering you now. What's the problem?"

"The problem is, it's not what you're offering. You just admitted you couldn't handle a casual affair with me. A few weeks ago, Tamara, I wouldn't have cared, but like I said, I like you, I don't want to hurt you."

She nodded and looked away, then she stood and reached for her purse and car keys.

"Tamara?" He stood and followed her.

"It's all right. I appreciate your honesty."

He wrapped both his hands around the back of her head, caressing her luscious lips with his thumbs. His body was silently cursing him right now. "You're Daphne's best friend, and I'd like it if you were my friend as well."

"I can't be your friend if you're going to look at me like that, Dale."

"Damn it," he muttered right before he pulled her head forward and pressed his lips against hers. He was too weak. He cursed himself over and over as he continued to kiss her. He was being too rough, bruising her lips with the pressure, but he couldn't get enough of her.

He thought of how she'd looked in that towel, how he'd wanted to take her budded nipples in his mouth, how he'd wanted to slip his hands under that towel to the top of her thighs, and touch her, stroke her, make her tremble with need.

Suddenly, Dale tore her blouse off, his mouth still pressed against hers. She moaned or was she protesting? He backed her hard against the wall, then lifted his head, staring into shocked eyes as she looked at her torn clothes.

He registered a brief glimpse of lacy bra and rounded cleavage before he ground out, "Don't say a word, dammit."

She didn't look like she could say anything. She was breathing deeply and her eyes were as large as saucers.

"No one has ever affected me like you do, Tamara." He knew it sounded like an accusation, like he was blaming her for acting like a savage, but he didn't know how to amend it. He braced a hand against the wall and dropped his head, fighting to regain control.

"I should be flattered then?"

He glanced at her torn top, cringing. Reaching for the Disney bag, he tossed the t-shirt at her. "Put this on. It's more your style anyway."

"I thought it might loosen you up a bit."

Dale shook his head. "I'll never be the guy you want me to be, Tamara. I'll always be too rich, too pampered, too damn upper crust for you. You would only hold it against me."

Cheeks aflame, she took off her torn top in sharp angry movements, and put on the extra large shirt. "And you'll hold my lifestyle against me."

The T-shirt drooped off her shoulders and the sleeves flapped around her elbows. She looked so cute he wanted to pick her up and take her to bed that second. "So the last thing we need is to get involved with each other," he said, pain twisting his heart with each word. Not only was he physically attracted to her, he genuinely liked her and he didn't want to end something which could turn out to be wonderful.

"We'd end up hating each other," she agreed and reached for the door knob.

Dale took her arm. "Tam, wait. Would it kill you to accept your heritage? Would being by my side, dressed like a lady, bother you that much?"

She smiled sadly, and he knew she was slipping through his fingers, and that he was losing something unique, something precious.

Her voice was gentle and full of regret. "I suppose it would, as much as wearing Mickey Mouse would bother you. I need to go, Dale."

He wanted to stop her, beg her to spend the night after all. To forget who they were and just enjoy each other, but he knew she wouldn't stay. Not now. "I'll walk you to your car."

When they got to the curb he looked for the beat up old VW bug, but didn't see it. She clicked the alarm to a shiny, clean, sleek, black Jaguar.

"Don't tell me this is your car?"

"All right, I won't tell you."

"Where's that mess of a car I saw you in when we first met?"

She smiled wide and winked. "That was my

work car. I don't like to take this one to the office for obvious reasons."

Dale smiled back. Damn, he liked her. And he wanted her so bad it hurt. So, why was she leaving? "Tamara, I'm sorry."

"I know. Me, too."

And just like that, she was gone. The perfectly engineered automobile glided away, stopped at the stop sign and all he could see were red brake lights.

He shook his head as he stood alone on the curb, knowing this soft breezy night could have turned out so differently. Why hadn't he just offered her whatever she said she wanted and slept with her? He had done that in the past with women. You say the love words they want to hear, and they drop on your bed quietly and willingly. None of it had to be true.

But, unfortunately, with Tamara, it was true. He shoved his hand in his pockets and headed back to his condo. Damn, why did he have to end up caring about her?

CHAPTER SIX

Dale didn't expect to hear from Tamara again, but much to his surprise, she called the following week to check on Raffi and to tell him Raffi would be celebrating his fifth birthday that week. Since he wasn't sure what to do for a child's birthday, Tamara gave him pointers.

Then she and Raffi spoke on the phone for about twenty minutes then Raffi handed him the line. Her tone was polite and professional, and she never brought up the awkward night which still nagged at his conscience. Dale decided to follow her lead and not bring it up either. But at the end of the call, he wished their conversation had been more personal. He replaced the receiver with a sense of longing, both foreign and unpleasant.

He and Raffi got along better each day, and Dale found he enjoyed having a boy in his home.

Dale spent hours helping him with homework, taking him to museums and on educational excursions.

Dale's mother, whom he had dreaded telling about Raffi, was actually supportive. As they sat on their backyard porch on a sunny Saturday morning, she encouraged Dale, but warned him about getting too attached. "Remember, he's only with you temporarily."

"I know, Mom."

"Will you help another child after this one is gone?"

Like Tamara? On to the next one? An odd pain that began in his heart and rose to close up his throat, made him uncomfortable. "No. This is a one time thing for me."

Edna rose a delicate eyebrow and took a sip of her tea. "Why this child, Dale?"

"He needed someone, and I just happened to be there."

"I see."

They watched Raffi play with Edna's two Dalmatians on the lush, green grass. With a twinge of guilt, Dale admitted to himself he had taken Raffi to please Tamara. He had set out to show her he had a heart, but she didn't seem to care.

He stood, leaned down and kissed his mother's cheek. "Maybe it's just the universe's way of telling me it's time I do something for someone other than myself."

Edna touched her son's face. "No," she said. "I believe it is quite the opposite. You have been a good son to both your father and me. You have dedicated yourself to the corporation at the cost of a personal life." She glanced at Raffi. "Perhaps taking time to help mold this young man will give you an opportunity to enrich your soul, to look at life a bit differently. Perhaps this is more for you than for the child."

"Perhaps." Dale smiled.

Of course balancing work and Raffi was no easy task. The next three months, which took him into the hot summer, became a test of endurance for Dale. He repeatedly had to juggle business meetings and commitments with Raffi's needs. His nights out with clients, nursing his double whiskeys and plotting how to get more money, were replaced with mundane activities such as cooking and bathing the child.

He hired two new assistants at work to avoid getting backlogged. Still some things had to be handled by him. He met with the marketing department to implement their new TV campaign. Quest Air needed to change their image from being solely a national airline to include their international routes. After the meeting he rushed to Raffi's pre-school to pick him up and drive him to Daphne's house.

"Why do I have to go to her house again?" Raffi complained.

"I've got to go back to work today."

"But you said we could see a movie."

"On Saturday. I said Saturday."

"You said last Saturday and then you had to work and I had to go to Daphne's and we didn't go, and -."

"We'll go." Traffic was a nightmare. Cars barely moved at ten miles per hour. The heat rising off the pavement was actually visible and Dale's temper flared as well. Just as he was about to cross the intersection, he caught a red light. He slapped the steering wheel. "Damn!"

Raffi eyed him, then lowered his head.

"Sorry, Raffi, I'm in a hurry."

"I know."

"I promise we'll do something fun this weekend, okay? Just the two of us."

He nodded.

Dale felt guilty, but he had to meet with the board today to discuss expansion of flight routes. His schedule couldn't be helped - not this week.

In the wood paneled boardroom, he and his father pleaded their cases for three hours. In the end, Dale felt confident the expansion routes would be approved, and funds would be directed toward this growth.

He accepted an invitation to dine with Weir, their corporate president, although he wasn't hungry.

"You've been scarce," Weir said during their shrimp cocktail appetizers. "Seeing someone?"

Dale laughed. Didn't he wish. "No, just busy."

"Well, I've got a woman for you."

Dale placed a shrimp in his mouth and chewed. He and Mike Weir had routinely gone out on double dates. They were the same age, and were friends as well as business associates. "I'm too tired for women these days."

"This one isn't like our usual." He pointed with his fork. "She's a record producer in Hollywood. A knockout."

"Sounds worse than our ususal." Weir's girlfriend was a brilliant model. Unfortunately, her friends never seemed to be as intelligent, although they were always fun.

"How about Saturday? We can take a trip to Catalina, stay the weekend . . . ?"

Dale smiled. Sounded good, but he promised Raffi this weekend. "Maybe some other time."

Weir leaned across the table and gripped Dale's forearm. "I'm telling you, she's hot. Take the weekend off. The board's going to pass your plan. Relax."

Dale studied Mike's face. "I can't make it this weekend. Personal stuff. Sorry."

Weir shook his head. "You should be."

Dale finally made it to Daphne's house about ten that night, and Raffi was already asleep. He placed him in his car seat and drove home. The boy continued to sleep even as Dale carried him into his room, and tucked him into bed. Boy, what he'd give to sleep that soundly.

In his living room, he poured himself a drink, hit his message machine, and sat on the couch with a heavy sigh.

Three messages. One from Tamara to see if everything was going well. She called every once in a while. Each time she let more time elapse between calls, and Raffi asked for her less and less. He had accepted she wouldn't be a part of his life, but Dale had a harder time accepting it.

As he listened to her voice he had an urge to call her at home, just to talk, just to see if her voice still made his heart beat quicker. He let his head drop on the back of the sofa and closed his eyes, picturing her face, the shape of her lips, the sparkle in her eyes.

His body stirred. *I need a woman. Any woman. Just as long as she helps me forget Tamara.* Maybe he should have taken Weir up on his offer. But he really didn't want to date.

What he wanted was a cute social worker with the voice of an angel.

Dale and Raffi had a great time at the matinee movies. Dale hadn't been to a movie theater since he was a teenager. He had been too busy, and besides the women he dated were more interested in a more sophisticated type of theater.

Afterwards he drove them to the country club where Raffi had a tennis lesson while Dale took care of club business.

As he was strolling back to the courts to get

Raffi enjoying the sun on his back and the smell of freshly cut grass, he saw Tamara running down the front steps of the administration office. Her hair was pulled up on top of her head, and she dressed casually in jeans and a yellow button up, sleeveless shirt.

"Tamara," he called out to her.

She stopped and smiled when she saw him. "Dale. Hi, you look wonderful. How are you?"

"I'm doing quite well. What are you doing here?"

She laughed. "Paying my dues. Can you believe they lost my check and were going to cancel my membership?"

"I didn't realize you used the club enough to care?"

"Well, I don't really. It's just that I know how long the waiting list is and if they cancel . . . I don't know, I've belonged for so long . . ." She shrugged.

"You look thinner."

"I've been working long hours."

To keep from thinking of me? Arrogant thought. Wishful thinking. "Raffi still asks about you."

"You're doing a great job with him, Dale. You should be proud of yourself."

He'd rather *she* were proud of him. "He's a great kid."

"Yes, he is," she agreed with a nod. "Well, I need to get back to work. I'll see you at Daphne's wedding next month?"

"Tamara." He reached for her arm. "Maybe

we could have dinner . . . before Daphne's wedding."

Tamara's eyes glazed over and wavered. "Why?"

Did he have to spell it out? He missed her. And still wished they could have worked things out and deepened their relationship. "I'd enjoy having dinner with you."

"I'm . . . ah . . . seeing someone, Dale."

Stunned, he jerked his arm back. Seeing someone? Here she was in his thoughts day and night, and she had gone on with her life as if Dale hadn't even exist. "In that case, I suppose . . ." He was at a loss for words. Had he just imagined that she cared for him?

"It was the only way I could stop thinking of you, Dale."

He watched as the truth flickered in her eyes. "You did the right thing," he said, although nothing felt right about her dating another man. She should be with him. Sometimes, the heart knows better than the mind. Sometimes two souls connect in a way that reason can't explain. Sometimes being with the wrong person is the only *right* thing to do.

She leaned forward and kissed his cheek. "I'd love a dance at the wedding. Save one for me?"

He wanted to grab her shoulders and kiss her for real, not accept just the soft peck she had given him, but he only nodded and smiled.

Tamara thought the shattering pain she'd experienced the first few months after she and Dale decided not to pursue their attraction was gone, but it wasn't. It still hurt. He looked so carefree with his feathery hair softly blowing, making him look handsome and young.

Long ago, she had stopped thinking of him as the rude ogre who guarded the country club. He was nothing of the sort. Everything Daphne had told her about her brother back in high school was true. Dale was kind and charming. He made you feel special with only a smile. How she wished they were more alike in their values and lifestyles.

He'd actually looked hurt to find out she was dating. But she hadn't meant to hurt him. She wanted him to face the truth just as she had. No matter what their minds, bodies, and hearts told them, they would never be together.

She hurried along the freeway to get home in time for her date with Roy. After her glimpse of Dale, she had to force herself to get excited about the date.

When she got home, Roy was already waiting for her, pacing in front of her door step, his baggy jeans barely clinging to his hips. He tossed his long, black hair. "You're late."

"Sorry, sorry, I had an errand."

He clutched the back of her head and kissed her sloppily. Tamara didn't know why she put up with him. He was rude, abrupt, and had a bad temper.

"Next time take care of your errands when we're not going out."

She didn't bother reminding him she was not late, he was early. She unlocked her front door. "I will. I apologize."

They walked into her apartment and he sauntered to her refrigerator and pulled out a beer she now kept to please him. "How long will it take you to get ready?"

"Where are we going?"

He shrugged and took a gulp from the can. "I'm low on cash. How about we grab a pizza and come back to your place."

Tamara stiffened, she knew exactly why he wanted to come back here. She had no intention of sleeping with him. "How about a movie?"

"Tamara, you gonna keep me waiting forever? I wanna be with you, you know?"

"Roy, I need to go slow."

"If we go any slower, I'll be a walking hard on. What's the problem?"

"I don't intend to be just a release for you."

He laughed and came toward her. "It'll be good, baby, trust me."

Roy's rugged good looks, long hair, and worn leather jacket were perfect - just the type of man she wanted. So different from the country club boys she'd grown up with, but rather than being attracted to Roy, she was indifferent to him.

His hands moved over her hips and bottom intimately, and she tried to enjoy it, but her body wouldn't respond.

"What do you say?" He nuzzled her neck.

She threaded her fingers through the hair she liked so much. "Let's go out, Roy. I want a wild ride on your bike tonight."

He laughed again. "You got it." He slapped her bottom playfully. "Let's go."

Roy went tearing through the streets, the bike actually lifting off the pavement at times as he flew over railroad tracks.

Tamara wrapped her arms around his waist and held on tight. She loved being on his bike, finding it exhilarating. The speed and the feel of cutting through the wind made her blood pump faster, made her feel alive. She was disappointed when they reached the pizza pub. If she'd had it her way, she would have ridden all night.

Roy got off the bike, shook his full head of hair, and gave her a lopsided grin. "Wild enough for you?"

Tamara sat on the bike watching him. No, neither the man nor the ride was wild enough. What was wrong with her? "I guess it's time to get off?"

He grabbed her hand and pulled her off the bike. "Yep, time to eat."

Roy ate almost an entire large pizza by himself. The two slices she ate were truly too much. She wasn't hungry. She wasn't in the mood to be on a date. The problem was, lately she wasn't sure what she *did* want.

CHAPTER SEVEN

Preparing for Daphne's wedding, took an entire day. She made an appointment for a manicure, something she hadn't done in months. When that was over, it was time for the hair and make up. Hair took a couple of hours. They cut and styled it in a swirled bun on top of her head, leaving wisps loose. Hair stylists loved to do that. After the details of nails and hair were over, her make up seemed simple. She chose a natural look which made her eyes stand out and accentuated her lips.

Daphne had helped select her dress months ago, but Tamara hadn't realized how beautiful it was until she had it on. She couldn't believe how well it accented her figure. The dress was a soft cream lavender with lovely beads, bordering on Victorian. The neckline was high with dainty, pearl buttons running all along the front. The long sleeves, in a more modern look, were completely transparent. As a finishing touch, a lavender hat accompanied the dress, which Tamara decided to leave off for the time being. She was pleased with her appearance reflecting back from the mirror.

Even though she wasn't part of the wedding party, Tamara arrived at the church early, because Daphne insisted she be included in some of the pre-wedding pictures.

The large church echoed with voices when she walked in, and right away she spotted the family and photographer.

Dale glanced over his shoulder as she approached, and much to her delight, did a double take and excused himself to meet her.

"Is it really you, Tamara?"

"It's me."

"You look . . . absolutely stunning."

"Thank you, so do you."

He smiled and her heart constricted - such a sexy smile.

"Daphne's a little hysterical today. We'd better let her know you're here." He offered her his arm and she took it, letting him lead her the rest of the way down the aisle.

Daphne's face did indeed look strained. "Oh Tam," Daphne said in exaggerated relief. "I can't go through with this," she whispered in a shaky voice.

Tamara took Daphne's cold, jittery fingers

and pulled her aside. "Calm down, Daph."

"You were right. I'm going to be stuck being Mrs. Adam Kingsley forever. I'll never have a life again. I'll--"

"Daphne. Slow down."

"I just can't do this. I just--"

"Daph! Stop, you love Adam." Tamara took both her hands and gazed into her friend's frightened eyes. "You look amazingly beautiful today, Daphne. You can't deprive Adam the joy of walking down the aisle with you."

"Tamara," Daphne whispered, her eyes unusually bright. "What if I'm just marrying him because I should, because my mother approves of his family?"

Tamara frowned. "Are you?"

"Well, he's gorgeous. He loves to travel like I do, and he promised we would go ski at a new resort every winter. He wants to be a father, and he makes me flavored coffee, Tam, and brings it to me in bed . . . ."

Tamara smiled. Daphne spoke so fast and incoherent, she was hard to follow. She hugged Daphne for a moment, then pulled back and looked into her misty eyes. "Remember when we stayed up at night in our dorm and dreamed up our perfect man? Was it Adam you described?"

Daphne sighed and her body slackened against Tamara. "I don't know."

Tamara narrowed her eyes and stared at her friend. "Let's see if I remember. You wanted someone cute and Adam is gorgeous as you've just said; supportive, even tempered, loyal, faithful, honest, rich, and willing to be a family man. Sound like Adam?

Daphne smiled. "Yes, I think so."

"I do too, Daphne. I don't know how, but you've found him. This is your day. You've been waiting a long time for it, preparing, putting up with your mother . . . ."

Daphne laughed.

Tamara pulled away and smiled. "Enjoy it, Daph. Marry Adam and be happy, okay?"

"I love you, Tamara."

Tamara swallowed through the tightness in her throat. She nodded and smiled at Daphne. "You made me dress up in this costume, and getting ready took me hours. You don't think I'm going to let you get away with canceling the wedding now, do you?"

Daphne laughed and hugged Tamara again. "If this marriage doesn't work out I can always move into the ghetto with you, right?"

"Absolutely."

With a glowing smile, Daphne returned to the picture taking session.

Tamara sat on the front pew to watch the camera snap pictures of the bridal party, then the family in a variety of poses. Then she was called to join the family. She felt incredibly self conscious being included in those pictures, but if Daphne wanted her in them, how could she refuse?

The ones where she had to stand next to Dale were the worst. He looked so formal and omnipotent. When he placed his hands on her hips or shoulders, she practically jumped out of her dress.

"Relax," he whispered in her ear, his warm breath caressing her skin and raising her body temperature.

Damn him, did he always have to appear so confident and in control?

She smiled and the camera flashed.

"One more," the photographer called.

Dale eased one of the curly wisps away from her eyes, running the back of his index finger down the side of her face. He winked. "One more."

He stood behind her, a hand at her waist, his breath above her ear. Torture. This was pure torture.

After the photographer finally excused her, she went to freshen up in the small restroom at the back of the church.

Dale stood waiting in the small hallway when she got out. "What did you say to her up there?"

Tamara glanced at him. "To Daphne?"

He nodded. "She looks ten times better. The anxiety is gone from her face. She now looks as beautiful as she should on her wedding day."

Tamara shrugged. "Just a little girl talk. Getting married is a big step. She's nervous."

Dale moved in so close she could see the exact shape of his lips and smell the spicy aftershave he had splashed on. "Who'd of thought," he said huskily.

Tamara tipped her face upward. They were

almost cheek to cheek. "What?"

"A few words from you, and my sister is magically transformed into a content, excited bride."

If she moved her face a fraction to the left and he to the right, their lips would touch. Tamara's face burned at the thought. "Daphne's like you, Dale, afraid of making a mistake."

He stepped back. "And you're not afraid?"

Through her lashes she saw him standing like a statue in front of her. "Yes, I'm afraid of everything - especially events like these."

"Yet, you were able to convince Daphne that getting married is the right thing to do."

"It is." Tamara drew a breath. "Have you ever watched her when she's with Adam? It's like she's walking on air. If she doesn't marry him, she'll regret it the rest of her life."

Dale's eyes narrowed, a seemingly unspoken question shining in their depths.

Faint footsteps sounded behind Dale, and they both looked around.

"Hello, Tamara."

She glanced down and saw Raffi in a Tuxedo with a perfect haircut, looking like a little man. Her heart swelled just like every time she saw this dear child.

"Raffi." She smiled. "How are you, sweetie?"

"I'm fine, and how are you?"

Tamara continued to smile and looked from Dale to Raffi and saw how Raffi tried to emulate Dale. She didn't know what to say to the boy. She wanted to reach down and touch him, hug him, but resisted. "I'm . . . fine."

"It's good to see you." Then he looked at Dale. "Can I go with Grandpa John to the limo? He said there's a T.V. in there."

Dale squatted to Raffi's height. "Sure, you *may*, but don't touch anything else. Remember, this is Daphne's big day and we want everything to be perfect."

"I understand."

"Good," Dale said and kissed the boy before giving him a soft pat on his bottom.

Raffi ran off without saying good-bye to Tamara, and she tried not to be hurt by the rebuff.

"Grandpa John?" She raised an eyebrow at Dale.

He stood and shrugged. "My dad told him to call him that."

"You should be careful--"

"Forget you're a social worker for one day, okay, Tamara?"

He left then, just like Raffi, without a good-bye.

Time dragged before the guests started arriving. Ushers seated them in the pews and they whispered among themselves. Tamara stood back against a wall and watched the beautiful people glide in with their perfect outfits, loaded with jewelry, smelling of expensive perfumes, and sitting stiffly to witness the union of two of *their* families.

Tamara sighed, the current scene reminding her of the weddings she had attended as a child and how she'd been forced to behave like a little lady. She had hated it then and still felt uncomfortable.

At that moment, her parents walked in, and she decided to sit with them for the ceremony. She hadn't seen them in over five months.

"Mother, Father, hello."

"Darling," Celeste said in her high pitched voice. She touched the side of her face to Tamara's and kissed the air. Andre, her father, gave her a real kiss at least. But then again, he wasn't wearing lip stick.

"I'm glad you were able to make it," Tamara said to both of them.

Her father grunted and sat. Her mother told her she wouldn't miss Daphne's wedding for anything. After all, she was like Tamara's sister.

Tamara nodded. *And you've probably spent about the same amount of time with her as you have with me.*

"What a delightful dress, dear."

"Thank you, Mother. You both look marvelous also. Any interesting trips lately?"

"We were in London a couple of months ago for a few weeks, but nothing special. We're planning a South American cruise for the Christmas holidays."

"Oh?"

"Unless you had plans to visit us, of course."

"No." Tamara shook her head and looked at her cream colored fingernails on her lap. "I, ah, I wasn't planning on visiting." She did her best to smile.

"Well that works out then."

A long silence ensued. Celeste was as uncomfortable with Tamara as Tamara was with her. Tamara's eyes began to blur. Why did people have children they weren't equipped to love? "I'd better go check on Daphne."

"How's your car?" Andre asked.

"Perfect, Dad." What could go wrong? He made her trade it in for the latest model every year. The car was already paid for, all she had to do was drive the old one in and drive out with the new. It was her birthday gift from him every year.

"Still happy with the Jags? We can change to a different manufacturer if you like."

"Jags are fine. More than I need, you know that."

He looked across at her for an extended gaze. "You look gorgeous today, Tamara."

"Thanks." She knew he was trying. Of her two parents he had always been the more caring, but part of her also knew he just felt responsible for her well being, and that was different than love.

"Are you taking care of yourself."

"Sure."

"Good. Good."

She escaped her parents, thinking she couldn't stand to sit with them another second. She'd survived the obligatory greeting, that was more than enough.

The smile on Daphne's face as she stood at the altar watching Adam filled Tamara with an inner peace and happiness. Her friend would make a great high society wife, and it would bring her the kind of happiness she deserved. Daphne had been preparing for this her whole life.

Dale sat beside Edna and held her hand while her husband, John, sat on her other side. Raffi sat next to John Curtis. Edna held her head high. There were no tears in Edna's eyes, only prideful triumph as she watched her daughter say her vows.

The ceremony was beautiful and brief. After Daphne and Adam walked down the aisle and exited the church, the family followed cheering and clapping. Then the rest of the guests hurried after to watch them drive away in the limousine.

As soon as she slipped outside, Dale took her hand. "Glad that's over. Come on." He grabbed Raffi with his other hand and led them both to his Mercedes.

"Dale, I've got my own car."

"We'll get it later."

Raffi climbed in and bounced on the back seat.

"Sit still," Dale ordered. Raffi did.

Tamara sat beside Dale and glanced back at Raffi, winking at him. Raffi smiled and buckled himself into his car seat.

Dale drove to the reception at Pacific Sands Country Club in silence. Raffi hummed. Tamara wondered what she was doing in his car with them both.

"She was beautiful," Tamara said to break the

silence.

Dale glanced at her then extended his arm and traced her jaw bone with the back of his index finger. "She wasn't the only one."

"Thank you."

"I know how difficult that was for you. I wish I could have sat beside you and held your hand."

Tamara found that just the thought of holding his hand through the ceremony eased the tension she'd been holding inside. The incredibly sweet sentiment clouded her vision, and she turned to stare out her window.

His hand slipped down and took her fingers, he squeezed and she squeezed back.

At the country club she lost track of him for a while. She told him she'd watch Raffi while he checked with the caterer.

As soon as they located a table and sat, Raffi said, "I'm bored."

"I'm sure you are. I didn't like these parties when I was little either."

"Oh, I like the parties, but only for a little while."

Tamara combed back his hair with her fingernails. "You sure do look good, young man."

"Distinguished."

"Oh, really?"

"That's what Dale said. 'We must look distinguished, tonight', that's what he said."

Tamara laughed. "Well, you certainly do."

"Know what else?"

"What?"

"I missed you," he said, changing the subject simply as only children can do.

"That's nice of you to say. I've missed you too." She wished she could tell him how much.

"Dale said you did, but you had res-pon-sa-blil-ties."

"Responsibilities." This little boy had a peculiar way of tearing her heart to shreds. "I needed to let you and Dale get to know each other alone, understand?"

"He missed you, too, he told me."

She straightened. Raffi had to learn to be more discrete. "Perhaps you shouldn't tell me what Dale tells you in confidence."

"In what?"

"It means secret."

"He don't care if I tell you."

"Doesn't. He doesn't care if you tell me."

"Nope, he doesn't."

Tamara smiled. Raffi was a dear boy.

"Can I go play?"

"Where?"

"Over there." Raffi pointed to the grassy hill.

What the heck, it was better than sitting here. "Sure, go ahead."

When Dale joined her and asked for Raffi, she pointed at the hill.

Dale's face hardened. "He's rolling on grass with a tuxedo on?"

"I told him it would be all right."

Dale frowned at her. "You had no right to do that. First of all, that grass is not meant to be trampled on, and second--"

"Dale," she said, and put a hand on his arm. "What is the grass for then, to just look nice?"

"Precisely, now excuse me."

But she stood and gripped his arm harder. "Isn't this where we started?"

His jaw muscle twitched. "How will it look if my kid is allowed to run around the grass when others are not? I'm a board member, and I know better."

She shrugged. "Who cares, Dale? He's a little boy. Let him have some fun." She hadn't missed the fact that Dale had called Raffi *his* kid.

He covered her hand with his. "When you look at me like that, so damn beautiful, how can I not let you have your way?"

She smiled, glad she'd convinced him in some way. "Can you sit with me for a while or do you need to go?"

"I have a few obligations, but there's nothing I want more than to spend some time with you, Tamara. I'll be back shortly."

She hoped her eyes didn't give too much away, but her disappointment was sharp and penetrating. She didn't want Dale to leave, but understood he had to. Just like she knew he'd be expected to sit with his family for dinner.

Much to her despair, she was seated with her parents and their friends. She longed to leave, to go have a beer with someone real, with her co-workers or even Roy's friends. Instead she listened to the older generation discuss the tragedy of current fashions, and how today's youth knew nothing of elegance and subtlety.

Tamara was relieved when the prolonged dinner was over, and the bride and groom approached the dance floor for their first dance. The pair glided along the parquet flooring, smiling, gazing into each other's eyes, and finally kissing. This earned them applause by the captivated audience. Daphne then danced with her father while Adam danced with Edna, then they switched to his parents. Brothers and sisters joined in, followed by grandparents, aunts, uncles, until the dance floor was crowded with elegant couples.

The most handsome man of all had to be Dale. He danced with his sister, then his mother, then his grandmother. He was a skilled dancer and a pleasure to watch. She stopped breathing when she saw him kiss his grandmother's hand and turn on his heels toward her.

He held out his hand. "Finally, I can ask the woman I've been dying to hold in my arms all night. Would you like to dance, Tamara?"

Her parents' shock was barely contained at Dale's choice of words.

"I'd love to." She placed her hand in his, meeting his charming smile with one of her own. Her heart seemed to expand and for some reason the aura of the evening instantly changed.

CHAPTER EIGHT

Out on the dance floor, Dale pulled Tamara against his long, firm body. Entwining his fingers with hers, and locking her in place with the other hand pressed to her lower back, he moved slowly to the music. "It's so good to hold you again."

"You're a good dancer, Dale."

"I'm good at a lot of things."

She laughed softly. "I don't doubt that."

"So . . . you didn't bring a date."

"To Daphne's wedding? Of course not."

"I thought you were seeing someone?"

She couldn't see his face because they were cheek to cheek. She eased her head back enough to look at him from the corner of her eyes. "Roy isn't the type of person who would feel comfortable in this kind of setting."

"I see. He's good enough to sleep with but not good enough to introduce to your friends and family. Sounds like you're getting a little snobbish, Tamara. That's not like you."

She noticed the tightness of his jaw and how the pressure of his arm around her waist increased. She couldn't resist and caressed the back of his neck with her hand which she'd placed around his shoulder. "I'm not sleeping with him, Dale. I just thought it would be a good idea to date so I could . . . ."

"Forget about me?" His voice was thick.

She looked away from him and pressed the side of her face to his again. "Yes," she whispered in his ear. "It hasn't been easy."

He sighed heavily. "For me either."

"I know, Raffi told me."

He pulled back suddenly and looked directly at her. "What did he say?"

Tamara smiled. "That you missed me."

"That little traitor." Dale chuckled. "Well, it's true. I don't know how I can miss someone who was never really part of my life, but I do."

"We're doing the right thing, Dale. Things would never work between us." *So why did it feel so wrong to be apart?*

He tilted his head, his eyes dark, penetrating. "Actually, things may work quite well."

"Dale."

"You smell exquisite. Your hair, your clothes, you look perfect tonight."

Perfect for him. That was the problem, she didn't feel perfect, she felt so unnatural - like a made up doll. But she smiled, glad she had managed to please him. "It was part of the dress code. On the bottom of my invitation it said, 'must look perfect'."

His fingers tightened around hers and his thumb caressed the sensitive skin between her index finger and thumb. "Well, you've met and exceeded the dress code."

"Anything for Daphne."

"Anything, yes." His eyes seemed to caress her, as he regarded her with undeniable tenderness. "You're a good friend."

"I try."

The music ended and he led her off the dance floor, keeping his arm around her waist. "Care to take a walk?"

She'd love nothing better than to leave this stuffy reception, but being alone on a moon lit walk with Dale was too dangerous to her heart, so she shook her head. "I don't walk well in high heels."

"Tamara, there you are. You have to grant me a dance."

Both she and Dale shifted their attention to Charles.

Tamara accepted his kiss on the cheek and made the obligatory statement of how wonderful he looked in his tuxedo.

Dale casually lowered his hands into his pockets. "I didn't realize you two knew each other."

"Sure," Charles boasted with a wide grin. "We

went out to dinner together once."

At Dale's uplifted eyebrows and questioning stare, Tamara shook her head. "Now Charles, that isn't exactly true. You're going to start rumors," she teased him.

Charles laughed. "Actually Dale, we were with Daphne and Adam, but I wished it was just Tamara and myself. Unfortunately she told me she was hopelessly in love with someone else already, or I would have pursued her shamelessly."

Dale nodded. "She has that effect on men."

Tamara gave Dale a murderous look she hoped would shut him up. "I'd like to accept that dance now, Charles."

"Wonderful. Excuse us, will you, Dale?"

Dale pulled one arm out of his pants pocket and waved it in front of him. "Please."

Tamara danced with Charles, trying to deflect his obvious flirtatious comments. After the dance, Dale was no where in sight, causing Tamara's lighthearted mood to plummet. She accepted a few more dances from other gentlemen, including her father.

The older folk sat after a period while the younger guests, along with the bride and groom, danced to faster, more modern music. Tamara enjoyed those dances much better, since they weren't as intimate.

For some songs the women danced together while the guys cheered, reminding Tamara of the nights she and Daphne had gone out to clubs and danced all night with whomever happened to be there.

Dale danced none of the modern dances. She saw him at his mother's table or with other relatives, always serene, charming, but with an air of authority.

Raffi, who earlier had found other kids to roll on the grass with him, now sat beside Dale, his eyes drooping.

Tamara wanted to join them as much for Raffi as for Dale, but she didn't want to seem too forward, especially since Edna was at the table. *Oh, what the heck, if Dale wasn't there, Tamara would have gone to Edna to congratulate her. Why not now?*

With her head held high, she approached their table. "Edna, what a marvelous wedding."

The older woman glanced at Tamara and smiled politely. "Thank you, my dear." There was a short pause, then she added. "Won't you sit down?"

Tamara avoided looking at Dale. "I'd love to."

"Sit by me, Tamara," Raffi mumbled, half asleep.

Edna eyed Raffi critically and turned a curious gaze back to her. "You've met Raffi?" she asked Tamara.

"Yes, didn't Dale tell you?"

Edna shifted her eyes to her son only momentarily. "I see. You handled the . . . paperwork?"

Tamara nodded with a smile. "Everything,

yes."

"I'm tired, Dale," Raffi whined.

"There's not much we can do about that now, is there?"

Tamara had to bite back a sharp comment at Dale's inconsiderate answer. "Come here, Raffi. Sit on my lap for a little while."

Raffi's eyes lifted to Dale for approval.

That angered her further. "Come on, sweetie. It's okay."

Raffi smiled and happily hopped onto her lap, and within minutes he'd fallen asleep. She kissed the top on his head and sat back.

"Looks like your dancing is over for the night," Dale remarked dryly.

She stared at him, finding him cold and cruel, and for some reason his attitude really hurt. "I don't mind."

"Why do you baby him so much?"

"Because he *is* a baby, Dale. Can't you see that?"

Dale's lashes lowered as he watched the boy sleep, then without answering he looked away to the dance floor.

Edna watched the exchange with interest, but offered no opinion, no advice. *Thank God for that.*

As she held Raffi for the next couple of hours and watched everyone dance until they could no longer stand, she wondered if she'd done the right thing leaving Raffi with Dale. It wasn't the first time she'd had that thought. Dale had no idea how to care for a child. He thought if he provided food, clothing, and material goods that was all Raffi needed. But Raffi needed love more than anything else. It broke her heart when Dale spoke to Raffi as if he were an adult.

When the time came for tossing the bouquet and garter belt, Dale turned to her. "You want to go? I'll hold him."

She shook her head. "Not interested in that bouquet."

"Or the marriage that goes with it, I take it."

"Definitely not. You go."

He shrugged, glanced at his mother, then winked. "About time I got married, huh, Mother?"

She smiled at her son. "Considering your younger sister has beat you to it, perhaps you should."

Dale lifted his large body and strolled to join the men when it was their turn. They hooted and called out, some curling their arms to reveal large muscles. Everyone laughed. When the groom flung the garter everyone jumped and lunged toward it. As if in slow motion it glided in a curve over everyone's arms and landed right in Dale's outstretched hand. He'd made no effort but simply stood in place and lifted his arm. He twirled the garter around his index finger then folded it into his pocket.

"Congratulations," Tamara said when he returned.

"I guess it's my lucky day." He smiled, making him look irresistible.

She wished he would smile more often.

"I suppose I should start packing Daphne's gifts." Dale stretched and waited for his mother's response.

Edna nodded. "Daphne will cut the cake and then she'll be leaving."

"Right. I'll be back."

Dale was gone for about thirty minutes. He came back in time to see his sister off in the limousine.

Tamara had to wake Raffi so she could also wish Daphne a happy honeymoon and hug her goodbye.

"Dale, you're taking care of the gifts?" Daphne asked nervously.

He nodded. "They're in my car, don't worry about anything. Have a great honeymoon."

When Tamara got to Dale's car she realized what they were talking about. Brightly wrapped and bowed packages filled Dale's trunk and back seat. "Where will Raffi sit?"

"Between us."

"What?" She couldn't keep the surprise from her voice. "He has to sit in his car seat."

Dale looked irritated, but he pulled presents out of the back and placed them in the front, leaving just enough room for he and Tamara to sit.

"Are you taking all these to your place?"

"We'll drop them off at Daphne and Adam's new place. It'll only take a while longer. Do you mind?"

"Not at all." She got Raffi belted in first then

slid into the passenger side.

What a night. She glanced over her shoulder and watched Raffi fall asleep again. Of course, the poor child was tired. Even she had to fight to keep her eyes open. Dale drove in an unusually quiet mood. She watched his profile, wishing she had the right to reach across and caress the frown on his forehead, and feel the stubble now apparent on his jaw. She closed her eyes, figuring it was better to shut out the image of what she couldn't have.

When they got to Daphne's house, Dale came around and lifted the sleeping Raffi out of his car seat. "Take the keys, Tam, and open the door."

"The servants . . . ?"

"Have the weekend off."

She removed his keys from the ignition and opened the door. Dale took Raffi to Daphne's bedroom. From the door jamb, she watched him place Raffi down gently on the bed and cover him with a quilt, the image warming her heart. How could Dale be so cold and unfeeling one minute and so tender the next?

He closed the door to the bedroom and led her to the family room. "It's chilly in here, isn't it?"

Tamara shrugged, although she had her arms hugged around herself. "I guess."

"I'll build a fire."

He threw a couple of logs in Daphne's fireplace and lay some kindling around the logs. He struck a match and the fire starter slowly caught, sending soft red and blue flames around the logs and flickering light into the room.

Then he stood and looked at Tamara. "That should take the chill out of the room. What do you think?"

"I didn't know we were staying long enough for it to matter?"

He dropped his hands in his pockets. "I have to bring the gifts in. You can sit here by the fire and relax until I finish."

"Okay." But she didn't sit. She stood by the warm fire, listening to the crackling and popping sounds of burning wood. Mesmerized by his grace and perfection, she watched Dale come in with his arms full of beautifully wrapped boxes, then go out for more. He placed them all on Daphne's dining room table.

"With the number of people at that ceremony it doesn't seem like there are many gifts."

He closed the front door and held up a basket full of cards with his other hand. "I think most people gave money."

Like Daphne really needed more money.

Dale walked across to her, rubbing his hands together.

She felt strangely vulnerable. "Now what, Dale?"

He lifted an eyebrow. "What do you mean?"

"It's late, you started a fire, and . . . we're all alone ."

"This is all true." He stepped in closer, bringing their bodies only inches from each other.

Her heart raced. "Is it also true that you don't intend for us to leave right away?"

"Tamara," he whispered and shook his head like he wished things were different. Then he cupped her face with both his hands. "You look like a princess tonight. I've been waiting all night to get you alone. Do you think I'm in a hurry to leave?"

Truth was, she felt like a princess. She no longer felt unnatural or uncomfortable in her dress. The night had taken on a surreal quality. She in her pearly gown, he in his black tuxedo, standing next to a crackling fire in this museum of a house. She stepped into his arms and lifted her lips to meet his. His hands were warm on her face and his lips hot and eager.

Dale's kiss was so tender and loving, her eyes filled with unshed tears. He let a out a shaky breath as he pulled back, then dropped his face to her shoulders. "You smell heavenly."

Tonight she was everything Dale desired, and that's exactly what she wanted to be. She wanted to see the passion in his eyes and the appreciation as he held her and made love to her. She wrapped her arms around his waist.

He tightened his hold on her. "Tamara, do you want to go?"

"Does it feel like I want to go?" Her voice was thick with desire.

"No, it definitely feels like you're willing to stay. Are you sure?"

She unsnapped his cummerbund and dropped it to the floor. "You're going to continue to dress in those boring suits all the time, aren't you?"

"I'm not going to change who I am."

"Neither am I."

He reached to the top of her head and began pulling out pins. Her hair flowed down to her shoulders. He ran his fingers through it and sighed. "That means you're going to continue to walk around in torn jeans and vulgar T-shirts."

She loosened his bow tie and unbuttoned his ruffled shirt. "You'll go to those boring dinners and expect me to go with you."

He kissed her chin and began undoing the neck high buttons of her dress. "You'll take me to loud diners with mediocre food and rude cashiers."

Tamara laughed. "I thought you liked that deli."

"Did I say that?"

"I guess not." She placed her hands over his, stopping him from his goal of disrobing her. "So we're both refusing to change."

"It appears so."

She looked at Dale's handsome face, her heart thumping, her breath lodging in her lungs, making it almost impossible to exhale. "We'll be making a big mistake it we continue then, won't we?"

"You think so?"

She finally exhaled. Afraid. "No, I don't." As terrified as she was of being with Dale, she was even more so of walking out of this house and never seeing him again. "I want to make love to you so badly, Dale."

He flipped his hands and caught hers, then he brought them to his lips. He kissed her fingers, one at a time. "Thank God, because Tamara, I intend to make love to you, right here, right now."

CHAPTER NINE

Tamara's dress came off, along with his coat, bow tie, and shirt. They dropped to their knees in the thick, lush carpeting, and facing the warmth of the fireplace, Dale began a cherishing process with his hands and mouth. He straddled her and gazed at her naked body. "You are *such* a stunning woman."

She couldn't believe they'd gotten to this point. Were they actually moments away from knowing each other in the most intimate, magical way possible for a man and a woman? She shivered with anticipation.

He brought his body against hers. "Cold?"

"Not anymore." Not with his hot body so close to hers.

"Frightened?"

"Not really." Yet she had never wanted to lose herself in a man, to be absorbed by his passion, as she did now with Dale. And that should scare the hell out of her.

He kissed her collar bone, running his tongue temptingly along the same lines. "Yes, you are," he said, his hands caressing her hips and coaxing her thighs to move along the outside of his so she had slowly wrapped her legs around his waist. "And you should be. This is no amusing diversion, something were going to easily erase come morning."

She placed her hands on his shoulders, feeling his strong body above hers, wanting him, needing for him to fill the vacuum inside her if only for just one night. "I won't want to erase it."

As with everything he did, Dale elegantly filled her in one majestic sweep that left her stimulated beyond belief. "Oh Dale."

"Open your eyes." He gazed at her, angling his head, a look of fire deep inside him. "I've never met anyone like you, Tamara."

And she'd never had a lover like him. Most wanted to get it over with. One, two, three and they were finished. Not that she'd been with many men in her life. They were college boys when she'd been stupid and reckless.

She caressed Dale's back, relishing the feel of him inside her. She met his eyes. "You don't have to do this. I don't need sweet words and loving looks."

He moved against her with as much finesse

as he'd shown on the dance floor. What a beautiful, graceful lover. He brought her to the brink of fulfillment and stopped. "Yes, you do," he said, breathless.

"What?" she gasped.

"You do need sweet words and loving looks and so much more."

She needed him to continue making love to her. She'd never before been left in this state of aroused energy. "Dale, oh Dale. Please."

He brushed her ear lobe with his moist lips. "Let me love you. Let me in your heart. Open up to me, Tam."

She felt her passion ebb and tears cloud her eyes. "Dale, don't make me cry." She wasn't used to letting anyone love her. She wasn't sure she knew how. But part of her knew he was right, she did need exactly what he was offering.

He gazed at her face, seemingly taking in every feature. "Cry if you want to."

Why did he want to tear her down, make her so completely vulnerable? "I don't want to." But it was too late, tears ran out of the corners of her eyes. Her heart felt as if it were being torn and rebuilt. In Dale's arms she felt completely cared for, totally loved. And yet, she was terrified.

He kissed her eyes. "Hold on to me."

She did and felt his body completely fill hers, his hands caressing her breasts, his lips roaming her face. "My sweet Tamara. I want you again and again."

"Yes," she said, as a staggering jolt shook her

body. She fought for a breath and to hear what Dale was saying.

"Beautiful," he said. "And all mine."

"Yes, Dale, all yours,"she whispered.

He drove into her repeatedly until he stiffened, then relaxed and dropped his weight onto her.

The room was silent, only the crackle of burning wood and their heavy breathing interrupted the quiet. Neither moved. Tamara could not think. She seemed to be on another plane.

Dale shifted. "I adore you, Tamara," he whispered. "Are you okay?"

She caressed his moist temples and kissed his chin. "I was more than okay, I hope."

He chuckled. "Did I overwhelm you?"

She met his loving eyes. "I'm not used to being. . . I don't know how to deal with . . . ." How did she tell him she'd never had anyone care about her feelings the way he just had?

He touched her lips with one finger. "It's easy. Let me show you how." He moved down her body and drove her wild as he slowly and luxuriously made love to her again like no one ever had before in her life.

Afterwards, neither spoke. Tamara dreaded facing him if he regretted what just happened. Words of love during sex couldn't be trusted. She knew her soul would shatter if she saw one sign that he wished they'd had more self control tonight.

He eased away from her and sat with his

elbows on his knees and his hands buried in his hair. Then he stood and added another log to the fire. Immediately he returned to her side and cleared his throat. "I've never made love to a woman on the floor before."

Was he apologizing? Her heart sank. "Does it make any difference where it happens?"

He lay beside her again, leaning his weight on his elbow. With his other hand, he threaded his fingers through her hair, gazing deeply into her eyes. "No darling, I'd make love to you on the moon if you asked me to."

Tamara laughed. She trailed her fingernail down the length of his chest and abdomen. "And I thought you were the conservative type." Then she pushed him onto his back and rolled on top of him.

He loved watching her. She looked so damn sexy hovering over him, the low fire light silhouetting her. He ran his hands up and down her back. "Tamara?"

"Yes?" she asked provocatively.

"I was just wondering . . . the man you told Charles you were involved with . . . it was me, wasn't it?"

"What?" He could barely make out her face, but he sensed her teasing smile had faded.

"You told Charles you were seriously involved with someone already. It wasn't Roy, it was me."

She tensed and shook her head. "It wasn't anyone. I told him that so he . . . ."

"Would back off?"

"Something like that."

"Is that why you told me about Roy, so I'd back off?"

She began to ease away, distancing herself from him, so he reached across and encircled her waist.

"Dale, I don't want to talk about this now."

"I can tell."

"Well, does it matter? I'm here with you, aren't I?"

"Yes, you are." He caressed her smooth hip. "I guess, I wish you had been talking about me. I'd like to have a serious relationship with you, Tamara."

She stiffened only momentarily. "Would you?"

He shifted and leaned over her so he could look into her dazzling eyes. "I would."

Tamara combed her long fingers into his hair, scratching his scalp, then pulled his head down. She kissed him vehemently, but he responded as lovingly as he could, massaging her sensual lips in a side to side motion. As her passion subsided he pulled away and gathered her into his arms. She lay meekly against him, stroking his arms.

"Could you handle it, Tamara? Will you let me get close to you?"

She sighed. "I might fall in love with you."

He kissed her forehead, understanding her fear. After all, had she ever really been able to trust anyone with her love? "I'd like that."

"I might already be in love with you."

He doubted it. "I hope so."

He dozed off with Tamara in his arms and awoke at some point as she crawled away from him. "Where are you going?" he whispered drowsily.

"I'm going to borrow a shirt from Daphne. I'm cold, and I don't want Raffi to wake up before us and find me naked."

He nodded. "Put on my shirt." Then he dropped his head and went back to sleep.

"Is he ever gonna wake up?"

"Shh, he had a long day yesterday making sure his sister's wedding turned out well."

Dale had been awake for the last few minutes but found the conversation between Raffi and Tamara interesting enough to fake sleep a little longer.

"What could go wrong ? It was just a party. There were like a million people there, huh?"

"Mmm, you're right, it felt like a million."

"I never saw so many people like that, Tamara. Have you?"

"Yes, I have, actually. I went to lots of weddings, birthdays, and other parties for people I didn't know because my parents felt it necessary to show up."

"Was it fun like this one?"

"No, after a while they stop being fun."

"Do you think Dale will be mad at me for dirtying my tuxedo?"

A pause. "No, sweetie, he won't be angry with you."

Dale decided to roll over and let them know he was awake. Tamara had astutely dropped a comforter over his nude body. He clutched at the comforter and sat, leaning his back on the sofa. "What time is it?"

Raffi sat on a bar stool drinking milk and eating toast. Tamara stood on the other side in the kitchen. They both acknowledged him at once.

"Late," Tamara said.

"Hi, Dale," Raffi greeted him.

Dale rubbed his stubbled face. "I suppose I better get up and get you two home."

Raffi shook his head. "That's okay, me and Tamara are getting some talking in."

Dale smiled. "Oh, in that case, there's no need for me to hurry." He got up with the comforter clutched around his waist, but his clothes which he'd dropped all over the room last night, were not around. He glanced at Tamara, hoping she'd see his silent plea and give him a clue to where she'd put his clothes. She impassively sipped from a steaming coffee mug.

"I'm going to go dress," he offered.

"Mmm, good idea," she said.

"Isn't it though?"

She took another slow motion sip, then smiled. "In the bathroom."

"Thank you."

He slipped on his pants, not worried about getting his shirt back from Tamara. He would enjoy watching her in his clothes. He had a feeling both Raffi and Tamara were more than happy to laze around Daphne's house a little longer. He settled his hands in his pockets to straighten out the lining, and found Daphne's garter. He pulled it out, staring at it like it held the secrets to his future. It had flown into his hand as if there had been an invisible tether between him and Adam. He smiled at that thought and shook his head. *You're losing it, pal. One night with Tamara, and you're already reading too much into it.*

The door bell rang as he walked out to the living room. He shot Tamara a puzzled look. Who would be visiting Daphne's house the morning after her wedding?

She shrugged.

"I'll get it." He opened the door.

His mother and father stood on the doorstep, smiling at him. "We rang the bell because we saw your car in the driveway, dear, and figured you had spent the night," Edna explained.

"Yes, ah, we did. What are you doing here?"

"Daphne asked us to drop off her wedding gown and few other things. Are you going to step aside and invite us in?"

"Of course," Dale said, allowing them to enter and intrude on his peaceful morning . . . and dreading it.

It didn't take more than a fraction of a second for Edna to notice Tamara talking and laughing with Raffi. She gave John an all knowing look then pegged Dale with cold censuring eyes.

"Oh, Edna, John," Tamara said, as she lifted her adoring eyes from Raffi and noticed them watching her. Her expression sobered. "Good morning."

Tamara wore only Dale's tuxedo shirt which just covered her bottom. She looked magnificently alluring to Dale, but spotted his mother's disapproval written all over her face.

"Tamara, we didn't expect to see you here this morning."

Tamara glanced at Dale, then back at Edna. Her face grew to deeper and deeper shades of red as the silent seconds ticked on. "I didn't expect you to see me either."

John cleared his throat. "I'll bring in what we came to drop off, then we'll go and leave you kids alone."

"Good idea, Dad. May I get you some coffee, Mother?"

"No, Dale." Her tone was cool. "What you can do is come and see me later today or tonight."

And he knew exactly what she would say to him when she saw him. "If I can."

She nodded stiffly. "Tamara, it was nice to see you."

"Edna, I . . . you don't need to leave."

"I believe I do, my dear."

Dale walked her to the door and when he returned, Tamara had on a pair of Daphne's beige shorts and a yellow, sleeveless top. It wasn't her style, and he was disappointed. "You okay?"

"I'm so embarrassed." She stood with her arms crossed and one hand on her forehead, rigidly staring out a large picture window.

"Why?"

"You don't understand, Dale." She turned and faced him. "She was like my second mother. Every time Daphne got into trouble in high school, it was my fault, and Edna would come to the school and punish us both. I felt, just now, like she was going to lay down another one of her laws and threaten to incarcerate me if I broke it."

"My mother is tough, but she's a kind woman."

Tamara dropped to the sofa. "She's always been able to make me tremble with just one look."

Dale sat beside her on the sofa, put his arm around her, and squeezed her shoulder. "Has the same effect on you as I do, huh?"

Tamara gave him a sideways look and smiled. "Not quite."

Dale kissed her temple. "Who cares what my mother thinks, Tamara. We're both adults, and we don't need her approval to sleep together."

Dale said it quietly, but Tamara still glanced at Raffi who sat happily making a picture on the table with his Cheerios. "Your mother's approval means everything, Dale, and you know that."

He didn't deny it. His mother's approval was important to him, and he'd go tonight and get it. He wanted Tamara to be part of his life for as long as she'd have him, and Edna needed to give him her blessing.

The moment his mother met him at the front door, Dale realized the last thing Edna would say was how happy she was for him.

She didn't even say hello as she ushered him into her study and sat behind her large cherry wood desk. This room always smelled like the furniture had just been polished with lemon scented oil. As a boy he'd loved it. Now it just irritated him because it reinforced her fanatical need for perfection.

"I am very disappointed in you, Dale. Out of all the women available, you choose to take advantage of your sister's best friend. I don't understand it."

He placed his hands on his hips, too agitated to sit. "I assure you, I didn't take advantage of her."

"Don't get smart with me. She's a very confused young girl, very vulnerable, and not someone for you to toy with."

"Toy with? Is that what you think I'm doing?"

"I haven't the slightest idea what you're doing." Her tone remained cool, and her displeasure was evident from how rigidly she held her body.

He approached her desk. "My first inclination is to tell you it's none of your business, but I won't do that." He planted both hands on her desk and leaned across. "I like Tamara, she's full of spirit and makes me feel alive. I plan on seeing a lot more of her?"

"To what end?"

"I don't know, Mother. Are you asking me to predict the future?"

"I'm warning you she's not a girl you *can* have a future with." Her eyes held his as if trying to make him understand what was incomprehensible.

"You don't know that and neither do I." He pushed off her desk. "Tell me you like her, just a little."

Her expression softened. "Dale, I happen to care for her very much, I just know she is not for you."

He walked around her desk, and kissed his mother's perfumed, refined cheek. "If you can love her, and Daphne can love her, why can't I?"

Edna lowered her eyes. "Love? I didn't realize you had fallen in love with her."

"I don't know that I have, but if I did, I'd want your support."

Edna didn't give him her support, but neither did she outright reject the idea of allowing Tamara to occupy a permanent spot in their family. For this Dale was grateful, because somehow, Tamara already occupied a permanent place in his heart.

CHAPTER TEN

Tamara had agreed to watch Raffi while Dale had his talk with his mother. As he drove to her place and watched the neighborhoods deteriorate more and more the closer he got to her apartment, he silently vowed he would convince her to move. It was dangerous for a beautiful, young woman like her to live alone in such a crime infested area.

He definitely didn't feel comfortable leaving his car in the street, but he had no choice.

She greeted him with a wide, warm smile. "You're still in one piece."

"Do you think my mother would harm her only son?" He kissed her cheek and strolled in. "Where's Raffi?"

"My room. I think he's jumping on my bed."

"Wonderful," Dale said sarcastically. Tamara

needed to learn how to discipline better.

She disappeared into her kitchen. Dale went to her bedroom and indeed found Raffi jumping as high as he could on her king size bed and dropping on his bottom only to bounce back up. He was enjoying himself like crazy. Dale felt a twinge of disappointment. All the toys he'd bought Raffi, and he didn't look even half as happy at home as he did bouncing on Tamara's bed.

He took a moment to glance at the rest of her room. It looked welcoming. She'd decorated it in soft, pastel colors, very feminine.

Raffi noticed him and when he landed on his bottom, he stopped. "Hi," he said self-consciously.

"Having a good time?"

"Ah, yeah."

Dale smiled. "Good. We've got to get going though. Tomorrow's a school day."

"Okay, Dale." He scooted off Tamara's large bed, and ran out of the room.

He was going to call the boy back to fix the mess he'd made on her beautiful, ruffled bedspread, but he'd escaped too fast. Dale sighed and began stretching out the comforter himself and arranging her soft, lacy pillows against her headboard. Lace. He smiled. He couldn't help smoothing his fingers over the fabric and thinking of Tamara's wild hair spread out on the pillow as she slept. He inhaled the sweet vanilla scent that seemed to cling to everything she owned.

"You don't have to do that," her patient voice came from behind.

His hand stilled on the pillow. Here he was, bent over her bed, having fantasies about her. Caught. *Well, there's the answer to your question, Tamara. Sleeping with you once, didn't get you out of my system, not by a long shot.* He stood and faced her. "Raffi . . . he, ah, messed it up."

"It's okay." She smiled. "Are you leaving so soon?"

Dale nodded. "I've got work to do tonight and Raffi has school tomorrow. He should go to bed early."

She shrugged, but looked hurt.

Damn it, why was he acting so cold with her when he didn't mean to? He just didn't want to end up sleeping with her again, before he had a chance to think about what Edna had said. He certainly needed to get out of her bedroom where her scent lingered everywhere and drove all reason from his mind.

Dale approached her, but she didn't move out of the doorway. "Do I at least get a good-bye kiss?" she asked.

Dale slid his hand along the side of her face, and she leaned into it and closed her eyes. His heart lurched. He continued to move his hand, threading his finger through her hair.

She opened her eyes. "What's wrong?"

"Nothing, darling. Don't look so sad."

"I think I am sad." Tamara's eyes were wide and brilliant.

"Because of me?"

"Because I want you to stay, and you can't wait to get away from me."

Dale took a deep, painful breath. She was right. How could he deny it? He bent forward and kissed her sweet lips. But he didn't really want to get away from her, only those feelings growing inside him every time he looked at her. "Last night was heaven for me, Tamara," he whispered against her lips. "I'm not leaving you, I'm just going home."

She shuddered, then leaned her forehead on his. "I'm sorry. It just felt like you were shutting me out."

"Tamara, forgive me." He let out his pent up breath. "If I'm closing up it's because I'm frightened. Everyone, including you, has told me you're the wrong girl for me, and yet I want you, all the time." Her hands felt so good on his hips.

"It's okay, Dale. I'm not expecting a wedding ring, in fact I don't know that I'd ever want that from you."

"That's exactly what scares me." He cupped her face and tried to see into her soul, but her eyes gave him no answers. "I'm not against going out and having a good time, but if I fall in love with you, I want to know you're willing to take it to the next level. You're skittish as hell, afraid of commitment, and I don't want to be just another fool you've left behind when you start feeling overwhelmed."

She inched back trying to loosen his hold on her. Dale held on. "I'm already overwhelmed, but I'm not the one running out of here because Mommy disapproves."

"I'm not running out. I'm leaving because I have to go home, put Raffi to bed, and get ready for work tomorrow." He tipped her chin. "And yes, I want to think things through and make sure neither of us gets hurt."

"Dale, it's a little late to worry about hurting each other, isn't it?"

"True." He released her. He was already in over his head.

"All right, then."

All right what? "Now, in the mean time, I don't want you seeing anyone else."

Her eyes widened. "Did you think I would? After last night?" She started to pull away.

He tightened his hold "What about Roy?"

"I'm not interested in going out with Roy or anyone else, Dale. I made love to you last night. Do you think I take that lightly?"

He released her with a curse. "I don't know, dammit. You won't tell me how you feel. I need more from you, Tamara. Tell me. Tell me right now that Daphne, my mother, you, everyone who's told me we don't belong together is wrong. Tell me that right now."

She looked surprised, speechless, but she nodded. "I want us to be together," she whispered. "I thought you understood how I felt last night. But I can't tell you they're wrong. I just hope they are."

"Aren't we leaving?" Raffi said, having approached unnoticed.

Tamara reached behind her and caressed Raffi's head. "You are, sweetie. Dale and I were just walking out to get you."

"No you weren't. You were talking and I–."

"Never mind," Dale said lifting Raffi into his arms. "Sorry I kept you waiting."

Raffi smiled, then laid his head on Dale's shoulders. Dale pulled the boy closer and his heart swelled. When he glanced at Tamara, the tender expression on her face was almost his undoing. "I'll call you."

She hugged her arms around herself and nodded. "Good-night, guys."

Dale had made love to her, touched her as intimately as another human being ever could, made her spirit soar, yet she hadn't been sure what she'd felt was love - until just now. The moment little Raffi laid his face on Dale's shoulder so trustingly, so content, Tamara knew she loved Dale. He had willingly taken this child into his home, into his life, and was giving him everything he needed, even love. And Dale was offering her love too. She wondered if she could accept it as easily as Raffi did.

Tamara's office was involved in its annual fund-raiser. Child Welfare office had a deal with the local minor league ball club which allowed them to set up a few booths the last two weeks of the season. They would sell candy, take donations, and disseminate information. She ended up leaving for work early everyday to get her normal work done, and arriving home after the ball games in time to drop into bed. She had about ten calls from Dale in three days on her answering machine. Thank God the team was on the road for the next three games and she'd get a break. She wouldn't have to return to the stadium until Friday night. She'd call Dale back tomorrow, she decided as she slipped into dreamland.

That annoying ring wouldn't go away, then it stopped and she heard someone talking. She heard *herself* talking. Tamara opened her eyes, frowning and attempting to sit up in bed. She looked at the clock on her night stand - 1:30am. She groaned. Who the heck was calling her at this hour? When she heard Dale's angry voice, she got her answer.

She reached for her phone. "Dale?" She cleared her voice. "I'm here, I'm here. What in the world -?"

"Where have you been?" He snapped.

She dropped back, her head cradled on her pillow. "Do you know what time it is?"

"About two hours later than the last time I called and you weren't home."

"No, I got home about an hour ago." She yawned. "What's up?"

"Tamara? Where have you been?" This time the question didn't sound so rough, only worried.

"Working."

"Until midnight?"

"Mmhhmm." She was so tired. She wanted

to talk with Dale, but she didn't have the energy.

"I'm coming over."

Her eyes which were drifting closed, opened. "Now?"

"Yes, now. Is there a problem with that?"

"Dale, I'm so tired. Can I call you tomorrow?"

"I said I'll be there within an hour. Bye."

He hung up and Tamara frowned. He couldn't be serious. She dropped the receiver next to her in bed, flopped around and went back to sleep.

This time, there was no ringing, only banging. She buried her head under her pillows, but the banging continued and Dale was calling her name. Dale? He said he was coming over. She pushed herself up as if she were doing push-ups. She squinted at the clock which now registered 2:30am. She let out a string of unladylike curses and stumbled to the front door. There stood Dale fully dressed and awake, and Raffi in his pajamas half asleep.

She bent, lifted Raffi into her arms, and took him to the guest room. "I guess your sleeping here the rest of the night."

"We was worried about you."

She kissed his soft cheek, and he drifted off to sleep immediately. She was going to kill Dale. Yep, kill him.

He stood in her living room with his hands on his hips looking indignant, and all of a sudden, she didn't want to kill him anymore, she wanted to take him into her bedroom and curl up next to him.

They stared at each other in the quiet of the early morning.

"I have to get up again in less than four hours, Dale Curtis. I should be furious, but I don't have the energy."

His gaze ran over her face. "Do you know how worried I've been about you?"

"Worried that I was hurt or that I was with someone else?" She had to ask. He didn't seem to trust her and she couldn't understand why.

He stared at her for a long time, then shook his head and slumped on the arm of her couch. "I didn't know what you were doing every night until midnight, Tamara. What were you doing?"

"Fund-raiser. I'll explain tomorrow. Come to bed with me."

At first, he looked like he was going to protest, but changed his mind. He took her hand and let himself be led into her bedroom. He stripped off his clothes and slid in beside her. "Your body fits so beautifully against mine."

"I'm so tired, Dale."

He kissed her forehead and pulled her against him. "You're so reluctant to let yourself love me, I'm worried you'll find someone else just to prove to yourself you don't really care about me."

She chuckled. Mr. Confident wasn't so secure after all. "That's something a man would do, darling, not a woman."

"Oh," he said. "That doesn't make me feel any better, Tamara. Are you laughing at me?"

"Shh, hold me." She couldn't believe she was

wrapped in Dale's arms, snuggled against his warm chest, and she was going to fall asleep, but that was exactly what she did.

When the alarm went off at 6:00am, Tamara wanted to stomp on it and throw it out her window. "I can't get up. I can't."

"I'll shut it off," a male voice said.

As a male figure leaned over her to turn off her alarm clock, her eyes flew open in terror. Until she remembered Dale had come over last night, or rather this morning.

Then he pulled her against him and kissed her neck and shoulders.

"Mmm, Dale, I love--" she caught herself. What was she saying? "I love waking up with you, but -"

"I'm glad to hear it." He moved his lips to her breasts forcing her body to wake up. Her nipples hardened, the rest of her chest tightened, and her arms slid to his shoulders on their own.

"I've got to go to work," she whispered hoarsely.

"Me, too," he said and slipped beneath her sheet, dropping precious kisses along her rib cage down to her belly button.

She had to get up. She couldn't make love to Dale this morning, there was no time. But when he touched her, all she could do was moan with pleasure. When he slid above her and whispered loving, soothing, sensual words in her ears, her arms and legs wrapped around him on their own. When he braced himself above her and stared down at her, she asked, "What are you waiting for?"

"Permission."

"Granted."

He grinned, and slowly they became one, one millimeter at a time until Tamara thought she would die of anticipation. The distance between them was fully bridged, yet he didn't move. Her heavy eyelids opened and she found him staring at her.

"Oh Dale, what is it?" Would he always torture her this way?

The emotions playing on his face said everything he seemed afraid to voice.

Tamara reached up and slid her shaky hands on his stubbled face. "It's okay," she reassured him.

He bent his head and kissed her almost shyly. "I love feeling this close to you."

Tamara took a deep, unsteady breath. Never had love making been this intense, this meaningful. She loved this man so much. She arched her back and he shook. The idea that he was as moved as she was hit her hard, and her eyes filled. "Just make love to me, Dale."

"I will, but I wanted you to know how I felt first."

"I know, Dale." She kissed his chin. "I love you too."

She couldn't believe she'd said it, but she had, and the satisfaction on his face was her reward. He began to move above her, and as she arched her back, Tamara could no longer think about anything but the glorious things this remarkable man of hers was making her feel.

CHAPTER ELEVEN

Tamara showed him where to find the breakfast items as she gulped her coffee, and got ready to leave for work. She also explained exactly where she had been since he still demanded to know.

"You're crazy coming home so late at night by yourself in this neighborhood."

She shrugged. "I'm careful."

"I don't like it."

She almost said 'tough', but bit down on her tongue. He was only being caring. "Well, I won't go again until Friday night, and you can go with me if you'd like. Raffi might enjoy a night of baseball."

"This Friday night? I thought I'd get a babysitter and take you out."

"Sorry. Come with me to the ball park, you'll have a good time."

He shook his head. "Not my idea of fun, Tamara."

She put down her coffee cup and wrapped her arms around his waist, dropping her chin on his chest to look up at him. "You don't have to go with me, darling, but *I* have to go."

He smiled at her and stroked her back. "Fine, we'll go out Saturday night then."

"Games are Friday and Saturday night, and Sunday afternoon."

He held her upper arms and pulled her away from him. "You're working *all* weekend?"

She nodded. "It's only a two week period. I do it every year." Why did she feel like apologizing again? "I'll make it up to you another time."

He crossed his arms. "Like having dinner at my parents' next Thursday night? They're hosting Dad's foreign business investors."

Damn, here we go, those lousy, boring dinners she hated. Tamara told him how much she disliked those social events. Why did he have to spring one on her so soon when their relationship was so fragile?

"Tamara?"

She tried to smile, honest she did, but her lips wouldn't cooperate. She stepped away from him. "Sure, Dale. If that's what you want." Her stomach clenched.

He didn't smile either, but at least he looked satisfied. "Raffi and I will be here Friday for your game, then."

Was his answer contingent on hers? A compromise. Yet it didn't feel like a compromise. It felt more like coercion and that hurt. Tamara tried to push back the resentment which began building. She picked up her purse, car keys, and headed out.

"Tamara?"

"Yes, Dale."

"Don't hate me too much, okay."

She sighed. "I don't hate you."

"No, you said you loved me and if that's true, you'll have to accept some of my obligatory dinners."

"And what about my obligations?"

"I'm trying to accept them too."

So, it was a compromise. God, why had she gotten involved with a guy from the stuffy, upper class circle? She'd spent years avoiding them, and now she'd fallen in love with one. "Don't push me too hard, Dale." She left before she said too much more.

Dale watched her walk out the door. Don't push *her* too hard? He was the one who had risked his car by sleeping here all night, and was now standing alone in her run down apartment. He was the one having to accept the woman he loved working out in the slums at ungodly hours. Couldn't she give a little? What was so damn hard about dressing like a human being and enjoying a nice dinner with clean, educated people? She was going to have to be a little more accommodating.

Dale woke Raffi and called him to the kitchen so he could make him breakfast. He decided to fry eggs. While he poured Raffi orange juice, he turned her old stove on to warm the pan. The smell of gas became evident seconds later. He turned the knob off, then on again, but continued to smell gas. Did Tamara know there was something wrong with her stove? He fed Raffi some cereal instead of eggs. Then before they left her apartment he called Tamara.

"My stove? Just jiggle the knob a bit, and the gas leak disappears."

"Tamara, that's dangerous."

"I've had it for years, it's fine."

"I'll get you a new stove."

"Dale, I don't want . . . just a minute." She began talking to someone at her office. "I don't need a new stove."

"I happen to think you do. You don't mess around with gas leaks."

"Really, I appreciate . . . just a minute."

Dale clutched the receiver, losing his patience. "Tamara."

"Yes, yes, that's fine," her voice was distant as she spoke to someone. "Honey, I've got to go."

Honey? He liked that. "All right, I'll take care of the stove, don't worry."

"I'm not, darling. I'll call you tonight."

But when she called, it wasn't to thank him as he thought she would. She was furious just because he bought her a new stove. Most women would be grateful. What was wrong with her? Did she want to blow up her whole apartment building?

"Next time you decide to change something in my apartment, I'd appreciate it if you asked."

"I did. I called you at work."

"And I told you I didn't need a new stove."

"No, you didn't."

"Dale, don't tell me what I said or didn't say. I could have had the old stove fixed."

"Did you have some strange attachment to that stove or something?" Her reaction baffled him.

"I like to live within my means, and I don't allow men to buy me things."

"You don't allow it? It's not like I bought you frivolous jewelry or something. Besides, you could afford to buy anything you want."

"I don't spend my parents' money unless I don't have a choice. I spend what my paycheck allows."

Dale definitely didn't understand her. Who willingly lived like a pauper if they didn't have to? "Look, Tamara, that stove needed to be replaced, and if you're so irresponsible as to keep a dangerous thing like that in your apartment, you left me no choice."

She gasped and hung up. Dale thought about it for a few seconds then started laughing. The woman was angry because he'd bought her a stove. Well, she certainly wasn't after his money like most women.

By Friday night, she appeared to have forgiven him for buying her the stove. She greeted both Raffi and Dale with a huge smile and sweet kiss.

"Nice jeans," she said and winked at Dale.

Dale laughed and admitted that she actually looked pretty good herself in tight jeans.

She handed both Dale and Raffi a T-shirt.

Dale held the shirt up against his chest. "What's this for?"

"Put it on. You're working with me tonight."

"Working? I thought we were going to enjoy a ball game."

"Well." She shrugged. "You are, but technically you're with me."

Dale wasn't even going to try and figure out what she meant. He slipped on his T-shirt with the Child Welfare logo on the front, and Raffi did the same. Then they all left.

At the stadium, Dale understood the need for the shirts. She drove in through special staff gates and their shirts were their entry pass. Child Welfare had a tented booth and as guests walked through the front gates, they bought candy for the game and left their donations.

Dale and Raffi stayed with Tamara for a while. Raffi helped pass out bumper stickers and other paperwork. Dale stood back and watched with admiration. Tamara was so good with people. She absolutely shone. Young people, older couples, everyone who came through the gate was drawn to her. All she had to do was smile and welcome them to the ball park, and they made a detour to her table.

Then one of her coworkers showed up with balloons and a helium tank. Dale volunteered to blow them up and asked Raffi to pass them out.

"Wow, Tamara, you've brought two excellent helpers," Lisa said.

Tamara glanced at Dale and treated him a spectacular smile. His breath actually locked in his chest. "Yes, it seems I have," she said.

Dale vowed that he'd help her every day, every night for the rest of his life if it made her look at him like that.

When the balloons were gone, and the majority of the crowd was already seated, Tamara sat back on the folding metal chair. She lifted her hair up and exposed her sexy, moist neck. Dale looked away, not trusting himself to keep his hands off her if he watched.

"You boys can go watch the game if you'd like. The excitement is pretty much over."

Dale watched Raffi bounce onto her lap. She kissed and tickled him. Raffi giggled and tried half heartedly to stop her hands. Then he reached up and stroked her face. They both stopped laughing and stared at each other. Dale suddenly felt like he was eavesdropping on a private moment.

"Thanks for helping tonight, Kiddo."

Raffi nodded. "Can you come see the game with us?"

Tamara lifted her eyes to Dale as if just remembering he was standing there. She smiled at him then returned her attention to Raffi. "I have to stay at the table for a while. Come get me in about an hour, okay?"

Raffi straightened, slid off her lap, and grabbed Dale's hand. His big brown eyes smiled at Dale. "One hour, Dale, then she'll sit with us."

Dale brushed Raffi's cheek with the back of his fingers. "Can we wait a whole hour for our girl to join us?"

"It'll be hard." Raffi nodded with a sincere look on his face.

Dale had to laugh at the adorable child. "Yes it will, but you're going to love baseball. Lets go." He eyed Tamara and she blew him a kiss. God, he loved her.

She joined them during the sixth inning. They bought hot dogs, sodas, and watched the rest of the game. Dale enjoyed watching the game since he hadn't been to a stadium in over twenty years. But mostly he enjoyed watching Raffi's eyes grow big at everything he saw. The child was so easy to please.

And Tamara, she was another one who seemed to be on top of the world. She cheered with Raffi, challenged Dale sing the baseball chants, and seductively licked the mustard off his lips when he bit into his hotdog and it oozed out all over his mouth. As the hot September day faded and cooled Tamara snuggled next to him and Dale marveled at how she managed to make her work night loads of fun for all three of them.

When they got back to Tamara's place, they put Raffi in the guest room where he immediately snuggled into a pillow and went to sleep. Dale closed the door, turned to Tamara , and lifted her into his arms. She wrapped her arms around his neck and brought her lips to his. He kissed her as he carried her into her bedroom. He couldn't wait to make love to her, and to his delight, it seemed she couldn't wait either. She was so responsive, so loving. They didn't even talk, there was no need. Not tonight.

Dale couldn't get to sleep that night. He watched Tamara sleep instead. Her chest, barely covered with a sheet, rose and fell rhythmically. Tamara worked and played hard, then slept just as soundly at night. Daphne was wrong, Tamara wasn't on a self destruct mode, quite the opposite in fact. She seemed to live every second of her life, and she seemed happy.

He reached for her hair, holding a handful in his fist then opened his hand so that it slipped through his fingers. She made a mumbling sound and cuddled closer to him. Dale wrapped his arms around her. He was in deep trouble. He loved this woman and wanted her beside him forever. He kissed her temple tenderly, happy that at least now, she appeared to want to be no where else.

CHAPTER TWELVE

The following week Tamara had her nights back, but it appeared the troubling cases had doubled and the free time she'd hoped to have with Dale and Raffi vanished. Someday, it would be nice to come to work and find there were no new cases to work on. Unfortunately, she didn't have much hope of that day coming.

She made a point of calling Dale every night this week. They spoke on the phone for hours like teenagers in love. Tamara went to sleep every night with a warm feeling inside her heart.

When the dreaded Thursday night came, Tamara rushed home so she would have hours to get ready. She wanted to be perfect for Dale and his parents dinner. The appreciative glint in his eyes when he entered her apartment sent a tremor through her and reassured her that she looked respectable and maybe even a little inviting.

"I was going to ask if you're ready, but I don't have to. You look marvelous, darling."

"I'm ready. Hi, sweetie," she said to Raffi.

"Hi," he mumbled, with a pout and red rimmed eyes.

Tamara tried to keep her alarm in check, staring immediately at Dale.

"He decided he didn't feel like dressing tonight," Dale explained with obvious irritation in his voice.

Then why not let him wear what he wanted? Tamara couldn't understand why adults always wanted to push their wants and desires on children. Just because it was a formal dinner for the adults didn't mean the children couldn't just be children. Although she didn't agree, Dale had made his decision and she wouldn't contradict him in front of Raffi. "I see," she said through the tightness in her throat.

"Shall we go?" Dale took Tamara's elbow.

"Yes, of course." She let Dale lead her to his car, and once they were all buckled in and Dale got onto the freeway, Tamara turned around to talk to Raffi. He sat with his head bowed.

"This dinner won't last long. Then you can take those tight, uncomfortable clothes off."

Raffi nodded, but said nothing.

"Hey, sweetie, how would you like to come over this weekend and help me bake some cookies. Then we can go see a movie."

"He's grounded this weekend," Dale interrupted.

"What?" Tamara frowned at Dale.

He placed one hand on her knee and squeezed gently. "We'll talk about it later."

She stared at his profile for a long time, not knowing what to say since he had effectively told her to shut up. She turned completely around in her seat and concentrated on the front windshield, perhaps unjustifiably angry with Dale, but angry just the same. They all sat in silence until they reached his parents' mansion.

There they were greeted by servants, led to an immense living room, given a list of drinks they could choose from, and told to wait for Dale's parents to arrive.

Tamara sighed. Weren't parents supposed to greet their children warmly when they came home? She walked to a tall, narrow window and looked out to the private garden illuminated by park lamps.

Dale walked behind her and placed a hand on her right shoulder, squeezing it slightly. "Thanks for coming," he whispered in her ear.

She didn't look at him. "How long will we be locked in this room?"

"Tamara, we're a little early."

"Oh, that explains it."

"What's wrong?"

She whirled around and whispered, "Raffi was crying."

"Of course he was crying, he didn't get his way."

"What did you do to him?"

"Do to him?" He grabbed hold of her shoulders with both his hands and stood in front of her. "Are you serious?

"Why is he grounded?"

"Because he *will not* throw a fit when he doesn't get his way, and he *will* mind as long as he's in my home."

She bit her bottom lip and rolled her eyes.

"And you have no right to question the way I discipline him," Dale continued, his voice rough.

"Oh, don't I?"

"No, Tamara. He lives with me. Would you like to take him back?"

"Is that what you'd like?"

Dale cursed. "I will not have this argument with you. Not tonight."

He marched away from her, accepted his drink from a tuxedoed waiter, and stood stiffly on the other side of the room.

Damn, Tamara sighed, she wanted this night to be perfect for Dale. *She* wanted to be perfect. She asked Raffi to sit on the sofa, and handed him a glass of orange juice. "Come on, Raffi, smile, please."

He lifted large, disappointed eyes to Tamara. "You first," he said with no apparent inflection, but looked so adorable she had to laugh. Then he smiled.

Two couples were escorted in next. Then three more entered and Dale graciously handled the introductions. His parents, of course, showed up last. They all spoke business, and Tamara tried to smile and appear interested. She moved among the people until she approached her hostess.

"Edna," she whispered.

Edna moved discreetly away from the others to speak with Tamara alone. "What is it, my dear?"

"It's Raffi. Is there somewhere he can play for a while?"

Edna looked pensively at the little boy sitting quietly on the sofa. "Well . . . play . . . I'm not sure. What do you suggest?"

Tamara knew toys were too much to ask for. "How about a television?"

Edna didn't react.

"Paper and markers?"

At this Edna lifted an eyebrow. Good sign.

"Upstairs, third door to your left."

Tamara smiled. "Thank you. I'll be right back."

She took Raffi's hand and together they climbed the stairs and entered the room Edna suggested. Inside she found a piano, Daphne's no doubt, and a desk loaded with everything imaginable. Raffi could entertain himself in here for a few hours.

She was pulling markers out of the desk for Raffi when Dale walked in. They both froze and stared at Dale for a few moments, then Tamara continued to arrange the desk top for creative drawing.

Dale closed the door and slipped inside with

his hands buried in his pockets. His gaze ran over the items in the room. "Daphne and I spent hours in this room."

Raffi sat on the chair, and Tamara stood behind him, leaning over his shoulder, both her hands full of pens and markers. She watched Dale through her lashes.

"This was the only room in the house we were allowed to run, jump, or scream in."

Edna had been as strict with him and Daphne as her parents had been with her. Yet he had accepted and embraced his place in life where Tamara had renounce it. Was it because at least Edna loved her children and kept them close? Tamara's mother had just sent her away to school for other people to raise.

Tamara lowered all the writing instruments onto the desk. "Here Raffi, draw me something." She kissed the top of his head and went to Dale. "This is the piano Daphne played for hours on end, isn't it?"

Dale's right eye twitched. "She told you about that, huh?"

"Daphne's gifted when it comes to playing and singing."

Dale nodded. "Yes, she is."

Tamara touched his arm. "God, I'm sorry, Dale." She wanted him to smile at her the way he had at the baseball park. She wanted to hear him talk as sweetly as he had over the phone the past few days.

He looked at her hand indifferently, then into

her eyes. "What are you sorry for?"

"I don't like to argue, especially not with you."

He pulled a hand out of his pocket and slid the back of his fingers along her jaw line. "Just give me a break. I'm trying with him."

"I know you are, I'm sorry."

They left Raffi to play. A servant came in to watch him, but they reassured him that they were down stairs if he needed anything. He seemed content, and only asked if he could play the piano.

"You can play with anything you want, pal," Dale ruffled his hair.

They allowed dinner to be served to Raffi separately. Luckily, Dale accepted her recommendation on that note. That left the adults alone at the picture perfect dining table. Dale was wonderfully attentive to Tamara.

"This is the first time a young lady joins you at one of our dinners, Dale." Mr. Rodille asked. He was balding man with red cheeks and silver rimmed glasses. "This is encouraging. Are you finally getting ready to settle down?"

Tamara tried not to cough outright. She swallowed her bite of red rose potato, and reached for her glass of wine.

To his credit, Dale grinned comfortably. "I believe Ms. Cassetti is much too intelligent to let herself get trapped into a confining entanglement like marriage."

Mr. Rodille laughed. "She's a free spirit, is she?"

Tamara groaned inwardly and visually

appealed to Edna.

Edna smiled. "Roll, dear?"

"Yes, thank you." She took a roll from the basket which was passed to her.

"Where did you meet?" Rodille spoke directly to her now.

"At, ah, Daphne's bridal shower."

"Tamara and Daphne went to college together, Anthony." Edna said with a poised smile.

"Really, how interesting." He winked at Dale. "You've got good taste, young man."

Dale's heavy hand took hers. "Thank you, I agree." He smiled at Tamara.

She wondered if she was supposed to be grateful for the compliment, not paid to her, but to Dale.

The formal dinner finally over, the men went to discuss business in the library, while the ladies went to the living room where the evening started, had coffee, and talked about their grown children. With nothing to add to the conversations, Tamara listened and took mental notes on what Edna liked and disliked, admired and despised.

Tamara and Dale stayed until everyone was gone.

"You did well," Edna complimented Tamara once they were alone.

"Did I?" *Had this been a test?*

"Yes, you did. I find it hard to believe you are the same girl who jumped out of dorm windows and hid beer cans behind bookcases."

"That was a long time ago, Edna."

She seemed relaxed as sat with her legs crossed on the sofa beside Tamara. "Are you telling me you are more like what I've seen tonight than what you used to be?"

Tamara shrugged. "You know what I do, what I believe, how I live, Edna. I'm not a rebellious teenager anymore, no, but neither am I a princess."

Edna gave a stiff nod. "Of course."

Tamara looked around for Dale to rescue her from his mother, but he'd disappeared. She sighed and looked at Edna again. "Honestly, in high school, I never thought I'd be attending a dinner party with you, Edna."

Edna smiled, a genuine smile. "My dear, I never doubted you were capable of acting like a young lady. I'm glad you did attend a dinner party with me."

Glad? That Edna put up with Tamara dining at her house as her son's escort was one thing, but to be 'glad' was quite another. Yet Edna was not one to offer niceties to ease a situation. If she said something, she meant it.

Dale and John entered the living room. Dale had a sleeping Raffi in his arms. "Ready, darling?"

Boy was she! "Good-night, Edna, and thank you for having me."

The older couple walked them to the front door and waved as Dale and Tamara drove away.

When Dale pulled into his own driveway, Tamara looked at him with a questioning stare.

"You don't mind spending the night, do you?"

"I've got to work tomorrow, Dale."

"I'll drive you home early tomorrow morning. I'd like you to stay with me tonight."

She got the feeling he wasn't asking but gave her consent anyway. After all, spending the night with Dale, wrapped in his arms, wasn't a sacrifice.

Dale put Raffi to bed while Tamara tried to make herself comfortable in his living room. She found it wasn't very easy. Everything was so neat and stiff. She had felt awkward all night at his parents' place, and now it seemed to be prolonged. She moved through his condo, her heels clicking on his hardwood floor, and she stopped at his bedroom. Last time she was in here, he'd told her she'd be spending the night if she ever walked in again, and now it seemed he had been right.

Dale snuck up behind her and she threw a startled glance over her shoulder.

"Go on in, Tamara."

She smiled and entered his bedroom. "I wasn't planning on sleeping here tonight. I didn't bring any toiletries or anything to change into."

Dale smiled. "I don't really want you to change into anything. As far as toiletries, I think you'll find everything you need in my bathroom."

Tamara noticed he had a cupboard full of feminine products, from deodorants to makeup removers to feminine napkins. She closed the mirrored door and looked in the mirror. What was she doing blushing? She re-opened the door, pulled out the makeup remover, a brand new tooth brush, and some skin sensitive soap. She scrubbed herself clean and took off all her jewelry before returning to

Dale's bedroom.

He sat upright on his bed, his back on the back rest, like a Greek God holding a pose. She remembered her sculpting classes and wished for just a second she had modeling clay so she could capture his pose for eternity. But she'd just have to rely on her memory to keep that image imprinted.

"What's wrong?" He frowned.

"Nothing. Why do you ask?"

"You've been standing there, staring at me for almost a minute now."

"Oh," she glanced away feeling stupid. "I, ah, need help with my zipper." She turned her back to him. "Do you mind?"

She heard him slide out of bed and felt his body heat move closer and closer. She bit her bottom lip, knowing full well she didn't need his help, but couldn't resist the opportunity to feel his fingers gripping her zipper and sliding it down her back. His hands returned to her shoulders and slid the dress off, his lips barely touching her skin as he bowed his head and followed the trail of the fabric.

"I know you don't want to hear this, but I love seeing you all dressed up like tonight. You looked marvelous."

Tamara turned and walked into his arms. "I don't mind hearing that. I wanted to look marvelous for you."

Dale groaned, lifted her into his arms, and took her to bed. Tamara decided the boring night had been worth the effort after all. If throwing on a dress with some fancy accessories, and eating dinner with a bunch of old people made Dale react like this, it was definitely worth it.

He took his time making love to her, whispering the entire time how much he loved her, wanted her, didn't want to live without her. Yes, she'd dress up for Dale every night if he wanted.

Later that night she lay in his arms thinking how different he was when they were in bed together than during the day when he seemed cold and business-like.

The bed moved as he leaned close, watching her in the darkness.

"What?" She whispered.

"You're awake?"

She laughed. "I guess so."

He sighed and dropped back on the mattress. "I need to ask you a favor, Tamara."

Tamara turned on her side, fluffing her pillow so she could see his profile. "Anything, honey, what is it?"

"My father asked me to take care of some business for him in France. I'll need to be gone for about a month."

Tamara swallowed. "Gone?"

"Yes, I'm afraid so. The negotiations will be lengthy. We're trying to get permission for a new route through Charles de Gaulle. My favor concerns Raffi."

"I see."

"I'd hoped you'd agree to move in here while I'm gone, Tamara. I know it's a lot to ask, for you to watch Raffi and all--"

"It's not a lot to ask, but--"

Dale rolled on his side and inched closer, taking her hands. "It's not? I'll make it up to you."

"Don't be ridiculous. I don't mind watching Raffi. I'll have to rearrange my schedule a bit, but I don't mind."

"Thank you." He nuzzled her neck and she felt his smile.

She placed her hands on his shoulders. "But I don't need to move in here."

His smile slipped and he inched back. "Yes, you do. Raffi's things are here. His school is in the area. And besides I'd feel much better knowing you're living here while I'm gone than at your place."

So that was it. Didn't he understand she'd lived in her apartment for years before she met him, and she'd always been safe? "Dale, I don't want to move into your home."

"It'll only be for a month."

"I'll have to bring a lot of my things over for a whole month."

"Fine. I have an empty closet."

She sighed. Dale just didn't let up when he wanted something. "You mean you don't have a closet stocked with women's clothes like you do your bathroom cupboard with female items?"

Dale laughed. "I'm afraid not."

"Why do you have all those things, by the way?"

Dale covered a breast and began making erotic circles around her nipple with his index finger. Tamara's breath accelerated along with her heart beat.

"Well," he said thickly. "I like my women to feel comfortable."

She didn't like his answer. "Just how many women have spent the night in this bed, Dale?"

He let go of her breast and took her hands, entwining his fingers with hers and holding her arms above her head, then he shifted above her. "Not one I loved half as much as I do you, darling." He kissed her neck, and captured her earlobe between his lips.

Tamara's body couldn't help getting aroused, still she didn't like to think she was part of a long string of women he'd brought to his bed. "Is that true, Dale?"

He lifted his head and looked into her eyes. "Is what true, that I love you?"

"Yes."

"Of course it is. Do you think I'd say it if it wasn't?"

"It's just . . . it's the first time you've ever said it."

He let go of her hands and cupped her face. "I love you so much it hurts. And Daphne stocked my shelves in there for me, just in case she or any other woman came over. I think you're the first to actually use any of it."

She smiled. "Make love to me again, Dale."

"I'd love to."

CHAPTER THIRTEEN

Tamara didn't realize when Dale said he was leaving that he meant the next morning. He got up, packed his suitcase, and called his airline to arrange for a seat.

Raffi seemed disappointed to learn Dale would be gone for a while, but glad to learn Tamara was going to stay with him.

Tamara felt no happiness. She didn't want to be separated from Dale right now. She had never felt so loved and wanted as she did now with Dale, and though she felt vulnerable and didn't like it, she also felt glorious. But Tamara smiled, wished him well, and promised to be at his home waiting for him to come back. She tried to be positive, it would only be for a month.

The first week in Dale's home was awkward. Tamara didn't know where he kept anything, and felt uneasy opening cupboards and drawers looking for towels or sheets or laundry soap. She tried to keep everything looking undisturbed. But she became more comfortable as each day slipped past.

Flowers arrived everyday both at work and at home. When she spoke to Dale on the phone at the end of the first week he admitted he'd arranged for a delivery everyday until he came home.

"Dale, what am I going to do with all these flowers? I appreciate it, but you should cancel the order."

"No, I can't do that. I want you to think of me everyday when you get your flowers."

"Dale, honey, I think of you everyday whether I see your flowers or not. Are you doing all right?"

"I'm lonely without you, but aside from that I'm fine. How about you and Raffi?"

"Raffi's fine, but I, well," she sighed. "I don't like sleeping in your bed without you, Dale."

His voice got deeper. "That's exactly where I want to find you when I get home - in my bed, naked and beautiful, and ready to welcome me home."

"Well hurry up and get here, okay?" Tamara surprised herself by how much she wanted him home, and even more so by the effect those words had on her physically.

Daphne returned home from her honeymoon the following week and that made things a little better. She went to visit her in the Palisades.

Taking advantage of the last hot days of summer, Raffi took his swim suit and a friend. They played in the pool while Tamara and Daphne sat sunning themselves on the patio chairs and drinking iced tea.

"My mom tells me you and Dale are pretty serious." Daphne had on dark sunglasses so Tamara couldn't see her full expression.

"We're dating."

Daphne lowered her sunglasses on the bridge of her nose to let Tamara see her doubting eyes. "And?"

"And nothing."

Daphne reclined in her chair and pushed her glasses back up. "You used to be a better liar."

"Things are going well, but your mother shouldn't start fearing for her son's birthright yet."

"From what she told me, she was more worried about you than him."

"Me? Why?"

"She thinks you're too unpredictable. God knows where she got that from, right? And she's afraid you'll either take Dale too serious or not serious enough. She can't figure out what he's after. What do you think?"

"My money," Tamara said and slipped on her sunglasses, watching Raffi make back flips into the pool. She just wasn't ready to discuss her relationship with Dale.

"Funny. Okay, you don't want to talk about it, but tell me, do we have a chance at being sisters someday?"

"I'm not even thinking past tomorrow, Daph, okay?"

She shrugged. "Okay, fine."

But Dale *was* thinking past tomorrow. He figured if he could keep Tamara at his place for a month she'd be used to it by the time he got home, and he'd have an easier time convincing her to stay. It had never been his intention to live with a woman or get that involved, but neither was it his intention to have a child and he had committed to that, so why not commit to Tamara as well.

He worked long hours trying to establish a Paris branch to Quest Air, arriving in his hotel late at night to sleep. Paris in October wasn't exactly as mild as in California. Half the days, showers dampened the streets, the gloominess matching his spirits. The temperature stayed in the mid fifties the whole time, and he wished for Tamara's warm, giving body to hold at night.

When he could, he called her. Her voice sounded so close over the phone lines, and he ached with the desire to see and feel her beside him again. This little forced separation made him admit how much she was coming to mean to him. Could she possibly be *the one?*

Damn! If it wasn't one thing, it was another. Tamara slammed Cindy Patterson's file down on her desk and dropped her hands on her hips. She worked her butt off to get this child into a safe home then a judge turns around and grants unsupervised visits to an irresponsible, unfit mother. Tamara spent half an hour calming down the foster mother. Now she'd have to spend the rest of the day on legal paperwork, and she had to pick Raffi up at school.

"What are you staring at?

Tamara's gaze darted up at the sound of a deep voice she'd dreamed of every night for the past three and a half weeks. "Dale, honey, what are you doing here?" she asked and smiled at the same time.

He lifted one leg onto her desk and leaned his weight against it. "Boy, do you look good." He shook his head.

Tamara wound her arms around his shoulders and kissed him. Then she smiled into his eyes. "I thought you weren't coming home until the weekend?"

He shrugged. "I worked extra long hours so I could get back early. I missed you."

"Oh Dale." She traced his sexy lips with her pinky fingernail. "No one's ever missed me before."

He frowned strangely and she thought maybe she shouldn't have spoken so frankly with him.

"Well, trust me, I have. When can you come home?"

She took a step back and dropped her arms off his shoulders. "Well, actually, not until late. I've got to take care of a pressing problem." She sighed. "I was just trying to figure out what to do with

Raffi."

"Don't worry about Raffi, I'll pick him up. I've missed him too, believe it or not."

"I believe it. He's a terrific kid.""

"I'll chill a bottle of champagne, and we'll have it whenever you get home. How does that sound?"

Tamara couldn't believe she was lucky enough to find someone as wonderful as Dale. He was too good to be true. "I'll hurry."

After Dale left Tamara's dark day suddenly became much more bearable. In fact, she knew exactly what she was going to do. She called a meeting with the legal team. Unsupervised visits were out of the question, and she knew exactly how she was going to have them recalled.

By the time Tamara left her office she could barely keep her eyes open. She was sure Cindy would be safe though, and that's what was important. She drove home, to Dale and Raffi, thanking whatever kind spirit sent them to her.

Raffi was asleep when she got home, but Dale sat in the living room, still in his trousers and business shirt, his tie loosened, but still hanging around his neck. He sat on the couch watching a late night show. In his limp right hand which rested on his leg, he held a remote control.

Tamara took the remote control from him, and turned the set off. "Hi."

"I thought you said you'd hurry."

"I'm sorry."

Dale looked at her from his sitting position on the sofa, expressionless. Then he held out his hand. Tamara took it. He pulled her down on the sofa next to him. "I'm going to take off all your clothes and make love to you right here. Any objections?"

"No," she whispered.

Dale didn't say another word, and though Tamara would have wanted to come home, talk about his trip, have dinner with him, drink some champagne, she realized Dale was past wanting any of that. And soon his hands and lips inflamed her to the point where she was past wanting anything but him.

She loved the way Dale made love to her. She loved Dale. After their lovemaking in the living room, he carried her to the bedroom where he made love to her a second time. She tried to stay awake afterwards. She had so much to say to him, but she was physically and emotionally drained so she rolled on her side, closed her eyes, and went to sleep.

Over the next couple of months which encompassed the Thanksgiving, Christmas, and New Year holidays, Tamara wondered if the kind spirit which sent her Dale was putting her through a test. From the moment she acknowledged her love for Dale, she'd felt pressured to prove just how much. First by moving out of her apartment and moving in with Dale. She hadn't wanted to move, she loved her apartment, but Dale had been adamant. His arguments all sounded logical. And since she *did* love him, and wanted to be with him, she agreed he was right and moved in with him. She tried to rationalize -- her life would be the same, after all, it was just her address which was changing.

But that too turned out to be wishful thinking. Tamara's schedule bent each day more to accommodate Dale, his work schedule, and his holiday dinner parties.

Although she was constantly frustrated and resentful about this change, she understood he was facing various problems at work that needed his attention. Maintenance workers were threatening to strike and it looked like the expansion to France was going to fail. Half the evenings Tamara saw more of Edna than Dale while he and his father talked business in the library. But every time she thought of protesting, she bit her tongue.

After all, Dale was wonderful, he came home with flowers or jewelry all the time. Despite his pressures at work, he called her at her office with loving messages, reminding her constantly how much he adored her. So, she told herself she would be a fool for complaining about his business dinners or a few little changes she had to make in her own work schedule. Compromise was a small price to pay for Dale's love.

But when he dropped the bomb of her having to organize one of his dinner parties, Tamara thought for sure she'd fail the test. "I can't do that. I'm completely incapable of organizing those elaborate dinners. And besides that, I don't have the time."

Dale smiled patiently across their breakfast table. "It won't take too much of your time, darling. It's my turn to host. It's only proper."

"Dale, you don't understand--"

"Just ask Daphne to help you. She won't mind. In fact, she'll love it." He put down his coffee cup, stood, leaned across the table, and kissed the top of her head.

Tamara grabbed his wrist. "Dale, wait. Hire caterers or something, I can't do it."

His eyebrows furrowed and he looked at her like she was crazy. "Well, that's what I want you to do. Hire the caterer, decorators, whoever you need. You didn't think I wanted you to cook, did you?"

"That's just it. I don't know what you want me to do." Her voice rose. "I haven't a clue. And why is your problem suddenly becoming mine. I didn't volunteer to take on any of this crap."

Dale straightened and his mood darkened. "Fine, forget it."

"Dale."

But he turned and walked out, leaving her feeling like a jerk. Why had she lost her temper? She lowered her head onto her arms on the breakfast table. She didn't want to make him angry, but hosting a dinner party just wasn't who she was, and she didn't have the time for all the extra work. She lifted her head and rubbed her temples. Deep down, she knew this would happen, didn't she? She'd grown up exactly in this type of atmosphere where you hand to wine and dine the right people and keep up appearances. Yet she'd chosen to love Dale – and that meant she had to accept his lifestyle, as much as she despised it.

She stood with a sigh. All she had to do was call Daphne, which was what she'd do.

Daphne agreed to take care of most of the planning. Tamara helped with each step, that way next time, she would know what to do on her own. Next time? Was she planning on doing this again? No, but she had a feeling she might have to. Dale's cold shoulder after the incident in their kitchen warned her that she had better learn to like this, at least a little.

Daphne seemed baffled by Tamara's interest. "I thought you hated all this stuff." She closed the desert selection menu across her patio table.

"Yeah, well, it's not so bad." Tamara took a drink of water.

"Why don't you tell Dale to do all this himself?"

"I tried."

"Tried? How do you *try* to tell someone something? You just tell them."

"Just drop it, Daphne. I told him I'd take care of it, and thanks to you, I am, so let's get it done. I've got to get back to work."

Daphne rested her elbows on the table. She propped her chin on the back of her hands, her eyes narrowed as she watched Tamara. "You know, Tam, he isn't going to stop loving you if you refuse to do something he asks."

Tamara stood upright. "You finish. I'm leaving."

"Listen to me a second." Daphne stood and reached across the table for Tamara's hand, but missed.

"I don't want, nor do I have time to listen to this nonsense. Are you telling me you wouldn't help Adam if he needed you?"

"Don't get angry at me when the person you're really angry with is Dale."

"I'm not angry with anyone," her arms flew up in emphasis, but she *was* angry with Daphne for pointing out Tamara's exact fears – losing Dale's love.

"You're going to wake up one day from this love haze, and hate who you've become, Tamara."

Tamara felt as if she'd been slapped by her best friend. She stared at Daphne, part of her wanting to stalk away, and part of her wanting to pull her into a hug and cry on he shoulder. "Why are you doing this to me? I need your support right now." Tamara's voice was weak.

"That's what I'm trying to do. Just remember he fell in love with you because of who you were. There were plenty of women who wanted to be by his side and look like a trophy wife. I thought you wanted something different in life."

"I do. I did. Daph . . . ," she sighed. "Everything is happening so fast, I . . . I'm trying to compromise. That's what love is all about, right? Isn't that why you gave up your music?"

Daphne shook her head. "I gave it up

because I didn't want to go through the work to become a professional. I *like* my pampered lifestyle. You don't like it, never have, never will."

"No," Tamara admitted and stared at the menus on the glass table. She sat and held out a coaxing hand to Daphne. "Come on, help me finish."

Daphne sat across from her.

"I'm sorry I snapped at you, Daph. You're right – about everything, but I *want* to be with Dale, I really do."

Daphne smiled. "I know you do." She seemed to want to say more, but remained silent.

The night of the dinner arrived. Edna and John were invited, as well as Daphne and Adam since Daphne had all but put the dinner on herself. They hosted two other families. Conversation at dinner centered around the airline since Dale's condo didn't have a large library they could retire to for after dinner discussions.

Tamara had Daphne to entertain her, but since she was the host, she needed to keep the other women engaged in conversation also. The whole mess was tiring, and she hated every minute of it. Her only reward was Dale's proud smile.

During desert everyone complimented her on the marvelous dinner which struck her as strange since she hadn't done anything but point at a meal choice when the caterer handed her the menu.

"It's her first dinner, so she certainly should

be commended." Dale smiled at her.

"Your mother tells me, you two are quite serious," one of the women said with a conspiratorial smile at Dale.

"Yes, we are. As a matter of fact, we'll be getting married soon."

Tamara would have worried about the absolutely stupid look coving her face, if Daphne hadn't almost spit out her wine and Edna hadn't nearly choked on her piece of rum cake. Tamara glared at Dale.

"Married?" Daphne finally spoke after swallowing the wine. "You didn't tell me you were going to marry my brother?"

Tamara wiped her lips on a linen napkin and closed her eyes, counting to ten so she wouldn't blow up at Dale in front of everyone. "No, I didn't."

"What's the surprise?" Dale said cheerfully. "We figured you'd suspect by now. I mean, she's practically my wife already."

Edna put down her fork and gave Dale a brittle smile. "I believe, it is still expected for you to formally announce an engagement, if that's what you have decided."

"Mother, you're absolutely right. When would you like to make the formal announcement, darling?" Dale looked at Tamara with a charming smile, but all she wanted to do was slap that smile right off his face.

She glanced at Daphne's still shocked expression, then at Edna, then returned her gaze to Dale. "There isn't going to be a formal announcement."

An audible gasp sounded around the table which Tamara ignored as she stood. "Excuse me."

She walked to the bedroom, shaking with anger and resentment. How dare he make an announcement like that in front of his family and business associates?

Two seconds after she walked into the bedroom, he came in after her. "What the hell do you think you're doing?"

She spun around and faced him. "It would have been nice of you to ask me if I wanted to marry you before you told everyone I would." The sarcasm was out before she could calm herself.

Dale's right eye twitched rapidly. He rubbed his forehead. "I assumed that's where we were heading."

"Maybe we were, but usually the man proposes and the woman accepts."

"Is that what you want, a formal proposal?" His voice was cold and sharp.

"I don't know, Dale. All I'm saying is that if you wanted to marry me, you should have asked."

"Fine." He placed his hands on his hips. "I'm asking. Will you marry me?"

Tamara wanted to cry. This was the craziest thing in the world. Wasn't a marriage proposal supposed to be romantic and exciting? She felt pressured to say yes now that everyone assumed she already had. She turned away from him and sat on the bed.

"Tamara?" His voice became gentle. "You say

you love me. You're living with me. Don't you want to continue along this path?"

"Yes, but--"

"Then let's do it. We love each other. We're perfect for one another--"

"Are we?"

He came around the bed and knelt in front of her. Taking her fingers, he raised them to his lips. "I think so, Tam. I love you so much I can't live without you."

The sincere look in his eyes made her anger evaporate, but the uneasiness wouldn't go away. She didn't like the way he'd put her on the spot. "I love you too, but -."

"Then what's there to think about? People wait their whole lives for someone they can love. We're lucky - we found each other."

And she didn't want to lose him. He made her feel special, adored, needed. She pulled him onto the bed. "Marriage is a big step, Dale."

He pushed her onto her back and hovered over her, kissing her jaw, under her ear lobe. "Take it with me, Tam. Take the step," he whispered.

"Mmm." When he touched her like this, she wanted to give him the world. "I want you, Dale. Can we send all those people home and get under these sheets?"

"Soon." He met her eyes. "But I'm not going to let you get side tracked. I want a serious commitment from you. We're going to go out there and tell them all that we're getting married."

She saw the determination in his eyes. He

wasn't waiting for her approval, he was demanding it - just as he had demanded she move in with him. For a split second she considered telling him 'no' but the feeling faded when she thought of the alternative - life without Dale. She threaded her fingers into his hair. "Kiss me, Dale."

He did, deeply, passionately, leaving no doubt as to how he felt about her.

They returned to the dinner table and Tamara reiterated that there would be no formal announcement. "I don't want a huge party just to tell people we're getting married. We'll skip over the engagement party and just begin planning the wedding."

"But, Tamara, dear –." Edna began.

"That's the way it's going to be mother," Dale interrupted.

"Great!" Daphne stood. "Let me be the first to congratulate you both." She kissed Dale.

Others around the table followed her lead, shaking Dale's hand and kissing Tamara.

Daphne pulled Tamara into an embrace and held her tight. "I'm happy for you if this is what you want," she said quietly.

Tamara squeezed Daphne. "It is."

Daphne pulled back and smiled. "Then this must be the happiest day of your life."

Tamara nodded, knowing full well she *should* feel happy, but all she felt was pressured and strangely vulnerable.

CHAPTER FOURTEEN

Dale cursed when his father told him about the European expansion set back. "What the hell's the problem?" He paced behind his desk.

"It's a matter of gates, you know that Dale." John sat with his legs crossed.

"Yeah, well I spent a whole month establishing our Paris base, and I met with those bastards at the Federal Aviation Administration and they assured me we wouldn't have any problems."

John nodded. "Well, we have one last chance to convince them. They agreed to let us fly them out a few representatives. They're going to tour our operation. We'll have them to dinner at our place and make our last pitch."

Dale rested his hands on his hips and shook his head. He wanted the damned European flight routes. They'd secured London. Paris was the obvious second most important city. Then the rest of Western Europe would follow naturally.

John stood. "Go get some lunch and relax for a while. This afternoon we meet with the maintenance union to see if we can finish negotiations with them.

Dale took a seat and lifted a pen. "That's one problem we need to take care before this meeting with FAA."

"I don't know, Dale. They're pretty adamant."

"So am I."

John left more and more of the decision making to Dale, but of course, Dale deferred to him before he finalized anything.

John nodded. "I'm going to lunch. Coming?"

"Hell no."

"It might do you good. Call that beautiful fiancee of yours and take her to lunch."

Dale was already going over the revised contract the union was now proposing. "Thanks, Dad, but I'll catch a bite here."

His father left and Dale began adding and crossing out sections of the contact, shaking his head and mumbling to himself.

His secretary buzzed and asked if he wanted to personalize a note for Tamara before she ordered the flowers.

"What flowers?"

"You said you wanted to send her flowers."

"Oh, right." The past month, since they'd announced their engagement, she had been distant, preoccupied. He just wanted to remind her how much he loved her. Dale himself had been so busy with all the problems at work, he barely had time to spend with her. "Write, 'To my gorgeous fiancee, I love you and I miss you'".

"That's sweet."

Dale chuckled. "Thanks. Tell them to make sure she gets it today."

"I will."

Immediately, his attention returned to his work. He worked through lunch until his meeting. Then he sat through three hours of heated negotiations, where neither side seemed to want to give in to the others demands. They hated Dale's changes and Dale was determined not to be bullied by what he felt were unfair demands.

He returned to his office agitated and unable to sit. Checking his messages, he noticed he had one from Tamara.

He dialed her office.

"Ms. Cassetti's desk," she said.

"Hey, Tam, it's me. You called."

"Hi, sweetheart. Yes, I called to thank you for the wonderful flowers."

He'd forgotten about the flowers already. "Glad you liked them."

"I loved them. And I love you."

He leaned his rear on his desk and stared at the wall size portrait of one of their airplanes. "Working late today?" He asked.

"Unfortunately. You sound distracted. Is anything wrong?"

"Same old stuff."

"I'm sorry." Her voice went down a few notches. "Want me to come over and relieve some of your stress?"

He laughed. "That sounds like the best offer I've had all day."

"It better be."

His smile remained. "So, tell me what would you do to release, I mean, relieve my stress."

"Got a lock on your office door?"

"Yep."

"Mmm, well then we have a whole range of possibilities open to us."

Dale realized his penis was growing and hardening. He opened his legs to give himself more room. His coat and tie suddenly becoming uncomfortable. "I'm listening."

"Well, you're a man who's always short on time, so what ever I did would have to be quick and furious."

He groaned. "You're going to make me bust out of my pants." She laughed, and the sweet ringing of her voice made him want her more. "I meant what I said on the card. I miss you."

"I'm sorry I've been so busy lately, Dale."

"Me too. But unfortunately, it doesn't look like it's going to ease up for me."

"Any news on the route expansions?"

He didn't want to discuss that now. "Nothing specific. But I better go. I've got lots to do before I have to go pick up Raffi."

"Okay. I'll see you tonight."

"You mean you're not really coming over for a quicky in my office?" He teased.

She laughed. "I'd like to, believe me."

"Not half as much as I'd like it. I need you."

Her voice became tender. "I need you too."

"Bye," he said, and heard only a quiet click on the other end.

Dale was already in bed when Tamara got home from work. The last three nights either she'd gotten home late or he had returned to his office after she got home and they hadn't been able to get to bed at the same time.

She disrobed and climbed in beside him, kissing his shoulder.

He turned and pulled her into an embrace. "You work too much."

"So do you," she whispered. She flipped onto her side and molded her back against him.

He wrapped his arms around her middle. Dale began to kiss her neck and shoulders.

She loved laying like this, fully enveloped in a cocoon of Dale's body. She felt his erection behind her, strong, hot, eager. She shifted a bit so he fit between her legs. As he filled her with his thick, pulsing arousal, she sighed.

"I've been waiting for you," he said in a husky, sexy voice.

"I can tell." She loved how Dale became instantly turned on at the sight of her.

He thrust into her, slowly, rhythmically. "Did you miss me today?"

"Oh, yes."

He chuckled. "I missed you too." His rhythm increased and his hand slid up her belly, along her rib cage, and cupped a breast.

Flames burned her body - inside and out. "Oh, Dale."

"I made you dinner."

She reached behind her and caressed his hip. "I'm sorry I missed it."

"That's okay. I've got a surprise for you," he said, his breath now coming unevenly.

"Ah," she gasped at the ripples of pleasure shooting through her body. "Another surprise? I'm not sure I can take anything else."

He squeezed her nipple and laughed. "You can take it."

"Ah," she whimpered, feeling as if she'd lose control any second. The stroking of his body against hers was so intense, so delicious. "What is it?" She gasped.

"Kind of an early wedding present."

She tried to concentrate on his words, but her body seemed to be over riding anything but what he was doing to her. "We-, wedding?"

His hands moved to her hips where he held her in place and moved to a wild, passionate beat. "I bought us a house."

Her eyes opened and her body stiffened. "A house?" She dragged her mind out of the sensual heaven in which it lay, almost drugged. Her body was aroused to such a fever pitch, she was barely able to process what he'd said, but slowly, she forced herself to mentally step back from their physical union to absorb the fact that he'd purchased a home for the two of them without consulting her.

"Oh, Tam . . . baby . . . yes . . . a house." He pulled her close as passion overtook him, and he convulsed against her.

Tamara waited a moment, still digesting what he'd said, still fighting her body's need to maintain the connection it shared with Dale. He'd bought a house? For them to live in after they were married?

His hand came around the front of her abdomen and slid between her legs, touching what was already inflamed, almost pulling her back into a sensual black hole.

She pushed his hand away and slipped out of his grasp.

"Tam? Was it . . . ? His words came out unevenly as he regained his breath. "Didn't you enjoy it that way? We can -."

"It was fine." She sat on the edge of the bed, her back turned to him.

"Fine?"

She turned and faced him. "Why did you buy a house?"

He still hadn't caught his breath, and he seemed disorientated. "Ah, well, so we'll have a place to live."

"We have a place to live."

"Here?"

"Yes, this is where we've been living."

He ran a hand through his moist hair. "Tamara. You didn't expect to live here the rest of our lives, did you? We'll need more space."

"Whatever for?"

He stood, walked to a wall dresser, and pulled a towel out which he wrapped around his waist, making him look regal. "I thought you'd be happy about this." He sounded baffled.

"Happy that you've made a purchase which will effect the rest of our lives without even asking how I felt about it?"

His features darkened and he shook his head. "This is unbelievable. It was meant to be a surprise, a gift, so no, I didn't consult you."

The irritation in his voice made her feel even more defensive. He hadn't done this for her. She didn't want a lavish house. This was just another way of manipulating, of dictating the manner in which they would live - his way. "Where is this house?" she asked, unable to keep the bitter sting out of her voice.

He cursed. "The Palisades. Overlooking the Pacific like Daphne's. It's got a gourmet kitchen, a library, media room, workout room, eight bedrooms, maid's quarters. It's a goddam palace."

Her life was quickly spinning out of control, and she didn't know where the brakes were.

He came around the bed, pulled her to a standing position, and glared at her. "And what you should be saying right now is, 'thank you'."

She met his scowl, so angry she could cry.

"Thank you," she said, full of venom, full of hostility.

"Oh hell." He stormed to his dresser and pulled out a small box. He opened it, gripped her hand, and placed a beautiful diamond ring on her finger. "I thought I'd make love to you, tell you about the house, and give you your official engagement ring."

She stared at the huge ring with tears in her eyes. Her heart pounding. She wanted to hate it but it was so beautiful.

"It's three carats. Too much for you, I know."

"Dale," she said, feeling miserable. Had she over reacted? Was he acting out of love and kindness, giving the only way he knew how? Was *she* the one unable to bend? "I . . ." She looked at him, not knowing what to say. "I'm sorry."

He shook his head. "Yeah." He turned and went to shower.

When he finished, he dressed.

"Where are you going?"

"For a drive."

No, don't go, she wanted to say. *Stay with me, hold me.* But she couldn't speak. She watched him walk out of the room.

Tamara curled on top of the bed, sexually and emotionally unfulfilled; physically drained, and mentally shattered.

Tamara wanted to forget about their fight. She'd apologized repeatedly. She told him she would live in the damn house, asked him to take her to see it, but Dale was determined to make her pay for her outright rejection of his 'surprise'.

He refused to talk about any of it, choosing to work late every night. He was cold, unyielding, unreasonable. And his attitude angered her all over again.

In contrast, with Raffi, Dale had become a model father. He picked Raffi up from school everyday, and helped him with his homework. Usually they were involved in some type of game when she came home from work. Then he would promptly kiss Raffi goodbye before returning to work and leaving her in control. Raffi adored him, she could tell. At least this relationship had turned out right.

After a week and a half of the cold shoulder treatment, Tamara grew impatient. Couldn't she disagree with him? She decided to take a more active role in making amends.

When he brought Raffi home from school, she made sure she was home to greet them.

"Oh, hi," he said.

She smiled. "Hi guys. I'm making dinner tonight, okay?"

Raffi grinned. "Macaroni and Cheese?"

"No, that's Dale's specialty, but you're close, it's lasagne. A family recipe I got from my grandmother."

Raffi wrinkled his nose. "Sounds strange."

She laughed. "Well, it's good, trust me."

"I can't stay," Dale said.

"Sure you can. I came home early so you'd be able to eat with us."

"Yeah," Raffi agreed. You haven't even helped me do my homework yet.

Tamara held her hands out to her sides and nodded. "Right, and dinner will be ready by then."

Dale eyed her suspiciously, but nodded.

She finished preparing the perfect dinner table in the dining room with elegant china, his best wine glasses, a vase with flowers at the center. Then she disappeared into their bedroom to put on a casual light gray satin dress, guaranteed to catch Dale's interest.

She wasn't disappointed when she called them to dinner, and he stopped in his tracks to stare at her.

She offered him a glass of wine, throwing all her charm into a smile.

"I've got to get back to work. I can't drink."

"One glass."

He took it and sat. They had a pleasant meal. Raffi chattered. Dale watched her silently.

Just as they finished their meal, Daphne and Adam showed up with tickets for the opening of a new Disney movie at El Capitan theater. "We thought Raffi might want to go," Daphne said, full of excitement.

"It's a school night," Dale muttered, but at

Raffi's drooping smile, Dale continued, "but he's finished his homework and has had perfect behavior in class. He deserves a night out."

Raffi hooted and ran to his bedroom to get his coat. "Thanks, Dale."

"Don't thank me, I'm not the one with the tickets."

Raffi smiled at Daphne. "Thanks."

She took his hand. "Are you kidding? I've been dying to see this movie. Come on."

Tamara walked them to the door and Daphne winked on her way out. Tamara owed her one.

Dale was clearing the table when Tamara came back. She placed a hand on his forearm. "Leave it."

"I'll help you clean up."

She wrapped her arms around his shoulders, linking them behind his neck. "I'll do it later."

He stiffened. "Tamara, what are you doing?"

"How much longer are you going to ignore me? Haven't you punished me enough?"

"I'm not ignoring you or punishing you. Don't be ridiculous."

"Then put your arms around me."

He heaved a sigh and loosely encircled her waist, his hands softly caressing her lower back. "I've got to get back to the office."

"No, you don't."

"I do."

"I called your secretary and told her you wouldn't make it back tonight."

"What? How could you do that?" He tried to

disengage her arms.

"I told her I planned on raping you and you would be in no condition to return."

He froze, seemingly fighting a smile.

She touched his lips. "Come on, Dale. You've made your point. I was caught off guard with the house. I should have been more grateful. But you're not going to deprive me of your body too much longer, are you?" She licked his lips. "Don't you know how much I need your touch? I'm dying a little everyday when you won't look at me, won't make love to me."

He pulled her closer and tipped his lips higher, just out of her reach. "Is that what you want? My body?"

She loosened his neck tie and methodically worked her way down his buttons. Opening his stiff white shirt, she found a nipple and kissed it. "That's what I want." She slipped the shirt off his shoulders. "And I'll accept no arguments from you. Understand?"

He laughed and ran his hands along her satin dress. "I think I do."

He allowed her to have her way with him until he came close to losing control, then he lifted her into his arms, carried her to bed and made up for lost time.

Tamara was happy. They were together again. He told her he loved her, brought her an explosion of ecstacy, yet she still felt as if their relationship had sustained a large fracture that had not been mended.

Although he kissed her and told he loved her as he dressed to return to work, Tamara felt a void inside. She tried not to cry as she waited in the living room alone for Raffi to return from the movies.

CHAPTER FIFTEEN

Standing in front of the bathroom mirror, Tamara finished locking in her diamond earrings, which Dale bought her last month to go with her engagement ring. She stared at the beautiful image of herself. She wasn't being egotistical - she looked perfect, sparkled in her black, sequined dress and expensive jewelry.

Yet Daphne's words kept echoing back at her, *one day you're going to wake up from your love haze and hate who you've become.* And she did. She didn't even recognize herself anymore. She closed her eyes and turned away from the mirror. She was so unhappy. What was she going to do about it?

Just then her beeper went off, cutting into her thoughts. She frowned, noticing the time on her watch said it was almost seven P.M. She sat on the bed, crossed her legs, and picked up the phone, dialing her office automatically. "Lisa? What's up?"

"Tamara. Thank God. Cindy's mother is at the foster parent's house with a gun. She's drunk and wants to take Cindy."

Tamara's back stiffened and her pulse raced. "Oh no. Have you called the police?"

"Yes, they're on their way. Hopefully she'll still be there when they arrive."

"I'm going over there." Her thoughts raced to that sweet little girl who must be terrified.

"No, Tamara, that's not why I called you. I just wanted you --"

"I'm going, bye." Tamara rushed out of the bedroom. "Dale, I can't go with you tonight. I've got to--"

"You're not going? Of course you are. Are you insane? You know how important this meeting with FAA is."

"Yes, I know, but I got called from work and I have to --"

"Damn it, work again! Let someone else handle things tonight, Tamara. I'm sick and tired of you rushing off every time there's the slightest problem."

She picked up her purse and car keys. "You don't understand. Cindy's in trouble."

"Someone's always in trouble and it's always your job to get them out."

"Dale, please. I'm sorry, I've got to go, I'll explain everything when I get back."

He placed his hands on his hips. "Tamara, I

need you tonight. Shouldn't I come first?"

"Honey, you don't *need* me to sit beside you at a dinner table, but Cindy's mother--"

"I don't even know why you're still working there, Tamara. We're going to be married for Christ's sake. You don't need to work anymore."

She had her hand on the door knob. She let it go and looked back at him. "I've never needed to work. I'm independently wealthy, remember? I work because I want to, because I think it's important. I thought you understood that."

"Don't leave, Tamara."

"Dale, I've got to." She opened the door.

"All right, that's it, I've had it. I'm not going to fight this any longer. Leave, but don't bother coming back. If you're going to embarrass me tonight when you know how important this meeting is then I don't need you at all."

"What?" What did he mean? He didn't want her anymore? How could he say something so cruel?

"You heard me!"

"I did, but I just can't believe you said that to me."

He looked ashamed for an instant, but then the determined look came back in his eyes and his face hardened. "I'm sorry, Tamara, but it's time for you to decide. It's either me or that job."

Tamara took a deep shaky breath. Was this her sweet Dale doing this to her tonight? She couldn't deal with him or his outrageous behavior now. She had to get to Cindy. She nodded. "Okay,

Dale." Then she left as fast as she could. She blinked back tears as she drove, because right now, she didn't have time to cry.

Dale was numb all over. She left. He loosened his neck tie. *Well, I guess I know where I stand in her life.* He'd given her everything he could think of to make her happy, and she'd just thrown it all away. Daphne had been right about her, she was self destructive.

Dale readjusted his neck tie, called Raffi, and went to his meeting. To hell with Tamara.

If only she hadn't wasted valuable minutes arguing with Dale, she might have made it. By the time she arrived at the foster parent's house, Cindy's mother had taken her. The police arrived just after Tamara. The flashing lights of the four patrol cars, the neighbors gawking, the foster parents crying - it was all like a terrifying nightmare. Tamara sat on the porch steps in a her evening dress, shivering against the penetrating night chill, looking completely out of place. She couldn't believe this was happening.

She watched the scene before her in a daze. Then there was a rush to one of the police cars. Everyone listened attentively, and three cars screeched away. Tamara stood. "What happened? Where did they go?"

Lisa rubbed Tamara's upper arm. "There's been an accident. They think it's Cindy's mother."

The rest of the night came at her like unbelievable waves. Cindy's mother had been drunk, in a hurry, she didn't see the street light. Both she and Cindy were killed instantly in the collision.

Tamara answered police questions then got in her car and drove. Somewhere in the back of her mind she remembered Lisa talking to her as she got behind the wheel, but she didn't pay attention to her. She drove and drove and drove along the coast. When she got low on gas, she refilled and turned back, driving all the way home, to Dale's home.

It was 5:00 am when she pulled into the underground garage and walked into the condo.

Dale sat on the living room sofa. He looked like he hadn't slept either.

She walked right past him to their bedroom and began packing her bags.

He followed. "Tamara, where the hell have you been?"

She didn't answer. She couldn't talk. She just threw her clothes in the suitcase as quickly as she could.

"You can't just ignore me. We won't solve our problems like that."

She moved to the bureau. They didn't have problems. They didn't have anything. She'd been fooling herself for months.

"Tamara." He sighed. "Stop that, will you?"

When she didn't stop he gripped her arm, and Tamara froze without looking at him. She was too angry to look at him. All she wanted to do was lash out and if he was the closest one then he'd be the one to receive the brunt of it.

"Look, you don't have to leave. I didn't mean it."

"Let me go," her voice was gravelly, as if she'd taken a shredder to her throat.

"You're not listening to me. Stop packing. I forgive you for not going with me last night. You don't have to leave."

"Forgive me?" She turned and glared at him. "You forgive *me*? How grand of you, Dale."

"I think so."

She had to fight the urge to strike out at that smug face. She should have known. From the beginning she knew it was a mistake to fall in love with him, but he was so gorgeous, so kind to her. "Let me go, Dale."

"You stay out all night without calling to let me know you're okay, and now you come home and start packing and you want me to let you go?"

"You told me to leave and I'm leaving."

He cursed. "I was angry."

"You had no right--"

"The hell I didn't. You're my fiancee," he shouted.

"Was."

"Tamara? Don't be a fool," he said in a quieter voice.

"I've been a fool for months thinking we had anything special. We don't belong together. We never did."

He released her arm, and swung his fist at her suitcase sending her clothes flying across the bed and onto the floor. "I won't go chasing after you."

"Good, then it'll be over, and we can each go on with our lives."

Dale's eyes were red. He actually looked like he might cry, but Tamara didn't feel sorry for him. She hoped he would hurt half as much as she was hurting.

He bowed his head then began picking up her clothes. He deposited them back in her suitcase then roughly grabbed her chin and glared into her eyes. "Why? I thought you loved me?"

"You ordered me to choose. I chose my job."

He winced. "How could you?"

She batted his hand away from her face. "The fact that you don't understand how I could is our major problem. I thought you understood why I do what I do. You took Raffi in, you've seen what it is I do. I thought . . . I hoped you'd changed, Dale."

"I shouldn't have to change."

"No, but I should, shouldn't I? You were working real hard to change me, to convince me to be your little prize doll. Now you expect me to leave a job where I'm helping others, where I feel useful, to sit beside you and look like a trophy."

His right eye flickered, but he said nothing.

She laughed though she felt no amusement. "Funny thing is I was willing to do it because I loved you so much, but you want me to give up everything I am. I can't do that."

Dale stepped back, one step at a time until he was at the door to his bedroom. "I never wanted you to be a trophy, Tam." His voice cracked, and he shook his head. "I wanted you to be my wife."

She could see that his hands were shaking and that he was on the brink of tears. She didn't think she could hurt anymore tonight, but her heart felt as if it were being flattened with a steamroller.

He wiped at his eyes angrily and looked at her. "But that's not what you wanted, was it?"

Yes, she wanted Dale more than she'd ever wanted anything in her life. "Not under your terms, no."

He nodded as if accepting her words. "Well, what are you waiting for? Go on. Don't let my love weigh you down another second. Take all your things and get out."

Tamara left the condo, carrying her suitcase full of her old clothes, none of the items she'd purchased since moving in with Dale, nor his gifts. But once she'd hurled the suitcase into her car and sat behind the wheel, she wondered where she would go. The easy part had been to say she was leaving, but she had no place of her own anymore, she had no one. Her vision blurred, and she shook her head. No, she wouldn't cry.

Tamara started the engine and drove to see the only friend she'd ever had, Daphne. Even though they were brother and sister, Daphne was nothing like Dale, and she loved Tamara unconditionally. If only Dale could have done that. Tamara had tried to be what he wanted, she really had. But she needed to keep the essence of what she was or she was nothing.

The second Tamara was escorted in and Daphne was called to meet her guest, Tamara lost all control. Her tears began to fall, and her body to tremble.

"Oh my God," Daphne said and opened her arms to Tamara.

Tamara clung to her and sobbed in a way she hadn't done since she and Daphne were in high school together. Daphne squeezed her tight against her body murmuring soothing words.

Adam came out in a robe, his hair tousled, and his eyes blinking in response to the lights. "What's wrong? Daphne, what happened?"

"I don't know." Her voice was choked as if she was holding back tears herself. "Go back to bed, and I'll tell you in the morning."

Tamara felt his hand on her back. "I'll have a room prepared for you, Tamara. Good-night."

Tamara's sobs began to subside. She lifted her head off Daphne's shoulder and nodded at Adam. She wiped her eyes and face with her fingers, then finally faced Daphne. "I'm sorry."

"Don't you dare apologize. Let's go to the family room."

Tamara followed Daphne into the room with the fireplace where she had first made love to Dale.

At the sight, tears threatened to return, but Tamara bit her bottom lip and blinked them away.

Both women sat on the sofa. Tamara sat Indian style, Daphne tucked her legs to the side. With her head bowed, Tamara began to tell Daphne how her life had just fallen apart.

Daphne listened without judgement.

"And that's it. I had no where to go. I, I didn't know where--"

"I would have been very upset with you if you hadn't come. Of course, you did the right thing."

Tamara arched her head back. She was so tired. She hadn't slept all night. Her head pounded. "It's my fault Cindy died. I gave her mother no choice. I denied her visitations and she had no options but to steal her daughter. I did this."

Daphne placed a hand on Tamara's shoulder and squeezed painfully. "Don't be ridiculous. You did what was best for that child."

Tamara lifted her head and began to shake it, but Daphne gripped her shoulders with both hands and gave her a jolt. "Stop it, Tamara. You're a professional, and you know you don't take the blame for a crazy, drunken parent who acted dangerously."

"Ouch." She pulled away from Daphne's hands. "You're right, I guess. But I feel responsible. I need some sleep."

Daphne nodded. "When you get up though, you should call Dale. He didn't mean--"

"No. That's over. I never want to see him

again." But her words rang hollow, because in her heart she knew she did want to see him and have him hold her and make love to her. She *did* want all those things, and she hated herself for wanting them.

Daphne flinched at the intensity of Tamara's statement. "All right, fine, calm down. Let's get you to bed."

Tamara dropped onto the bed in the guest bedroom and slept all day, and most of the night. She awoke at 4:00am, having slept twenty-two hours straight. Daphne and Adam were still asleep. Tamara walked into the family room and sat cross legged on the sofa in the darkness staring at the fireplace.

Of course Daphne was right, it wasn't Tamara's fault Cindy's mother was a lunatic, but their deaths sat heavily on her shoulders. She needed to take some time off from work. Tamara picked up the phone and made airline reservations. She'd go to her parents' place in Greece for a couple of weeks. Her parents wouldn't be the there so she'd have the place to herself.

When Daphne woke, Tamara told her she was leaving.

"You don't have to, you know? You can stay as long as you want."

"I need to get away. I appreciate your offer, but I need to be alone."

Daphne nodded. "Do you want a ride?"

"I called a limo, thanks."

Dale spent a week alternating between anger and hurt. Anger at himself for pushing her and anger at Tamara for giving up. The rage inside him was easier to handle than the hurt. Still, he couldn't avoid it, pain seemed to wrap itself around his heart until every beat was excruciatingly difficult.

He also had to deal with Raffi who made it no secret he blamed Dale for Tamara leaving. How could Dale argue with him? It *was* his fault. He told her to go. But how could she leave so easily? She had to know people say things in anger they don't really mean. He'd been an ass to issue an ultimatum, but he never expected she would take it to heart.

Maybe she'd just been waiting for an excuse to leave him – to get out of an engagement she'd only half heartedly accepted.

Even if leaving Dale was acceptable to her, how could she leave Raffi? He'd die if someone separated him from the boy.

Dale off turned the TV at that troublesome thought - he wasn't watching it anyway. What would he do when Raffi was taken away? Just like Tamara, Raffi was temporary. Dale had only agreed to watch him until they found him a permanent home.

Dale had his elbows on his knees. He curved his back forward and hung his head. Would he lose Raffi too some day soon? The pang in his gut was too much to handle. He didn't want Raffi to be adopted by another family, and he wanted Tamara to come home. The three of them were a family.

The phone on his coffee table rang and he jumped, then reached back and picked it up. "Yeah?"

"Dale, it's Daphne."

"Yeah, what is it?"

"It's been a week since you threw Tamara out, and you haven't called. Dad says you haven't been to work either. The aviation mechanics will be striking, you know?"

Dale shook his head. This year was off to a perfect start, he thought sarcastically.

When he didn't answer Daphne continued. "I was wondering how you were."

He'd been sitting on his couch, watching moronic shows on TV, and nursing his double whiskeys. The only thing he managed to do was take Raffi to school and pick him up. "I'm alive."

"Not very from the sound of you. You haven't tried to call her."

It wasn't a question, but Dale answered it as if it was. "No, what's the point? She's gone."

"You two sure do give up easy. If you had tried to call her you'd have found out she took off for Greece."

That got Dale's attention. "Greece?"

"Said she wanted to be alone. She came to me that morning you two fought, you know?"

Somewhere in the back of his mind he remembered she didn't have an apartment anymore.

"I didn't even think of where she'd go. I was too upset. But why Greece?"

"Her parents have a home there."

"What about her precious job?"

"Under the circumstances they understood her need to get away from there for a while. I called in for her."

Dale rubbed his temples. "Under what circumstances?" Tamara wasn't the first woman to break up with a guy.

"Cindy, of course."

"I don't know what you're talking about, Daph."

"The little girl that was killed. Didn't you ask Tamara why she had to cancel out on your dinner party?"

"She got an urgent call from work and left. That's all I know." He rubbed a hand down his face. "When she came back, she packed her bags and left. Who was killed, and -?"

"Oh . . . My . . . you don't even know."

"What!" His patience ran thin.

Daphne told him about Cindy's mom and the accident. Dale stood and began to pace as he listened, gripping the receiver harder and harder the more Daphne spoke.

Tamara had been in an incredible amount of pain and all Dale had thought about was himself and pleasing business associates who shouldn't have mattered a fraction of what Tamara mattered to him. He had done the very thing he accused her of doing. He chose his work over her. She'd cried on his sister's shoulder, rather than his. He'd thrown her out.

"Dale? Dale say something."

He took in a shaky breath. "She must hate me."

"Didn't she tell you any of it?"

"No, I didn't give her a chance. I ordered her to go with me to the dinner or not come back home at all."

"That's pretty much what she said."

He dropped back on the sofa and held his head in one hand and the receiver in the other.

"Dale?"

"Yes, I'm here."

"Maybe this is all for the best –."

He lifted his head. "Meaning what? That were better off apart?" He asked, angry that she'd say something so insensitive.

"Listen, don't get upset. I warned you before you two got involved that her chosen life style was very different from ours. Maybe you'll both be happier now, is all I'm saying.

"Daphne, I won't be happy without her." He dropped back against the backrest of the sofa and squeezed his eyes shut. "I *loved* her, don't you understand that? I wanted to marry her, have kids with her, grow old waking up to her beside me every morning."

His throat threatened to close so he stopped talking. He inhaled deeply and opened his eyes. "You know what she accused me of? Wanting her around as a trophy. Can you believe that?"

"Yes."

Daphne's quiet reply surprised him. "Yes what?"

"Yes, I can believe she said that, and yes I can understand how she felt that way. I said the very thing to her."

He shook his head, unable to understand women. "You told my fiancee I only wanted her around as a trophy?"

"I told my best friend to open her eyes and be true to herself."

He cursed, feeling a new sense of betrayal. "Let me get this straight. You warned the woman I love, the one who was already afraid of commitment, to be –."

"No, Dale, it wasn't like that." Daphne's voice came across as truly regretful. "But you claim to love her and you couldn't see how miserable she was. I've known her a long time and I've never seen her completely bend to please a man before as she did for you. Can you honestly tell me you didn't realize you were forcing her into a lifestyle she was uncomfortable with?"

He squeezed the receiver harder as renewed pain washed over him. "I knew," he said. "I just thought she had leftover bad feelings from her childhood, and once she lived with me she'd feel differently. I thought if she . . . ."

"Loved you enough?"

She'd change for him. Just what Tamara had said. "Ugh, Daph, I think I'm going to be sick to my stomach."

"Don't be too hard on yourself."

How could he not. "You know what I thought? I thought I could wean her away from her job as if it were a pacifier or something. I actually thought I was doing her a favor, rescuing her from that terrible line of work. Ah, hell, Daphne, what have I done?"

CHAPTER SIXTEEN

Tamara didn't feel any better in Greece than she had in America. Fully dressed and wrapped in a blanket, she laid on the beach for hours staring out at the Mediterranean Sea, listening to the squawk of sea gulls, with absolutely no thoughts going through her head. She couldn't think anymore and worse, she couldn't feel.

At the end of her second week she called in to work intending to quit. This 'vacation' had proved to her she was a pampered socialite after all. What other social worker had the luxury of going to the island of Crete when the going got tough. Tamara couldn't cut it, this was proof.

Lisa was appalled. "You can't quit, Tamara. What happened was terrible, but you have to go on. There's plenty of other kids out there who need you."

Tamara shook her head even though she was on the phone. "I can't do it anymore."

"Bull. Stop feeling sorry for yourself and come back home."

"I'm not feeling--"

"Yes, you are. Do you think you're the only one who's ever lost someone, Tamara? It happens all the time, not to that extreme maybe, but we win some and we lose some. You just have to try to win as many as you can. If you give up on the rest of the kids, then everyone's lost, don't you get it?"

Instantly, Tamara knew Lisa was right. She'd said the very thing to others in her office when they'd had painful experiences. Those type of tragedies happened in her line of work. But somehow it felt different now that it happened to her. She had pull herself together, go back home, and face her life. "Give me another week, okay?"

"One more and that's it. Come home."

Home? Where was that? She called her parents next and told them she needed a place. They enthusiastically offered one of their homes.

Tamara didn't really want to take one of their elaborate estates. "I'd like my own place. Something small." At least, small by her parents' standards.

"Do you want us to buy you a home?" Celeste sounded surprised.

Tamara sighed. "Yes, mother. If I don't use some of the money you keep depositing in my name it's going to grow to such outrageous numbers I won't even be able to count it."

"Just tell me where and I'll have our realtor buy something right away."

Tamara looked out to the sea trying to absorb some peace from the calm waters, but she felt nothing. The cool, salt air filled her lungs. "By the ocean. How about a small place in Santa Monica?"

"Consider it done, dear."

"Mom?"

"Yes?"

"Small. A couple of bedrooms, a garage, and as close to the ocean as possible."

"I understand, Tamara. How are you liking Greece?"

It was lonely, so lonely. "Same as always. You know."

The realtor was able to make a cash deal and Tamara moved into her three bedroom, two story home as soon as she got back to California. It was definitely bigger than she'd envisioned, but she liked it. She could see the Santa Monica pier from her bedroom.

She walked through the empty rooms, hearing the echoes of her shoes on bare floors. This was her new home. She would fill the rooms slowly with furnishings and decorations. Everything from her old apartment was in storage, but she would throw most of it out except for pictures and those terrible pottery statues she made. Somehow, she no longer felt like the girl she had been before Dale.

Getting back into a routine at work was easier than she thought. Cindy's file had already been removed. She dove into the latest cases, doing her best not to get emotionally involved with anyone.

What she wasn't prepared for was a call from Dale.

"What do you want?" Just hearing his voice threatened to overwhelm her. How could she enjoy listening to his voice when he'd used it to tear her heart out.

"I'd like to get together and talk, Tamara."

"That's not necessary, is it?"

"Don't you think so?"

"Dale, I've got work to do."

"Why didn't you tell me about Cindy?"

Tamara bit her bottom lip, unable to answer.

"I didn't know, Tam."

"You didn't listen."

"Maybe you're right, I didn't. I'm sorry."

"I've got to go, Dale." She slammed the receiver down. She couldn't talk to him now, and not about Cindy.

The next four times he called, Tamara refused to talk to him as well. He'd hurt her too deeply. No one had gotten as close to her as he had, and he'd thrown her away like garbage. No, she couldn't deal with him, the pain was too raw.

Dale's frustration level was reaching the boiling point. Tamara wouldn't talk to him, and he couldn't get over her. Worst of all, he couldn't understand why. Every other time he'd ended a relationship with a woman, he'd been able to decide it was over and go on with life. Not so with Tamara. *It's because you love her, pal.*

The woman was unconventional, completely extraordinary, and making love to her had been like entering a whole new plane. When she held him, when she touched him, life became as close to perfect as was possible on earth. He reached an exalted state, a place where the human spirit could only be lifted by love.

"What are you doing, Dale?" Raffi asked.

"Ah, damn." He'd broken half a dozen eggs into the pancake batter. He tried to scoop out the extra yokes and poured some of the white out.

"Is it ruined?" Raffi stood on a step ladder, leaning over Dale's arm to help.

"I don't think so."

"Want me to stir?"

"Yeah, buddy. You stir."

Raffi smiled, took the bowl and whisk and stirred happily. Dale propped his rear on the kitchen counter and watched Raffi. He was so cute with his hair perfectly combed.

"Am I doing a good job, Dale?" His big brown eyes were bright with anticipation.

"Are you kidding?" Dale took the bowl from the boy and gave him a manly pat on the back. "You did a great job. We're ready to make those pancakes now."

Raffi jumped off the step and hurried to set

the table, forks on the left, knives on the right, napkin under the knife.

"You do that very well."

"Thanks. Tamara showed me how."

Dale flipped the pancakes and pursed his lips. "Tamara, huh? I'm real sorry things didn't work out with her, Raffi. I know how much you liked her."

Raffi shrugged. "I still have you."

Dale's throat constricted. He placed Raffi's pancakes on his plate. "Here you go. Eat up."

"Dale?"

"Yeah."

"Did you cry when Tamara left?"

"What?"

"I did. Does that make me a wimp?"

Dale pulled up a chair and sat across from the boy. "No, Raffi. It doesn't make you a wimp to love someone enough that you cry when she leaves."

The boy's big eyes were glued to Dale's as if seeking some mysterious truth. Dale felt so incompetent.

But then Raffi smiled as if he understood. "Is it okay if I love you, too?"

Dale's eyes misted. He leaned across the table and kissed Raffi's forehead. "It's the most wonderful thing anyone's ever done for me."

Raffi smiled and dug into his pancakes without another word. Dale ate with him, but his appetite had disappeared. His throat, his stomach, and his heart seemed to have constricted.

Raffi finished all his food and placed his plate

in the dishwasher. "I'll go play."

"Hey, Raffi."

"What?" He stopped in mid skip.

"I love you too."

He smiled sheepishly and ran off.

That evening Dale took Raffi to Daphne's house. He had to go see Tamara, except he didn't know where she lived, and not even Daphne knew. He talked to Lisa at Tamara's work, but she wouldn't give him her address.

"Please, Lisa. All I want to do is talk to her."

"Sorry. If she wants you to have it, she'll give it to you." She paused. "But she told me she was going to Ricky's pub in Santa Monica tonight. Catch her there."

"Ricky's pub. Okay, thanks."

Dale walked into the energetic, well lit pub, but rather than the small bar he expected to find, it was a spacious, two floor establishment. The lower level had tables where people were eating their dinner, and a long bar barely visible from the people crowded along it.

He swept his gaze from corner to corner but didn't spot Tamara. He waved a suited waiter away. "Just looking for someone."

Dale crossed the room and climbed the stairs hoping to find her upstairs. As soon as he rounded the corner at the top of the steps, he saw her. She was leaning over a pool table with a cue stick in hand, dressed in tight jeans and an even tighter stretch top which enhanced her chest. Her hair was bunched up on her head, held together by some gadget that looked like a butterfly.

Tamara hit the white ball, then laughed at the long haired man standing beside her. He placed his arm around Tamara's waist, his fingers slipping into her back pocket. Dale's jaw tightened and his breathing deepened. He didn't like the familiarity between them.

He marched over, grabbed her elbow, and pulled her away from the other man's touch.

"Dale," she said in obvious surprise.

"What the hell . . .," the long haired moron said.

Tamara put a hand on his chest. "Roy, this is a friend of mine."

"Oh, cool."

"Friend? I'm your friend now, Tamara?"

"Excuse us," she said and smiled at the other two couples who where standing around the pool table. Then she moved toward a more private wall next to another, less crowded bar. "What are you doing here?"

"I came to see you. But I can see your busy with your old boyfriend. Didn't take you long to get back together with him, did it?"

"Look, I'm enjoying an evening out with my friends. I don't need you here to ruin it."

"I'm not here to ruin anything. You won't talk to me when I call your office. I don't know where you live. This was the best I could do."

"Dale, we have nothing to say to each other."

"How can you say that? Tamara, you said you loved me. Do you say that so easily that you can walk away when the going gets tough?"

"You know damn well I don't."

"And what about Raffi? You left without even a second thought about him."

She closed her eyes as if she were experiencing extreme pain, and Dale was immediately sorry. He'd hurt her enough, he didn't want to inflict anymore pain.

He touched her arm, prompting such longing for her that he could barely stand it. "I'm so damn sorry, Tamara."

She looked at him silently then her long lashes dropped over her eyes. He felt as if she'd closed a door on his face. "I've made a mess where Raffi's concerned. I allowed him to get close to me, because I was selfish and wanted to be with you. That was a mistake."

"You're telling me that being with me was a mistake?"

Her stare was cold and direct. "The biggest I've ever made."

He placed his hands on his hips, hurt and anger wanting to make him pick up a billiard ball and throw it at the wall. But before he said something he'd later regret, he took a deep breath. "You don't mean that."

"I'm not the one calling and chasing you around, am I?"

He shook his head. "No," his voice was thick with defeat. "You're not."

Tamara almost lost her strength to go on. Dale looked so sad, and she sounded like such a cold bitch. But she had to do it. She had to convince him their relationship was over. They were poison for each other. There was no way it could have ever worked. She swallowed the dryness of her throat. She wanted to touch him, to take away the mean things she'd said, but instead she crossed her arms across her chest. "I've still got your engagement ring. I'll mail it back to you."

His eyes were shining brightly, and they flashed at her words. "Throw the damn ring in the trash. What the hell do I want with it?"

"Fine, consider it done."

His right eye flickered. "I want you to come get all your other things from my place."

"I took what I wanted."

"I bought those clothes and jewelry for you, Tamara."

"So what?" She squared her shoulders. "People have been buying me things my whole life. What I wanted was love. Not only if I jumped through the right hoops, but love because I was me. You don't love me, Dale. You only loved what you wanted to create."

"No, Tam, that's not true. I did love you. I still do."

She shook her head, not wanting to hear him say those words again. Listening to his sweet words of love was how she'd gotten pulled into his web in the first place. "Bull. I was a social worker who lived in a run down apartment and was happy to dress in thrift store clothes and eat off paper plates. Is that the Tamara you loved?"

He swallowed and blinked rapidly.

"I rest my case. Go find yourself a Barbie doll to love, Dale, and leave me the hell alone." She left him standing where he was. She couldn't bear to talk to him anymore.

"I'm sorry," she told her friends. "I need to go."

Roy frowned. "Now?"

"Didn't I make myself clear?"

"Sure." He shrugged, put his arm around her, and walked out. She didn't want him touching her, but she was beyond caring. She snuggled close to him and let him lead her out.

Dale felt as if he'd been in a collision with a brick wall. He clenched and unclenched his hands at his sides, trying to control the tremors attacking his body. It killed him to watch the woman he loved walk out in the arms of a hoodlum, and to know she didn't want to be anywhere near him.

For the first time he noticed the laughing people playing pool and darts and the couples chatting intimately at corner tables. Music played, but not overbearingly loud, the sound of glass touching table tops was more noticeable.

He'd done everything wrong when it came to Tamara, but she was mistaken, he did love her. He loved her enough to let her go. She wasn't happy with him. Every dress she'd put on, every dinner she'd attended on his arm had been a strain on her. He didn't want her to be unhappy when she was with him. If places like this pub were what made her happy then Dale had to step aside. He walked out of the pub without another look at his surroundings.

CHAPTER SEVENTEEN

For the next month, Dale concentrated on the only two things he had left in his life, Raffi and his work. Raffi had his sixth birthday which they celebrated with his friends from school. Dale kept it to a simple pizza party, remembering Tamara's advice from the previous year, and wishing this year they could have all celebrated together.

He gave all of Tamara's things away to charity. He thought of mailing them to her work, but she didn't want them, he knew that. Besides he swore he wouldn't bother her again.

But instead he was surprised when he got a call from her. "This isn't a personal call, it's about Raffi," she said.

"Okay." Just the sound of her voice did crazy things to his heart. "Is something wrong?"

"I'm calling to notify you that Raffi might be selected as an adoption choice."

Choice? Raffi was more than a choice. He was his son. "What the *hell* does that mean?"

"It means there's been a match, and if he's selected, he could be adopted."

"I don't understand," he said. "Is he going to be adopted or isn't he?"

"Possibly."

Her vagueness made him want to shout into the phone. How dare she use that same patient, dispassionate, social worker tone with him as she did with others! No matter what happened between them, she loved Raffi too. She had to feel *something.*

"What are we going to do, Tam?"

"There will be a visitation. Then we wait to see if the couple decides to proceed with the adoption."

He stared at the white walls and felt as if they were closing in on him. The anger inside him faded and was replaced by fear. "But . . . I don't want to lose Raffi."

She cleared her voice, and it became tender. "Dale, foster parents aren't meant to keep the children forever."

"I know, but . . ." His words failed him. The pain inside was overwhelming.

"We talked about this remember?" If you wanted to adopt him, you–?"

"I do."

"Dale." She sighed. "It's too late now that we've gotten notice of his possible adoption. There's nothing you can do."

"Nothing? Tamara, for Christ's sake, help me."

He heard her breathing on her end. After a pause, she said, "Let me call you back. Will you be home?"

"I'll be sitting by my phone."

"Okay. And Dale, you might want to contact your lawyer also."

He didn't like the sound of that, but he told her he would.

About an hour later she called back.

"What did you find out?"

"Basically that until whoever wants him makes their decision, you have no claim on Raffi."

His lawyer had said something similar. This couldn't be happening. Why was everything of any importance in his life being threatened?

"Dale?"

"What?" His chest tightened.

"Did you hear me?"

He slumped on his sofa. "Yes. Sure, I heard."

"I'm sorry."

"Are you? And why's that?" Dale was convinced the world was all mixed up, starting with these crazy people who were supposedly doing what was best for kids.

"I know you've gotten attached."

"Attached? I love that kid. I know you think I'm incapable of loving anyone, but--"

"I never said that."

He laughed harshly. "Oh, didn't you?" He tightened his hold on the phone. "And you're not fooling me, Tamara. You love him, too."

The line remained silent. When she spoke, her voice was weak, filled with as much emotion as his. "Of course I do. This is what we've been waiting for, isn't it? For Raffi to have a family with two loving parents."

"He's *our* son."

"He deserves so much better, Dale." Her voice was no more than a whisper.

He shook his head, refusing to believe anyone could love Raffi more than he did. "Listen, I'm not giving up on him. I'll call my lawyer back and start my own adoption proceedings."

"If you knew you wanted to do this, why didn't you do it earlier?"

"I planned to, but . . . I was feeling sorry for myself . . . because I lost you." He cleared his throat. "I won't lose him too, Tamara. If you won't help me, I'll find someone who will."

"I'll do what I can, but I won't make any promises." Her voice was so kind and sincere. God, he missed her.

He cut the connection before he ended up begging her to come back to him.

Later that day, Dale sat beside Raffi in his bedroom, playing with race cars, as he prepared to discuss what was happening. It was only fair Raffi be included in the decision since he had the most to lose and gain. Dale wanted to approach the topic carefully, but there was really only one way to say what needed to be said, and that was honestly.

"I received a call from Tamara today notifying me that there's a possibility you might be adopted, Raffi."

He was rolling his small matchbox car on the track he and Dale had built, and he stopped. He sat back on his heels. "By who?"

"Well, it's all preliminary right now. I'm not even sure you will be, but it's possible."

Without speaking, he pinned Dale in place with big, questioning eyes.

Dale forced enthusiasm into his voice. "How do you feel about that. It's good news, isn't it?"

"I don't know."

"You'd have a forever mom and dad."

He looked at his car again and rolled it back and forth. "That's true."

This was so hard. Dale didn't know what to say. He felt everything he did say was wrong. "Look, I don't want to get your hopes up, but I intend to contest it, so you can stay with me. Do you understand what that means?"

Raffi shook his head. He looked like he was about to cry.

"It means I don't want you to go, pal. I'd like you to stay with me forever, but only if you want to."

Raffi's shiny eyes beamed. "Yeah, I want to stay with you, Dale. We love each other."

He grinned in answer to Raffi's comment. "Yes, we do, and that's what I'm going to tell the social workers. But if it doesn't work and you get to be adopted, I want you to know it's a good thing, Raffi, even though I'll miss you."

The gleam in his eyes dimmed. "I won't be happy."

"You didn't think you'd be happy with me, and you have been, haven't you?"

"Yes."

Dale reached out a hand and rested it on Raffi's shoulder. "Well, then, either way I want you to know you'll be loved, okay?"

"Can I talk to Tamara?

"Now?"

"Yes, please."

"Raffi, I don't know her number. I could try her at work, but she might be gone by now. Why do you want to talk to her?"

"I just do."

Dale recognized the stubborn set of his jaw, and knew that whatever was driving Raffi at the moment made it useless to argue. Dale dialed Tamara at work.

"Hello," her tired voice answered.

"Tamara?"

"Yes."

"It's Dale."

"Oh, hi." She sounded exhausted and he wished he could tell her to come home where he could tuck her into bed and make her rest. "I didn't recognize your voice."

Yeah, right. He didn't believe her. How many hours had they spent talking to each other on the phone? But he ignored her comment. "I talked with Raffi regarding what's going on."

"I see. But you really don't know what's going on yet."

"I told him what I know. He asked to speak with you."

She groaned. "Dale, I can't."

"Why not?"

"What does he want with me? I can't do anything for him, for you, for either of you."

"I don't know, Tam. Should I tell him you won't talk to him. Is that what you want?"

"No, of course not. Put him on."

Dale called Raffi to the phone.

"Hi," he said timidly.

"Hi, sweetie." She couldn't believe the wave of emotion that shot through her at the sound of his voice.

"Dale said I might have to leave."

"Yes, I know."

"I won't." His little voice sounded so strong.

"Honey--"

"I want to stay with Dale. And I want you to come back home."

She sighed. "Raffi things aren't that simple."

He breathed heavy as if he were getting impatient. Tamara smiled.

"Just come home," his voice pleaded. "We could live without you, but it's not the same, and if you did, we would be happier."

"Raffi, right now, let's worry about keeping

you with Dale, okay? Not about me. I'll do what I can to make sure you can stay with him."

"That's good for now."

"Good. Now let me talk with Dale."

"I want to see you."

Tamara was surprised at how assertive he'd become. Dale was definitely rubbing off on him. "No, Raffi."

"Yes, I want to see you."

She sighed. "Let me talk to Dale."

"Tell him to take me to see you, or I'll call you back tomorrow."

Tamara laughed. Yes, he sounded like Dale. "Good night, sweetie."

"Well, he's really becoming something, isn't he?" she said to Dale when he got on the line.

"I'm sorry." Dale's deep voice made her skin get goose bumps. "I'll explain to him why you can't see him."

Why, because she was afraid to see Dale? That wasn't fair to Raffi. "You can take him to the club on Friday afternoon. We can get a bite to eat, and I'll talk to him."

"Are you sure you want to do that?"

"I think I should. In the likelihood that you lose him, Dale, he has to understand that it's not something terrible happening to him."

"I explained that to him. At this point I think he just wants to know that when he loves someone, it doesn't mean he's going to lose them. I'm not sure you're the one to make him see that."

Ouch. But, in a way, she deserved that. "If

you don't want me to see him--"

"It doesn't matter what I want, it's what he wants. If it's to see you, and you're willing, then fine."

She could hear Dale's pain in his voice. They were both hurt, and Tamara wished she could make all that misery go away. Why was love so painful and complicated? She wished she could be what Dale wanted her to be, but she'd tried and she'd failed. "Friday, then?"

"Friday."

Raffi tried to hide his excitement, but Dale noticed it in everything he did that morning, from getting up early, to picking out his favorite clothes, to helping fix breakfast. Today was the day he'd get to see Tamara.

I feel the same way buddy. I'm sorry I ruined it for both of us.

Tamara wore a cute light purple sun dress with delicate sandals. Her hair hung loose, with soft curls touching her shoulders. Dale swallowed through the thickness in his throat. He hoped he could get through this meeting with some dignity. He couldn't help wondering if her agreement to meet them meant she was softening toward him, and he had a chance to make things right again. No, he shook that thought away. He couldn't keep getting his hopes up. She told him very clearly that it was over.

Raffi walked straight toward the table where she sat, but at the last instant he ran and threw himself into her arms. She stood to catch him, gathering and holding him against her breasts, rocking him slightly from side to side. When she put him down and gazed at Dale, she had tears pooled in her eyes.

"Hello, Dale."

"Let's sit." He motioned her back in her chair. What he really wanted was to pull her against his body as she'd done with Raffi. He missed the feel of her skin against his.

They ordered their food and made small talk throughout their meal. Dale caught her up on family news, announcing that Daphne was pregnant.

Tamara's eyes locked with his. "She is?"

"You haven't called her recently?"

"No, I haven't."

"What happened between us has nothing to do with her, Tam. You were her friend before we got together, you know?"

She looked down at her salad. "Of course, I understand that. It's just . . ."

"What?"

"I had this need to get away from everyone and everything. It was the only way I could deal with . . ." She looked into his eyes again but didn't continue. The truth was in those deep brown eyes.

His guild cut straight through his soul.

Would he ever be able to make amends. "God, Tamara, I'm so sorry. You know that, don't you?"

"Don't." she held up a hand. "I didn't come here for this."

"I know, but won't you let me apologize?"

"You have." She smiled at Raffi. "How's your food?"

"Okay."

"I'm glad you suggested we meet because I want to explain what could happen now that you've gotten good news."

He shook his head. "I just wanted to see you 'cause me and Dale miss you."

Her smile slipped a bit, but she seemed to be able to firm it up again. "I've missed you too, but--"

"Then why won't you come visit us?"

She leaned back in her chair, glanced at Dale, and took a deep breath, looking for the first time, irritated. She usually was so good and patient dealing with her cases. But Dale knew Raffi was no longer just a case to her. She loved the kid.

"You're right, Raffi. I'll come and visit with you if you'd like or you can come to my house. If the adoption goes through, you have to promise me you'll try to be happy with your new family."

He nodded. "Okay, I promise, but only Dale can adopt me."

She smiled. "Go play on the grass, Raffi, I want to talk with Dale."

"Okay."

As soon as Raffi was gone, she turned impassioned eyes to him. "All right, Dale, I'll help you keep Raffi. This is why you two called me."

"It was part of it."

"It's the only part I'm willing to help you with."

"Fair enough."

She outlined her plan and his part in it. She had switched gears to her business persona, which caught Dale off guard, but he was impressed with her proposal. He found himself listening intently to what she said, because as she pointed out, his happiness depended on how this all turned out.

Tamara met with Dale and his attorney the following week, and they filed adoption papers. She told him to be prepared to state in a deposition his desire to adopt Raffi and why. Raffi should also be prepared to explain what he wanted.

Dale signed everything that was put in front of him. He didn't understand all the issues Tamara and his lawyer discussed, but he trusted them to know what they were doing.

As they walked down the steps from the lawyer's office, Dale admired her stylish business suit and her terrific legs.

"I can pick Raffi up and take him to get a burger tomorrow night," she said.

Dale was momentarily thrown. After so many weeks of keeping her distance, he was surprised to learn she wanted to see Raffi again. But then he remembered she promised to spend time with him. "Sure, that'll be fine."

They reached the bottom steps and she faced him with a warm smile. "Okay, then . . ."

"Yes . . ." he nodded. "I'll have him ready."

She turned and walked away. He watched her place her briefcase in her trunk and climb into her Jag. He lifted his coat and folded his hands into his pockets. At least she was talking to him.

But the following night, her conversation was just as sparse. She looked cute in casual jeans and a white, cotton, button up shirt. She waited at his door and when Raffi came skipping over, she took his hand and said good bye.

"Have fun," Dale said, trying to sound cheerful.

"We will," Raffi called immediately.

Tamara waved her fingers in the air and they left. To fight the feeling of loneliness, Dale sat at his desk to get some work done. A few hours later, they returned. Tamara had taken Raffi to Universal City Walk. They had a burger, fries and a chocolate shake, then walked around looking at the shops full of 'cool stuff'.

Dale listened to Raffi's hoarse voice, and his heart swelled. He was such a precious little boy. Everything made him happy. Dale was sure Tamara could have taken him to play in a sandbox, and he would have enjoyed himself just as much.

"Well, say good night and thank you, Raffi."

He gave Tamara a hug and kiss, and went contentedly to bed.

"Want some coffee?" Dale offered.

"Oh, no." She rubbed her hands on her jean

clad legs. "I better go home, it's late."

Dale didn't want to push. "Well, thanks for taking Raffi out. He had a great time, it seems."

"Yes, we both did." She stood by the door making no move to leave. "I'll, ah, call you . . . about the adoption . . . and, ah, stuff."

"Yes, please keep me posted."

"Okay." She opened his front door, hesitated a second at the threshold, then smiled at him. "Good night."

Suddenly he thought he should walk her downstairs to her car. In his cautious attempt not to spook her, he'd forgotten his manners. "I'll see you to your car," he said immediately.

He walked her down stairs and when she was safely buckled inside, he waved and went back into his quiet, lonesome condo.

The next few times he saw her were carbon copies of the first. They talked about Raffi, about their case, she was very polite, Dale tried to remain distant. But the void in his life haunted him. Though he searched for some kind of meaning in his daily existence, he found nothing but a beautifully embellished shell.

CHAPTER EIGHTEEN

The only day Dale and Tamara came close to discussing anything personal was when she did a home study on him. They met at Daphne's house, so Raffi would be entertained while Dale and Tamara sat in the library together to conduct the interview.

She asked incredibly personal questions about his childhood, his family, his schooling, his social life. He answered honestly and she listened without any reaction. She took notes, asked more questions, then scribbled his responses on the paper again.

Dale sat on a couch, and Tamara on a wing back chair. He leaned back, watching her, thinking how ironic it was for her to sit with such cool professionalism after what they'd shared together.

"What did you do after high school?"

He shrugged. "I dated a lot."

She glanced at him from her notes. "I mean, did you go to college, or get a job . . .?"

"Oh, that. Yes, both."

"Tell me about it."

"Not much to tell. I studied what my father wanted me to, worked for him to learn the business. Whenever I got a break, I'd vacation with friends."

She wrote on her notepad.

He wanted some reaction from her. He felt like he was talking to a shrink. "How about you?"

"Excuse me?"

"I said, 'what about you'? Why did you go to college?"

She stared at him like he had said something vile. "I don't know. I was supposed to. Why?"

"Just wondering."

She shook her head. "Let's get back to the study, shall we?"

"Whatever you say."

"Did you enjoy working with your father?"

"I did."

"How do you think you're similar to your father?"

"I'm intelligent, driven, extremely good looking."

That got a smile out of her. "How about kind, nurturing . . . ?"

"My father's kind. I don't know about nurturing."

"I have to ask," she hesitated. "How about your mother?"

Dale smiled. "You mean, is she nurturing?"

"Yes."

"You know the answer to that."

She nodded and looked at her papers. "If neither of your parents were very nurturing, do you think you will be able to be with Raffi?"

"Yes, I already am."

She wrote furiously. Then she paused, and began her questions again. "After college you went to work with your father full time?"

"Yes. Now you answer a question, Tamara. Does it bother you to ask people so many personal questions?"

She laid her hand on her notepad which rested on her lap and looked at him. "There's nothing personal about this, just questions on a form. The state requires it."

"I know that, but *you* have to ask."

"It doesn't bother me. But if you're getting tired, we can stop for a while."

Dale shook his head. "Let's finish."

She picked up her pen again and began firing off a new set of questions that brought them to the present time. After a few questions about discipline and parenting skills, she pronounced them finished.

He took a deep breath. "Finally. Are you sure they don't want to know how many showers I take a week or how many orgasms I have?"

She gave him a stern look. "Don't be crude, Dale."

He laughed. "You sound like my mother."

Tamara placed her voluminous notes in her

briefcase and sat back in her chair. "I definitely don't want to sound like her."

"Now what happens to all those questions?"

"I type them up and put the package together with your file and it all goes to the state. That's when we'll get notified that you can't adopt because Raffi is already being adopted."

"But he's not."

"Don't worry, I'll deal with that part of it. Your part is over for a while."

He leaned forward and peered into her eyes. "Does that mean I won't see much of you, again?"

She looked uncomfortable. "I'll keep in touch." She stood. "We're finished here."

He stood as well. *Yep, pal, she's finished with you, all right.* "Don't want to look at my sorry face anymore then, do you?"

She gazed in his eyes. "I'm doing this for Raffi, Dale. Remember why I'm here."

"How could I forget? You've got icicles for pupils."

She ignored him and exited the room.

Daphne offered a meal of barbequed hamburgers and corn on the cob. Outside, spring was in full bloom, the ocean blew a warm wind into the Palisade Hills.

Tamara looked longingly out the window. "I can't stay."

"I don't want to hear it, Tamara. You're staying. It's bad enough you buy a house and disappear for weeks without even calling me."

"I said I was sorry about that."

"Good, then don't argue about staying and let's go out to the yard."

"Really, I –."

"You don't have to sleep with Dale, just have a burger. Come on."

"Oh, jeeze, Daphne." She shook her head and went out to the patio.

Daphne smiled at Dale. "You can thank me later."

Dale smiled back. His sister was probably the only one who could manipulate Tamara. Well, maybe Raffi could too, since he purposely sat Dale next to Tamara.

Tamara pretended not to notice Raffi's blatant attempt at pushing Dale and her together. His insistence that Dale take the seat right beside her would have been cute if she wasn't so aware of Dale's every move.

That interview had been excruciatingly difficult for her to do. To have to delve into Dale's past and ask all those personal questions made her so uncomfortable she could barely look him straight in the eyes. She noticed *he* was even getting bothered near the end and giving her flippant answers.

Adam placed a plate heaping with burgers in the middle of the table. "Serve yourselves."

Tamara reached for a patty at the same time as Dale. "Excuse me. You go first."

"No, you go ahead. I was going make a burger

for Raffi."

"So was I," she said.

"Well, one of you do it so the rest of us can eat," Daphne interrupted.

Tamara stabbed a burger patty, placed it on a bun, and handed the fork to Dale. He took it, brushing her fingers, and making her stomach plummet. She felt as foolish as a teenager.

As hard as she'd tried to stay angry with Dale these past weeks, the feeling had faded. All she seemed to remembered was the love they'd shared. The love she still felt inside for him. But what she couldn't get past was the hurt. He'd failed her when she needed him most, and she couldn't find it in her heart to forgive him.

She prepared Raffi's burger and put it on his plate. The child made a show of thanking her and ate with gusto. Tamara glanced at Dale. He had a smirk on his face that told her he also noticed Raffi's exaggerated attempts at showing how happy he was when Tamara was around.

Every time she saw Raffi, she felt guilty. Even if Dale won custody, she had no claim on the boy. She'd never be the mother Raffi craved so much, which perhaps was the most painful part of this whole thing, because she truly wanted to be. They had gotten so close while she lived with Dale. How many nights had he fallen asleep on her lap?

She busied her hands with her food to keep from reaching across and pulling him against her now. Every time she had to meet with Dale and Raffi, she suffered the pain of their separation again. But she forced herself to go through with it, because she was a professional. Raffi would be one child she would do right by, no matter what the personal cost.

"So, now that you've studied my brother, what happens next?" Daphne squeezed ketchup on her bun.

"We wait for the state to reject his request for adoption."

"To reject? Why?"

"They will. Then there will probably be a hearing where both Dale and Raffi have to appear and plead their case."

Daphne glanced at Raffi then back at Tamara. "Is it possible that . . . ."

They'd lose? "Anything is possible," Tamara stated flatly.

They ate their burgers without further discussion about the subject.

"Well, what now?" Dale patted Raffi on the shoulder when they were finished.

He gazed at the pool. "I sure wish I could go swimming."

"Well, we didn't bring your suit."

"Let him go in his boxers," Daphne said.

"No." Dale gave his sister a stern look.

"Oh, come on, if Tamara could swim in the nude, a small boy could go in his underwear."

Tamara couldn't believe Daphne. What had gotten into her? She actually felt her face warm, and she never blushed. "Are you purposely trying to embarrass me?"

"You swam naked?" Raffi's eyes were huge.

Of course he'd seen her wrapped in her towel that morning, but had no idea what she'd done. "It was a long time ago, sweetie. Come on, let's get you in that pool."

Dale let them both leave without a word, but he turned to his sister as soon as Tamara was out of earshot. "Cut it out."

"What?" Daphne said innocently.

"Leave her alone, Daphne. You're not helping."

"I'm just trying to get her to loosen up. If she hates you she should just say so and get it over with. This false politeness is making me sick. But of course she doesn't hate you, she's still crazy about you, I know her."

"Well, I happen to know her too, and I want you to stop pushing her. She knows I'm here if she wants me, but she doesn't."

"So you're giving up?"

"Right now, all I want is her help in keeping Raffi."

"He's right," Adam squeezed Daphne's hand. He'd sat quietly through the whole meal, wisely staying out of the discussion, until now. "Tamara should be focusing on this case now. You don't want her concentration diverted by personal matters."

Dale nodded. Tamara had to feel comfortable to do her job. Dale had to be just another case to her. He'd better keep reminding himself of that, as well.

Daphne agreed to butt out temporarily. Dale watched both Raffi and Tamara jump in the pool.

"Hey, she's wearing my swim suit," Daphne protested. "And she looks fantastic in it, darn it."

Adam laughed. "Are you feeling big and unattractive again?" His arms encircled Daphne's pregnant stomach.

Dale tuned them out and watched Tamara's athletic body swim three laps, then splash around with Raffi. Just looking at her made his body ache. He positioned his chair so he could see them better and folded his hands on his belly. If all he could do was watch her then he'd be grateful for the opportunity and consider it a gift.

Daphne picked the plates off the table, and Adam cleaned the grill all the while teasing each other, and kissing as they passed one another. They looked so happy together. An unexpected longing for what his sister enjoyed swelled inside him. How wonderful it would be to have his own wife, with her expecting his child.

Tamara's laughter drifted from the pool gripping Dale's attention again. Raffi was doing somersaults into the water. Everything he wanted was in that pool, he just didn't know how to get it.

"You'd better take them some towels. The sun is going down," Daphne said, as she sat beside Dale.

He looked at his sister from the corner of his eyes, then stretched and stood. "Right."

He brought them towels and crouched down

at the edge of the pool. "Time to come out, you two."

"A little longer," Raffi pleaded.

"Dale's right, sweetie. We need to get out."

Raffi doggy paddled to the edge of the pool and Dale lifted him up by his arms and wrapped him in a huge gray towel. He didn't want the boy to be cold.

"I'll take him inside and get him dressed," Daphne volunteered.

Dale handed the wrapped boy to his sister, then held another towel. "Your turn," he said to Tamara.

She swam to the edge of the pool, much like Raffi had, and folded her arms on the rim. She looked at Dale, and he crouched down again, stuck by her grace and beauty.

"I'll be out in a minute, but Dale, I just wanted to tell you not to worry about anything. I'm going to do all I can to make sure you don't lose Raffi."

He wanted to reach down and touch her face. Beads of water clung to her lashes like little diamonds, but her eyes were red. He smiled. "You're good at your job. I'm not worried. Come on out."

She climbed up the ladder on the wall of the pool, breaking through the water swiftly and cleanly. She took the towel, and wrapped herself in it too quickly. "I can see how much you love Raffi. I won't let you down."

Unable to stop himself, he pulled her cool, wet

body into his arms. But immediately he stepped back, remembering what Adam had said. "Thank you. Keep me posted." Then he went inside to get Raffi and leave.

Just as Tamara had predicted, they rejected his adoption papers until Raffi was cleared as a possible adoptee. Tamara filed for a hearing date and received one two weeks later. Dressed in their best suits, Dale and Raffi headed to the court house. Dale told Raffi not to be nervous, but found it impossible to follow his own advice. Tamara hadn't explained exactly what she intended to say, but he had confidence in her.

She met him at the door as he and Raffi were making their way inside. She wore a conservative business suit, looking fabulous but so unlike the casual woman he loved so deeply. She took Dale's arm and walked along side him to their designated court room.

Then she stopped before a door, pivoted, and faced him. "Just follow my lead on whatever I say." Her face was serious, matching her formal attitude.

"All right."

"You know, even if we don't convince them today and you receive a denial, you haven't really lost. Raffi still might not be adopted out."

"Just give it your best shot, Tamara."

She blinked and gave him one brief nod. Then she smiled at Raffi. "Ready to tell them where you want to live?"

"Yep," Raffi said.

They entered the room which looked like a mini court. Dale's lawyer, Tamara, Dale and Raffi sat at one table which faced a team of government employees with bland expressions on their faces.

His lawyer began by stating all of Dale's legal rights, but it was Tamara who got their attention. She presented his home study, raved about the excellent care Dale was already providing for Raffi, and described the love she'd witnessed between them.

They asked Raffi how he felt.

"I want to stay with Dale."

"Even if there's a family that would love to make you a part of their life?"

"I already have a family with Dale. I have grandpa John, and aunt Daphne, and uncle Adam. My aunt's going to have a baby and I'll have someone to play with. I'll even be real careful with him when he's little" He looked at Tamara, then stopped talking.

The main official took notes, then smiled at Raffi. "I'm glad to hear you're so happy. I guess Dale's been doing a good job taking care of you."

Raffi nodded. "Dale's my dad now. We cook together, and he teaches me things, and we play, and I know he loves me because sometimes late at night when he thinks I'm sleeping he stands by the door and watches me. One time I even heard him cry." He ducked his head, then sat up straight. "But Dale says you're not a wimp if you cry 'cause you love someone."

The official smiled. "That's right, young man. He shifted his eyes to Tamara. "Do you have anything to add?"

Tamara seemed to have a difficult time tearing her gaze from Raffi, probably just as stunned by his statement as Dale was. She met Dale's eyes momentarily then turned back to the panel. "Yes, but I'd like Raffi to wait outside, if possible."

They nodded, and Raffi was escorted out.

"This was all my mistake," she began. "Mr. Curtis had mentioned his desire to adopt Raffi long before he received your letter. But, I, ah, had some problems with another case that failed miserably, and I wasn't able to handle my responsibilities. I left work for a few weeks, lost contact with all my cases, including Mr. Curtis'. It was my fault. The paperwork should have been filed, I should have completed the home study. I didn't do my job properly, and now Raffi could end up being hurt by my mistake. I don't want that to happen."

Dale straightened in his chair, the muscles on his neck tightening. What was she saying? It simply wasn't true. She was an incredibly competent social worker. He couldn't let her tarnish her record this way. "Ah, can I say something?"

Tamara flashed him a warning look. "It's not necessary, Mr. Curtis."

The official frowned and rubbed his chin. "You don't need to add anything, Mr. Curtis. I understand the situation."

CHAPTER NINETEEN

Dale followed Tamara to her car. "Why did you do that?"

"What?"

"Lie."

"I stretched the truth."

"You lied and it could get you into trouble."

She shrugged. "Not really. They'll research what I said and see that I really did leave the country for a while. It'll all blow over, but I wanted to get it on the record that you were the first to petition for Raffi."

He dropped his hands into his pockets and stood beside her. "I don't know what to say."

She opened her driver's door. "Just keep your fingers crossed. I'll know their decision in a couple of days."

Dale stepped closer. "How can I ever thank

you?"

She shook her head. "No need. I've got to get going."

He pulled out a hand and touched her arm, needing to feel her warm skin on his fingertips. "Wait."

She stiffened and her efficient business-like mask fell. "For what?"

"I do need to thank you. Because of you I have a wonderful son whom I love more than anything, Tam."

"You don't have him yet."

"I will." He looked at his feet and shifted uncomfortably. "At least I hope I will, but even if something terrible happens and I lose him . . . he's changed my life. You've changed my life." He met her stare, wondering what the frown on her brow meant.

"I'm, ah, glad, Dale."

He ran a hand through his hair, feeling completely helpless. "I know I messed up. I know I promised to take you as you were, and instead did everything in my power to manipulate you into living my way –."

"Dale –."

He held up a hand. "No, listen, please."

"It doesn't matter anymore."

"Yes, it does. I know . . ." He took a step back and shook his head. "What you do for kids . . . to help people become families . . . it's priceless, Tam."

He glanced at the tears in her eyes, and

offered a small smile. "You're priceless."

She wiped under her eyes, drying the tear stains. "Thank you."

"I didn't see it before because I refused to look. I was afraid to look . . . that I'd have to admit my perfect world wasn't as perfect as I'd always told myself it was."

"Dale -."

"But I know now." He cleared his throat. "I know if I lost everything tomorrow, the only thing I'd miss, is that little boy waiting up there with my attorney."

She smiled.

"And you Tamara, I'd miss you. I literally ache inside for you everyday."

"Dale, you're a good man. Really. But you and I . . . we're too different."

"I know. I'm not asking you to come back, Tamara. But I do love you, I've never stopped, and I never will. You've got to know that." He took a chance and reached for her hand, holding her long, delicate fingers in his. "And I . . . I would do it all differently if I had an opportunity to remedy the past."

Her tears returned. This time she took a step forward and embraced him.

He held her lightly, trying to control his emotions. "I'm sorry I was such a bastard that night when you needed me so badly, Tamara."

"Shh," she said. "Hold me."

He did, cherishing this moment, drinking in her warmth. *Hold me.* Two simple words - all she'd ever asked of him, that and his love. Why had it been so difficult for him to give?

When she pulled back, he let her go.

"I'll call you soon. Keep your fingers crossed."

"I will."

She got in her car, buckled her seat belt, started the engine, then brought down her window. "Dale?"

"Yes?"

"The times I spent with you were some of the happiest of my life. I just wanted you to know that." She stepped on the gas and her Jag tore down the road, proving it was capable of going from zero to sixty in a matter of seconds.

The state took a week to make their decision. Tamara left work early when she received notice.. How was she going to tell Dale he'd lost the hearing?

When she got home a large package waited on her door step. She dragged it inside, found a pocket knife and slit the tape along the edges of the rectangle box.

As she lifted the lid and eased away packing peanuts she saw a beautiful painting of her grandmother in an antique frame. Her mouth drew open and she stared at the precious gift in awe. She found an envelope with Celeste's handwriting.

What in the world? She unfolded the note

inside. A housewarming gift, the note said, then one line that left her baffled - *follow your heart.*

"Follow my heart?" she said, curious about what her Celeste meant. In all the years she'd needed the advice of a mother and never received any, this was a peculiar way to start.

Tamara thought of a blond gentleman and a dark haired little boy who belonged together, and wondered if Celeste knew Tamara was in love with them both and had been living with a broken heart for months. No doubt, Celeste had spoken with Edna and did know. She shook her head. Funny her mother should worry about the state of her heart when she'd lived with a fractured soul since birth. She folded the note, caressing the crease, and put it away in a desk drawer.

She lifted the cordless phone and dialed Celeste in New York.

Her mother seemed surprised to hear from her.

"I got the portrait, Mom. Thank you *so* much."

"I'm glad you liked it. I thought you might want it for your new home. "

"It means a lot to me."

The line was quiet for a few seconds. "Do you like the house?"

"Mmm, yes. Thanks for arranging that also."

"You don't have to thank me. I was glad to help."

Tamara sighed. "I guess I haven't given you

an opportunity to do much of that, have I?

Again a prolonged silence. "You're an independent young lady. I've always been proud of that fact."

Tamara closed her eyes and took a breath. "I had to learn to be independent at a young age." Used to keeping her feelings to herself, Tamara found those words hard to say.

"I know," her mother's voice was faint.

"I'm not trying to make you feel bad," she said quickly. "That's not why I called –."

"No, it's all right, Tamara."

Why wasn't she ever able to have a normal conversation with Celeste without feeling awkward? "I . . . I guess I better let you go. I just called to thank you for the portrait . . . and the note."

"You're welcome."

Was that all she was going to say? No insight on what she'd meant by those three short words - *follow your heart*? "I supposed Edna told you I was engaged to marry Dale?"

"She did."

"I should have called and let you know myself, but . . . ." It had never crossed her mind. When Tamara had been in Greece, she assumed Celeste thought it was only because of Cindy.

"It's okay."

No, of course it wasn't okay that her mother never knew what was going on in her only daughter's life. Not even something as important as an engagement. It wasn't okay that she and Celeste didn't even know each other. "Not that it matters anymore since we . . ." Tears came out of no where, and Tamara tried desperately to control them. "Since it didn't work out." Her sobs came in shuddering bursts. "I'm sorry."

"Tamara, are you okay?" Her mother sounded distressed. "Sweetheart?"

"I'm sorry, it's just . . . . Have you ever loved someone so much you cry yourself to sleep at night because they're not with you?" She bent over her desk, her forehead on the palm of her hand. "Have you?"

"Yes . . ." Celeste sniffed as if she too were crying. "You."

"Oh, Mom . . . ." Tamara's sobs racked her body and her thoughts switched from the pain of losing Dale to the pain of not having her mother's love. After she calmed she apologized. "I can't believe I'm doing this."

"Perhaps this will give me the courage to say what I've wanted to for so long. Will you listen?"

"Of course." Tamara dabbed at her eyes and nose with a tissue.

"I know you felt abandoned as a child. You had every right to feel that way. We did. I did abandon you in a way. Since I knew nothing of raising a child, I justified sending you away to schools. I told myself they would do a better job."

Tamara shook her head. "How could you believe that?"

"Because I was young, and insecure, and selfish." She sniffed again. "Sometimes I tried to put you out of my mind completely to keep from feeling guilty about not raising you myself."

Tears streamed down her face, but she gave a shaky laugh. "You're not making me feel any better, if that's your intent."

"But it's the truth and you deserve that from me."

Tamara felt she deserved much more than that, but she didn't say it. "I already knew the truth."

"But I was wrong, Tamara. If I could do it again, I would do things differently."

This was the second time this week someone had said that to her. Celeste and Dale. But neither could make up for injuries of the past. "What does that mean, Mother? What's done is done."

"I understand that. By the time I matured enough to realize what I'd missed, you were an angry teenager who hated me. I suppose I'd like to know if you still do?"

"Hate you? No, I don't hate you. I don't even know you."

Celeste cleared her throat. "I *am* sorry. At least that I can remedy, if you give me a chance."

"Are asking if we can have a relationship now?"

"I'd like that, darling. I really would."

It was a little late. Tamara didn't need a mother now. But a friendship? With Celeste? Maybe. "So would I."

The line was quiet, but not uncomfortable.

"May I ask one more question?" Celeste seemed hesitant.

"Sure, anything."

"If you are truly crying yourself to sleep over this failed relationship with the Curtis boy . . . shouldn't you do something about it?"

Tamara sighed, feeling drained from all the tears and emotions already spilled. "I'm . . . afraid."

"Of . . .?"

"Of getting hurt again. He . . . we're so different."

"Can't you be different and still be together?"

"I thought we could once, but Dale wanted me to be someone I'm not." And it still hurt how he'd tried to change her.

Celeste cleared her throat. "So will you do as I did and suffer silently all your life, every time you see him, wishing you had the courage to ask for the relationship you wanted?"

How long had Celeste wanted to connect with her and held back for fear of rejection? All those times Tamara thought Celeste had been cold and dismissive, had she just been afraid?

"Tamara?"

"I don't know," she said quickly. "I mean, I love Dale so much. But what if I trust him again and he . . . ."

"What if you talk to him and tell him how you feel?"

Tamara smiled. Maybe she and Celeste would be able to build a friendship after all. "That's good advice."

"Thank you."

They both laughed.

"Call me and let me know how the talk goes."

"I will. When will you be in California again?"

"Next month. Your father is meeting with the board of Cassetti Cultural Center."

"Really? I wanted to talk with you and Dad about attending the next board meeting."

"You did?" Celeste sounded completely astounded.

Tamara didn't blame her since she'd always refused to have anything to do with the self serving museum and institute. "Yes, I have a request."

"Which is?"

"I want to add a section dedicated to the poor children of Los Angeles. A place where they can get information, help, scholarships, those type of things."

"Your father will certainly welcome you to the meeting. Whether they'll choose to allocate money for something of that nature –."

"I want to use my money."

"Your money?"

"What you've been sending me for years. I don't need it. I'd like to donate it."

"Well . . . ," Celeste paused. "It seems reasonable to me. I'll tell Andre to call you."

Before Tamara could call Dale with the state's decision on the adoption petition, he called her.

"Any news?"

"Nothing firm," she lied and hit her forehead

with the palm of her hand for the lie. What good would it do to prolong the inevitable?

"Is no news, good news?" His voice was hopeful.

"I'll let you know soon." She swallowed hard. "I'm a bit tied up right now, can I call you back?"

"Sure, I understand," Dale said.

Lisa waved at her frantically. "Hold on, Dale."

She pushed the hold button. "What?"

"Raffi is available for adoption again."

"What? How?" An electric excitement began to bubble inside her.

"The couple chose the little girl."

"Oh my G-." She placed her trembling fingers over her lips. "So Dale can re-file adoption papers?"

Lisa smiled. "Well, what are you waiting for. Call him."

Call him? He was on hold. "Thanks, Lis." She lifted the receiver and hit the flashing hold button. "Dale, you still there?"

"I'm here."

"Listen, can you and Raffi come to my place tonight?"

"Your place?" He paused. "You mean your office, right?"

"No, my house. Let me give you directions." She rattled off her address.

"Santa Monica?" His voice sounded surprised.

"Middle ground. Not the ghetto as you and Daphne say but not the Palisades either.

He laughed. "Is this about Raffi?"

It was about all their futures. "Yes."

"Tam, do you know? I can't wait, is it good or bad news?"

"Both."

She heard him exhale. "All right. We'll be there."

CHAPTER TWENTY

Tamara blew out the match. A gentle lavender incense began to suffuse the room. Then she arranged plastic plates and bowls on her round dining table. From her refrigerator, she pulled out the assortment of sandwiches she'd prepared, and a tossed salad, placing both at the center of the table.

She stared at the table. Boy, she was getting as bad as Daphne and Dale. Did it matter how the table looked? She just wanted everything to be perfect.

The door bell chimed and Tamara drew a breath for courage. When she opened the door, she had a smile in place. Raffi hugged her, Dale smiled.

"Come in."

"Wow, you're right next to the beach," Raffi

said.

"A block, not bad, huh?"

Raffi's bright eyes danced. "Wow, one block? This place is way better than that dumpy apartment you had."

"Well, thank you . . . I think."

Dale laughed. "It's great."

She shrugged. "Bigger than I wanted, but leave it to my mother's realtor to find me a home."

Dale raised an eyebrow. "You accepted help from your mother?"

She smiled and shrugged. "Well, they put money in an account for me every month whether I use it or not. The balance was getting obscenely large. I decided to empty it a bit."

"I'm glad," Dale said.

"Me too. I decided there wasn't any shame in accepting who I was. I've spent too many years wishing and pretending I wasn't my parents' daughter. At some point, you have to accept your heritage, don't you?"

Dale stared at her. "Accept it, not embrace it."

She met his eyes and knew he understood she would never embrace it whole heartedly, but she had decided to use her money and status to make both her life and the lives of others richer. In her bank account, it helped no one. "Want to see the back yard?"

"Yeah!" Raffi ran to her sliding glass door and dashed outside before she and Dale made a move.

They both chuckled and she glanced at Dale.

"I guess I should give you the bad news first."

He closed his eyes momentarily and quaked as if a shiver ran through him. "I guess I lost."

"Well, the hearing yes."

"Damn it." He turned away from her, his hands on his hips.

"Dad, come out here," Raffi called from outside.

"Dad?" Tamara placed a hand on his back.

"He started calling me that after he found out I could lose him. Maybe it's his way of pretending it wasn't happening." He shook his head. "I don't know."

"Dad." Raffi peeked inside. "You comin' or not. She's got a swing on this big tree, and –."

"Come in, Raffi. I was just about to tell your dad the good news."

Dale's eyes were red when he faced them. "You mean there's good news somewhere?"

She nodded. "The couple that wanted to adopt Raffi chose not to proceed. Meaning he's still your foster child."

"Yippie," Raffi yelled.

Dale frowned. "I don't understand."

"You can now file for adoption."

"But they said I couldn't –."

"You couldn't because someone else was already in the process." She shook her head dismissively. "It's a bureaucratic technical thing. But now that they've dropped out, Raffi is . . . well, available."

"Cool," he said, taking Dale's hand. "Now, will

you come out here and look at the swing?"

Dale grinned, lifted the boy, and kissed him.

"Ah, Dale, man, don't do that."

"Raffi, I love you, kid. I was so scared I'd lose you."

Raffi looked seriously at Dale, then at Tamara. His arms flew around Dale's shoulders and he buried his face in his neck. "Don't be scared, Dad. I'll never leave you."

Dale squeezed him tighter, and Tamara had to fight tears.

"Okay," Dale said, his voice loud and cheery. "Let's see this back yard."

They all went outside, Raffi running and laughing and Dale watching him proudly. Tamara folded her arms on her belly and leaned on the house, envious of their closeness and ecstatic that they'd found each other in this world. Funny how she'd never realized how perfect they were for one another. Raffi had transformed Dale, and Dale had turned the scared little boy into a confident, happy child who had learned how to give and receive love.

She mentally crossed them off her list. Case closed. "Guys, let's eat."

They all hurried inside and washed their hands. They sat at the table to eat their salads.

"You know," Tamara said. "The adoption should be a no brainer now."

Dale chewed and nodded. He wiped his mouth with a paper napkin. "I've recently cut my work hours in half, you know?"

"No, I didn't"

He nodded. Lifting a butter knife and a slice of bread, he occupied himself with the spread. "I decided I had more important things to enjoy in life than work."

"What did your dad say?" She reached for her lemonade glass.

"He cut my salary in half."

She stopped short of taking a drink. "You're kidding?"

"No." He grinned. "Considering we had to settle with the union at a less than favorable contract to get the aviation mechanics back to work, and we were told to petition again next year for the expansion to France, I'd say he was more than fair."

Tamara forced herself to keep her mouth shut, and her temper from flaring. Dale was his son, not just an employee, and after all the hours Dale put in . . . it didn't seem fair to her.

"But he decided Raffi needed an expense account curiously close in dollar amount to what I used to make."

She smiled.

"The state will look favorably on the extra time I'll be spending with Raffi, won't they?"

"Most definitely."

"Will the fact that I'm single and male hurt my chances?"

"Well, I was thinking of that," she said, purposely letting her sentence drop.

Dale stopped eating and gazed at her.

"If you were married, you'd practically have a

guarantee."

"Yes, I guess that would make sense."

"And since I'm the one that got you involved in foster parenting and well . . ."

"Introduced us," Dale supplied.

"Right. I was thinking . . . I was wondering . . . how I could help you out."

Dale rubbed his chin and watched her with a curious look on his face. "Actually, if Raffi had a house with a nice yard like this, it would look good. My condo is a bachelor's pad. I'm surprised my social worker didn't point that out during the home study."

"Well," she shrugged. "She was probably being lenient."

He nodded.

"Besides, she knew you had another house in the Palisades to move into eventually."

He shook his head. "Not anymore. Sold it."

Raffi stopped eating and shifted his attention from Dale to Tamara as if he were watching a tennis match.

"Can we have the sandwiches now?" Raffi asked.

"Of course," she said.

"I don't know where I'm going to find someone to marry on such short notice though," Dale said.

"You know, Dale, I've got plenty of room here."

"That's true. But I couldn't impose on you."

"You could." Her eyes locked with his and a silent message full of hope and forgiveness passed between them. Besides, I already know you both, and I *do* love Raffi."

Raffi put his sandwich down. "What are you guys talking about?"

She took the boy's hand and decided to be serious. "Raffi, I'm proposing to have you move in and the three of us be a family. Would that be okay with you?"

"I've always wanted to live with you."

She smiled. "Okay, then Dale. I think you both should move in, and we should get married."

Dale winked. "But Raffi wouldn't want to move out here and change schools and everything."

The boy nodded. "Yes I would." He shifted all his attention to her. "Tamara, I wouldn't mind."

Dale shrugged. "Well okay. If that's what you both think we should do, I'm all for it."

Raffi seemed pleased, but Tamara's heart played an erratic beat against her rib cage. She loved Dale, but could they really do it this time? Could they compromise enough to make it work? All she knew, was that she wanted to try.

They finished their meal.

"That was delicious," Dale said.

"Can I go outside and play now," Raffi asked.

"Excuse me? Where are your manners?"

"Oh, sorry. The meal was great, Tamara. May I be excused now?"

She laughed. Was this the same little boy who could barely string two sentences together when she'd met him? "You may. In fact, you both may. I'll pick this stuff up, and I'll join you in a few minutes."

Dale watched her disappear into the kitchen. "Go ahead and go. I'll be right out, Raffi. I want to talk with Tamara a second."

"You *are* going to marry her this time, aren't you?"

"As soon as possible."

"Okay." He smiled. "Don't mess up."

Dale laughed. "Thanks a lot for the vote of confidence."

Most of the dinner plates were disposable so it didn't take her long to clear the table. She was making coffee when he walked into the kitchen. Dale took a moment to admire her backside before stepping behind her and wrapping his arms around her middle.

She angled her head and smiled. "Hi."

"You won't regret this."

She turned and placed her hands on his hips, something he'd grown to love. "You mean marrying you?"

"You know that's what I mean. What made you change your mind?"

She shrugged. "I decided to follow my heart. And it's yours, Dale. It has been since the time you fell on me and knocked the wind from my lungs."

He chuckled. "Liar."

"No, you're right, not that long ago. I wanted you when you kissed me outside the deli, I liked you when you took Raffi in, I cared for you when you sent me away in that Mickey shirt, too honorable to take advantage of me when I was feeling sad and lonely." She stopped and took a breath. "But love - I loved you that night you took all my clothes off in front of the fireplace. When you kissed me with such passion and held me like . . . ."

"I loved you."

She nodded. "And I lost my heart."

"And then I stepped all over it." He placed his forehead on hers."

"Yes."

"I didn't mean to. When I told you to leave, I . . . ." He looked into her eyes. "I was trying to be a tough guy. I never thought you'd go. I didn't know about -."

"Cindy. But, you did. I told you it was an emergency and you didn't -."

"Care."

"Right."

"I guess I thought if you loved me enough, you'd change for me."

"And I guess I thought I had."

He nodded. "You had. You did." He released her. "My world was way different than yours, Tam. I had a lot of growing to do, and I didn't want to do it. I figured it was easier for you to mold to my life than me to yours. Yours was so foreign to me."

She laughed. "You poor little rich guy."

He laughed as well. "I was a pompous ass. Let's face it."

She arched an eyebrow and nodded. "But

such a sexy one."

"Well, thank God for small favors."

Her expression sobered. "Will you mind moving out of your fancy condo, into a middle class neighborhood?"

He shook his head. "I'll live where ever you want me to."

She inched close and slid her hands along his sides. "Are you really reformed, Dale Curtis?" She gave him a sexy, teasing smile that melted his heart and stirred his libido.

"I'm still the same guy. I'll still inherit my father's company, I'll still have business dinners and trips I'll have to go on. But I love you, Tamara and you'll never have to do anything that makes you uncomfortable. You'll always come first with me."

Her arms were now wrapped all the way around his back, and her body pressed against his. "I can live with that. Can you live with my lifestyle, my work?"

"Absolutely. I'm impressed as hell with you, lady."

"Well, then." She kissed his chin, sliding her lips along his jaw to his ear. "I only have one more question?"

"What?" He groaned.

"How long will it take you to drop Raffi at your sister's house and come back?"

He cupped her jean clad bottom. "No time at all."

"Good, I'll be in the tub. Take my key."

While Tamara ran the bath water, her door bell rang. Boy, he *was* fast.

She opened the door and found a delivery boy. "I didn't order."

"Ms. Cassetti?"

"Yes."

"I've got flowers for you."

"Oh, well okay, bring them in."

He went to his truck, then he and another man carried two immense wild flower arrangements each. They placed them on her coffee table. "There's more," the man said.

They went back to their van three times, leaving her with a dozen wild flower bouquets and one card from Dale.

She opened it, read his words, *To my wild flower*, and smiled.

She soaked in the tub until she was practically shriveled, but no Dale. So she dressed in an intimate satin negligee and lay in bed to wait for him, until exhaustion took over and she fell asleep.

She was awakened by soft kisses on her neck. Slowly, she opened her eyes and saw Dale hovering over her.

"What took you so long?" she asked, not wanting to wake up.

"I had a few errands to run."

That wasn't terribly romantic since he knew

she was waiting for him, but she let it slide. "Well, get in bed."

He handed her one violet. "I picked this one from the country club flower bed."

"Why, Dale, you vandal you. She smiled. "I love it. Thank you."

He nodded, and began taking off his clothes. Then he drew the covers back, took her hand, and pulled her out of bed. She glanced at his body and smiled. He wore Micky Mouse boxer shorts.

She laughed. "What are those?"

"Like them?"

"Dale, you're crazy."

Then he dropped to his knees. "I am. About you. Will you marry me?"

She took the small velvet box he offered. "I've already said yes."

"This time, I wanted to ask you the right way."

She looked at the beautiful, modest ring, then back at him. She dropped the ring on the bed and pulled him to his feet. She wrapped her arms around his neck and brought her lips against his. "Well, let me answer you the right way."

They shared a soft, loving kiss, drinking in all their pent up passion.

He groaned. "Was that a yes?"

"Yes," she whispered. "I'd be proud to be your wife, Dale Curtis."

He reached for her then dove onto the bed, surprising her, and eliciting a scream.

He laughed. "I love proud women."

"I love *you*," she said, before Mickey came off and Dale made her forget everything but the joys of being a woman.

As she cried his name and gripped his shoulders, she heard him whisper his own words of love, and Tamara knew at last, that her loneliness would forever be a dull memory of the past. She had love. She had a family. And nothing else mattered.

Here's a special advance preview of:

WINNER TAKE ALL

By Lara Rios

Coming in January 2002

WINNER TAKE ALL by Lara Rios, forthcoming book to be published January 2002 by Encanto Books, an imprint of Kensington Publishing Corp. Printed by permission of the publisher.

WINNER TAKE ALL

July

Multicolored race cars ranging from fire engine red to metallic green raced round and round the track, some fast, some slower. They created a dizzying blur of color in the scorching heat typical of the Bakersfield desert. Occasionally, a car pulled off to the side or onto the middle of the track, and a driver popped out of the window.

Graciela Alende walked slowly to the chain link fence separating the public seating from the race track and placed her forehead on the hard metal, closing her eyes. She wanted to shut away the memories also, but they weren't going to be as easy to block out.

Is this why you left me the car, Dad? So I'd think of you every time I saw it, every time I walked onto a speedway? She opened her eyes and stared absently at the cars tearing across the track as dust from the surrounding area drifted in the air. Just the sight caused a tightness in her throat, suffocating her. What kind of solace had her father gotten from these loud, dirty tracks? Graciela drew a deep breath and eased back a wisp of light brown hair which had worked loose from her orderly

French braid.

She turned and looked behind her. The stands were empty, but by tonight families would be occupying almost every seat. The race crowd was different from that of other sports. Maybe due to the noise level, or the fact that so many kids attended and ran around waving flags, but the atmosphere was comparable to that of a carnival more than a sporting event.

The fun actually began hours before the race started. Only after buying food and memorabilia of their favorite car and driver at the various vendor trailers, would the fans sit and enjoy the race. How many times had she witnessed the same scene? The last time had been three years ago, when she and her father had parted ways. She shook her head. In some ways, it felt like just yesterday.

"Track's not open yet." A deep female voice called. "Can I help you?"

Graciela turned in her direction, squinting at the bright sunlight. She drew a second steading breath to mentally bring herself back to the present. The smell of exhaust made her nauseous. "My name is Graciela Alende. I'm –."

"Oh, yes, Miss Alende. I'm very sorry about your father." The tall, athletic woman stopped in front of her.

Graciela nodded. The last two weeks she'd had to endure an endless number of phone calls and visits from people who were sorry. She was sick and tired of hearing those words. What exactly were they sorry about? All she wanted was to get past it -- go on with her life. "I received the beautiful bouquet from the speedway with all your condolences. Thank you."

"No problem. I'm Billie, by the way, the announcer." She held out her hand.

She took it and shook. "Hi, Billie."

"So what brings you here?" Her eyes seemed to stray to Graciela's clothes as she released her hand.

She wore a lavender sun dress, nylons, and a two piece platform sandal with a two inch heel. She obviously wasn't dressed for a day at the track. Billie probably wondered why Graciela had shown up dressed in a fashion better suited for a stroll through a museum. Maybe, this was the last way she could rebel against her father. Or perhaps merely a way to deny what she was about to face.

"My dad ran a car," she said.

"Yep, number 58."

"I'd like to speak with the driver, Cruz Ortega. Know if he's here yet?"

"Should be in the pits getting ready for tonight." Billie looked at the track. "He's not out practicing yet."

"Can I get into the pits on my own?"

"Come on, I'll take you. You're not pulling the car from the circuit, are you?" Billie led her to the pit area.

She wasn't sure what she was going to do. Of all the crazy things for her father to leave her - a race car. "I need to talk with Mr. Ortega. He probably knows the car better than anyone."

Billie nodded. "You're right there."

She followed Billie behind the track where some cars were in various states of being repaired while others were simply parked.

They stopped beside a shiny, royal blue Ford Taurus with the white number 58 painted on the side. The hood was up. Three men with grease on their hands, were pulling things in and out of the engine.

"Don't change the spark plugs until after the first race," said the one bent over the engine of the car.

"Cruz." Billie tapped the man's solid arm.

Cruz looked over his shoulder, keeping one arm on the car. Graciela got her first glimpse in years of his rugged, heart stopping good looks. Dark, thick eyebrows, casting a shadow over his eyes; sultry, pink lips; short, wind tossed black hair. He straightened. "Hey, Billie." His eyes flickered over Graciela and he frowned. "What's up?"

"You've got a visitor."

He glanced at Graciela again. "What's she want?" he asked Billie.

Why was he acting as if she weren't standing right in front of him? Graciela stepped closer. "I need to speak with you."

His frown remained, his forehead full of creases, and his eyebrows drawn together. "All right. Speak."

Graciela looked around. Somehow, she'd pictured being able to discuss her predicament in different surroundings. How could they hold such a personal conversation with engines revving and roaring to life – with so many people around? "It concerns this car."

"I figured it did, Miss Alende."

So he remembered her. For the first time since walking onto the speedway grounds, she felt a spark of pleasure. "The car has become my responsibility now that my father is gone."

"I expected as much."

She inhaled, irritated by his cold, dismissive words. "We'll I didn't. It's the last thing I expected him to leave me." Especially since he knew how much she hated the track.

Cruz crossed his arms and leaned his backside against the car door. He'd filled out very nicely. She noticed the fabric of his shirt stretched tight around the thick bands that formed his upper arms. And how his large torso narrowed to sexy, powerful, definitely manly hips.

"Beggars can't be choosers," he said after staring at her for several moments. "An American saying, isn't it?"

She wasn't sure what he meant by that, but she didn't like his attitude. "I need to figure out what to do with this car."

"Yes, you do."

"I hoped you might be able to help me."

"How?"

Graciela swallowed. "I don't know much about racing."

"No." He uncrossed his arms and placed his hands on the car behind him, repositioning his hips slightly, distracting Graciela momentarily. "You didn't exactly hang out at the track when your father was alive."

Oh, yes she had, more than she cared to remember. Every weekend for twelve years she spent trapped at these speedways while her father ignored her. But, the moment she turned eighteen and went away to college, she hadn't gone anywhere near a race track. Of course, Cruz probably didn't remember, and she wasn't here to argue with the driver. Let him believe what he wanted. "Which is why I need your opinion on--."

"My opinion?" He laughed. "How about a fact? This was a game to your father, but it helps pay my bills. Opinions aren't important here." he said.

"I understand."

"So now what? *You* tell *me*."

"Well, okay, we keep racing, I suppose. I'll learn whatever I have to to keep the car on the track."

He raised an eyebrow. "You mean you're going to keep running the car?"

"Yes." Was she? She wasn't sure what she wanted to do, how could she sound so decisive? Maybe because he seemed to be challenging her and she could never resist a challenge.

He smiled. "Great. So, I can still count on a pay check." He pushed off the car and stood.

"Mr. Ortega --."

"Cruz."

"About paying you . . . ." Graciela shifted on her feet, uncomfortable, unsure how to tell him.

"What about it?"

"Well, it might be a little difficult at first. You see, my father left me this car, nothing else."

Cruz's eyes widened. "Nothing? What do you mean nothing? Your father was a millionaire."

"Nothing. This car is my entire inheritance."

Cruz lifted his chin as if understanding. "He left you a hundred thousand dollar car without the means to maintain it." He shook his head. "That's funny."

"I'm glad you think so." She adjusted her purse and straightened her back. "Look, what I'm trying to say is, I have no extra money, just the car."

The frown reappeared. "What about maintaining the car, traveling, my salary? How do you intend to pay for those things?"

"I don't know. It can come from what we earn, I suppose."

Cruz glanced at Billie, then behind him at the guys, now listening with interest. He took Graciela's arm. "Let's go for a walk."

She walked beside him, out of the pits, where he turned under the bleacher stands, then stopped and faced her. They were all alone. And instantly, the difference between them became starkly apparent. She dressed neatly, in a clean dress, not a wrinkle in the fabric, not a stain. Cruz's T-shirt was ripped at the collar, and grease smudges soiled his chest where it looked like he'd wiped his fingers. She wore a light lavender scented lotion that kept her skin soft, delicate. His face was dark from car exhaust and moist from perspiration. He smelled of grease and cedar aftershave. But Graciela suspected the difference between them went deeper than the clothes they wore or the artificial scents they'd acquired.

"A racing team costs money," he said.

"I know –."

"And you don't have any?"

"No, but-."

"Then you better forget about racing the car." He lifted a foot and placed it on an iron bar and leaned his back on a support beam, looking at ease with himself and his surroundings.

"But, you'll make money, won't you? In fact, I'm counting on it. If you win a few races, we'll have enough to maintain the car, and I can pay my personal bills."

He shook his head. "Doesn't work that way."

"Why not?"

"Just doesn't. If you aren't prepared to dump lots of money to keep the car running, this is our last race."

Graciela didn't have a penny, didn't he understand? "Cruz, I'm not going to spend money on this car? I want it to make me money."

"It won't."

She pressed her fingertips to her forehead, where her freshly manicured nails scratched her skin lightly. Her temples began to throb. All those years she spent attending races and she never bothered to learn the sport, or what her father actually did to run his car.

She assumed that as the owner, her father sat back, watched the races, and cashed a big check at the end of each night. It wouldn't make sense for him to pay for a car that was draining him financially. Not only didn't it make sense, it wasn't in his nature. Carlos Alende never in his life did something that lost him money. Obviously, Cruz didn't know what he was talking about. "Why can't you just keep racing and making money?" she asked.

Cruz laughed. "Oh, I can, and with that you'd be lucky to buy the guys a beer at the end of the night, and refuel the car."

"You're telling me there's no profit?"

He stood upright and came closer to her. "I'm telling you the expenses are tremendous. I'm also telling you that if you expect that car to win many races, you're out of your mind."

"But why can't it? Aren't you a good driver?"

This time he frowned. "The point is," his voice turned cold. "The car is old. It constantly needs replacement parts. It's not a winner, it's a racer."

Graciela sighed heavily. "Replacement parts?"

"Engines, tires, and that's just for starters."

"Well, the car must make more than enough to cover those kinds of expenses."

He rolled his eyes, looking upwards, then swept his hand across his sweat drenched brow and into his scalp, moistening his coal black hair. With obvious irritation, and fading patience, he faced her anew. "This is the Southwest Series. We don't make money, Miss Alende, it's just fun."

"No, this is a business. I've driven three hours in the desert heat to get here, and what I want to hear is that you'll win, and make money."

He shook his head. "Have you heard anything I've said in the past ten minutes?"

"You don't understand. I don't have anything else to fall back on. This is it." She swallowed the lump in her throat. The past few weeks were beginning to take their toll on her. Reality was setting in - she had nothing now, no one. She needed just one person on her side.

His eyes narrowed and he stared hard and cold at her. "Am I supposed to feel sorry for you, Graciela?"

"No, I --."

"You asked for my opinion. Here it is. Sell the car, take the money, and run." He gave her body an intimate scanning. "This is positively not your thing, *Querida*." He turned and began to walk away, ending their discussion without a care to what would happen to her.

"Cruz, wait." Graciela reached for his arm,

desperate to make him understand. At twenty-four years old, she never worked a day in her life. The last six years, she'd spent in college becoming an Art major. She supported herself with a few thousand dollars her father deposited automatically in her bank account every month.

But all that was gone. She had used the money to live on, travel, have fun with, always figuring she was young and had plenty of time to decide on a career and get a job. Now, she wished she had been more responsible. But she never dreamed her father would die so young, and give his entire estate away to charity. If this car didn't make money for her, she didn't know how she'd survive.

Cruz looked from her hand on his arm to her face. "What?"

"As long as I own that car, and you're under contact to drive it, you have to do what I tell you."

His eyes hooded and the color on his face darkened. He turned completely around and faced her, looking like a thunder cloud hovering above. "Graciela, you're a young woman, a child still. You are not going to hang around a track full of men, and you are definitely not going to tell me what to do. Understand?"

She stiffened, lifting her face to meet his eyes, unwilling to let him intimidate her. "I will be at every race from now on, Cruz. You'd better get used to it."

He moved closer. One arm shot out and he

gripped one of the bleacher criss-cross supports over her head. Just as she took a step back, his other arm hooked around her waist.

"Hey," she complained, but the rest of her words remained locked inside as she stared at his handsome face.

"Remember when your dad hired me, Graciela? Seven years ago?"

"Y,yes." She frowned into his eyes. Her arms had bolted up in a defensive movement, and she now used them as a brace to separate herself from Cruz.

"Do you also remember that when he walked away, you kissed me? Remember that?"

"No."

Cruz smiled cruelly. "No, huh? Probably because it was your way to tease me. You were just having a little fun with one of your father's lowly drivers. Isn't that right?"

"No, Cruz, I–."

He tightened his hold around her waist. "Quiet."

She could only stare into his challenging black eyes. She did remember kissing him. She remembered being only seventeen and thinking Cruz was the sexiest, most masculine man she'd ever seen. Just arrived from Mexico, he was different, exotic, tempting. And he'd only gotten better with age.

His face was just above hers. Their lips almost touched. She saw the film of moisture on his temples and brow; smelled his aftershave; felt the heat from his body.

Then all of a sudden he lowered his head and took her lips. He administered a hard kiss, parting her mouth with his own sensual, full lips, without inserting his tongue. He slid his lips against hers, opened his mouth as if he were going to enter, but instead left her with the longing for his taste. Just as abruptly he lifted his head, keeping a firm hold on her body.

"If you don't remember the other kiss, then remember this one. I'll tell you again, this is no place for a beautiful, young, pampered girl like you. Good bye, Graciela."

When he released her, she practically lost her balance. She watched him retreat, too stunned to react. She touched her lips. Had she heard him correctly? Had he said she was beautiful? She closed her eyes and tried to clear her mind. What did it matter if he thought she was attractive? She should be angry. He not only had the nerve to tell her what to do with her property, but also to kiss her without her consent.

She turned and headed to her car. She wasn't angry at Cruz. Her normal life had suddenly turned upside down. She felt fear, anxiety, desperation . . . not anger. Above all, she was disheartened that the race car would not be the save all money maker she had expected it might be. What would she do now?

* * *

Cruz returned to the car and reached for his gloves in the tool box.

"What did she say?" Danny asked.

He slid each hand into a glove and squeezed his fingers open and shut. He shouldn't have touched her, damn him. "Nothing."

"What do you mean nothing? Is she still going to race the car?"

Danny was young and energetic and had a passion for cars, but he was also a pain in the rear at times. Cruz shrugged and moved past Danny, trying to remember what he was doing under the hood.

Dan leaned on the car beside Cruz. "Man, is she hot. I mean, if you can get past that miss hot shot attitude. Did you check out her -?"

Cruz straightened and hit his head on the inside of the hood. "Shit," he yelled. "Don't you have anything to do?"

Danny gave him an innocent look. "You're in lousy mood."

"I'm racing today, in case you've forgotten, and I'd like the car to run. Do you mind?"

"All right, all right." Danny went around the car to finish his work.

Cruz tried not to think of Graciela as he labored with the engine, but found it impossible. After seeing her again, touching her, feeling her soft lips against his, his mind and body wanted nothing more than to remember.

He'd seen Graciela maybe a dozen times in the past seven years, usually arguing with her old man. As the years went by and she'd changed from an immature seventeen year old to a woman in her twenties, he'd often daydreamed about kissing her again. In his imagination, it certainly never happened the way it had today.

He'd always pictured her smiling, inviting him to kiss her, then to undress her, begging him to make love to her. He pushed away from the engine, and yanked off his gloves.

"What's the problem, Cruz." Danny wiped his brow and drew a grease stain on his forehead.

Why was he doing this to himself? Graciela Alende was not the kind of woman he'd ever want. She wasn't nurturing or compassionate. Her tastes were completely different than his. She dressed in clothes he imagined were so expensive, he couldn't afford them even if he spent his entire salary. Besides, he knew she was a cold, heartless bitch.

All she did was use her father for money. A man Cruz would have walked through fire to please. But not Graciela. The only thing she was close to was his wallet. "I guess that Alende chick got to me more than I thought."

Danny shook his head and laughed. "Heard she can do that. Yep, heard some really good stories about her and the old man."

Cruz frowned. And they were all true. He still didn't understand why she didn't adore Carlos

Alende as much as he had.

"Heard she flirted with the drivers, conned them out of beer, drove the old man crazy," Danny continued. "Did you know her then?"

Cruz shook his head, and thought about the kiss she'd given him years ago. She'd done more than flirt, but he wasn't about to tell Danny, and add to the gossip.

"I've got a headache," Cruz moaned. The back of his head was throbbing. "I'm going to get a drink, okay."

"Hey, relax, Cruz. I'll finish this, and Flip will be back soon - went to get us some burgers."

Cruz nodded. As he strolled away, he lit a cigarette. He blew out a puff from the side of his mouth, relaxing. Between his late night racing schedule, janitorial work, and morning college classes, he was physically drained. He couldn't wait for the race season to be over so he could rest. He'd be out the extra pay, but at least he'd catch up on his sleep. Of course, with Graciela Alende being the new owner, he would probably be out of a racing job soon anyway.

He missed Carlos Alende already. The pep talks he would give him, the pats on the shoulder. . . a man who understood hard work and loyalty; a man Cruz had admired like no other. That was precisely why Cruz would never be able to comprehend that distance between Graciela and Carlos Alende. Didn't the woman realize what a treasure her father had been? Didn't family mean anything to her?

Cruz was profoundly close to his parents. He never would have treated them with disrespect, the way she did Mr. Alende. In Mexico, Cruz helped his father at the auto shop every night. After going to school all day, he would put in another five or six hours working on cars so that his father wouldn't have to hire a helper. He'd missed out on some of his childhood and teenage years, but he didn't mind, because he was making life easier for his father. He would always go out of his way to please both his parents.

With Graciela and Mr. Alende that wasn't the case. Even at his funeral, she stood with no emotion on her face during the service. Immediately afterwards, she walked away without listening to or acknowledging anyone's condolences.

What kind of woman didn't cry at her father's funeral?

He reached the concession stand which was not yet open, but the girls always let him buy something before the race. He peeked inside the booth. "Hey beautiful. Sure could use a large coke."

The cute teenager bent over getting paper cups from a plastic bag, lifted her head and smiled. "One soda coming right up." She filled a large cup, placed a lid on, and handed it to him.

He gave her a couple of dollars and winked. "Gracias."

She didn't speak Spanish, but seemed to like

to practice with him. "*Muy gusto.*"

Cruz laughed. "*Mucho gusto.* Although, what I think you mean is *de nada.*"

She shrugged sheepishly. Her mother walked in then. She and her three daughters ran the booth. "Still trying to pick up on my daughter, Cruz."

He smiled. "Naw, just buying a coke. Your girls are too smart to get involved with a guy like me."

She smiled and hustled around the grill, setting frozen hamburger patties at equal distance from each other. "If they were a little older or I was a little younger, we'd snatch you up in a heartbeat, and you know it."

Cruz laughed and turned away. He was starting to feel better. He didn't know why he let someone like Graciela Alende get under his skin. Just because the car now belonged to her, didn't mean his life had to change in any way. His driving record was pretty good. If things didn't work out with her, he could find another team to drive for, and keep that badly needed supplementary income.

Of course, keeping the woman out of his thoughts would not be so easy. He'd been fantasizing about her for so many years, it would be difficult to stop. The Graciela of his dreams was gentle and loving. The impression of the sweet seventeen year old still stayed with him, and he found that for some reason, he had always wished their paths would cross again some day. Now that they had, and he was faced with reality, he wished Graciela had stayed in his fantasy world.

ORDER FORM

Name:________________________________

Address:______________________________

City:__________________________________

State:____________________Zip:__________

Phone:________________________________

QTY	BOOK	COST	AMOUNT
	A Family For Raffi	$12.95	

SUBTOTAL	
SHIPPING & HANDLING $4.00	
CA residents add 7.5% sales tax	
TOTAL	

Mail to:
Pristine Publishing
P.O. Box 10816
San Bernardino, Ca. 92423
Visit our web site:
http://www.pristinepublishing.com